Fever in
the Dark

Fever in the Dark

ELLEN HART

MINOTAUR BOOKS ✖ NEW YORK

FEVER IN THE DARK. Copyright © 2017 by Ellen Hart. All rights reserved. Printed in the United States of America. For information, address St. Martin's Press, 175 Fifth Avenue, New York, N.Y. 10010.

www.minotaurbooks.com

The Library of Congress Cataloging-in-Publication Data is available upon request.

ISBN 978-1-250-08863-5 (hardcover)
ISBN 978-1-250-08864-2 (e-book)

Our books may be purchased in bulk for promotional, educational, or business use. Please contact your local bookseller or the Macmillan Corporate and Premium Sales Department at 1-800-221-7945, extension 5442, or by e-mail at MacmillanSpecialMarkets@macmillan.com.

First Edition: January 2017

10   9   8   7   6   5   4   3   2   1

How did I know that by the end of this book, you would
be gone? When I started writing this dedication, you were with me,
curled snugly in my lap and dreaming your doggy dreams.
I have so many memories, but that seems
cold comfort now. And so, this book is for you.
For my sweet, beautiful, loving Rocket, the best dog ever . . . except
when you weren't. I hope I see you again, if not in
heaven, then in some remote part of the universe, in a bar,
me with a bourbon, you with a marrow bone. Let's talk it over,
understand each other better, and cherish our time together—
time we were never granted in this life.

Cast of Characters

Jane Lawless: Owner of the Lyme House restaurant in Minneapolis. Part-time PI at Nolan & Lawless Investigations.

Cordelia Thorn: Owner of the Thorn Lester Playhouse in Minneapolis. Creative director. Jane's best friend.

Fiona (Fi) McGuy: Stage manager at the Thorn Lester Playhouse. Married to Annie.

Annie Johnson: Law student. Married to Fi.

Bridget Foster: Business owner. Annie's sister. Noah's wife.

Dr. Noah Foster: Psychiatrist. Bridget's husband.

Sharif Berry: High school football coach in Hammond, Ohio. Annie's old friend.

Roxy DeCastro: Assistant stage manager at the Thorn Lester Playhouse.

Charlotte Osborne: Production assistant at the Thorn Lester Playhouse.

Phil Banks: Retired banker. Annie and Fi's neighbor.

Mimi Chandler: Patient of Dr. Noah Foster.

Ted Johnson: Retired businessman. Annie and Bridget's father.

Willow Lewis: Nanny for Tyrion Foster, Bridget and Noah's son.

Draw your chair up close to the edge of the precipice and I'll tell you a story.

—F. SCOTT FITZGERALD

1

Noah Foster was a patient man, a doctor of psychiatry with a highly educated grasp of human nature. He thought of himself as forgiving, a live-and-let-live kind of guy, able to put the world and all its vagaries in perspective. But tonight he was at the end of his rope. His wife's scorn, her family's contempt, had finally burst into the full light of day. He was done with all of them. He wasn't a perfect man, but they weren't perfect either.

Wasn't it the Bible that said only the innocent were allowed to cast the first stone? A huge boulder had come crashing his way this afternoon in the form of a fist to his face. Noah didn't think his nose was broken, just bruised and badly swollen. He should probably be visiting an emergency room—or a police station—instead of heading back to Cordelia's mansion, but that's where his suitcase and clothes were, and most importantly, his son. He would march in, pack up, get his little boy out of bed, and tell Bridget that she and her dad could find another way back to California. He was taking the van and going home. He expected a fight and he was more than ready for it.

In many ways, the idea of divorce had been circling inside

his mind for months. During the eight years he and Bridget had been together, he'd discovered that monogamy wasn't for him. He didn't beat himself up about it; he simply accepted that he had a wandering eye and a hard time being faithful. He still loved Bridget, that's what was so sad. In the early years of their relationship, back when they were both in college, he'd fallen in love with her family as much as he had with her. But that was over and done with now. He had to accept reality and move on. The conclusion was liberating.

As he drove along Hennepin Avenue, he adjusted the van's vents. The air-conditioning didn't seem to be working. It was a sweltering July night in Minneapolis. For a city with a reputation as one of the ice capitals of the planet, this was a bit too Amazon rain forest for his tastes. His stomach was acting up, too, no doubt a response to all the stress he'd been under. He popped open the glove compartment looking for a roll of Tums. Finding none, he considered stopping at a convenience store to pick up a pack, but as he sailed along searching for one, he felt a sudden urge to vomit. He pressed a hand to his mouth. The van was new. The interior in perfect condition. Pulling over to the side of the road, he opened the door. Thankfully, the urge passed.

Back on the road, he turned right onto Twenty-Sixth and then another right onto Cordelia's street. Sweat dripped from his face. The pain in his stomach was growing worse by the second. It didn't feel like anything he'd ever experienced before. Was it his appendix? Something worse? Wiping his eyes, doing his best to focus, he pointed the van into the circular drive in front of the house. As he hit something hard, he stomped on the brake and threw the van into park. The next thing he knew he was throwing up all over the seat next to him. His throat burned and his mouth tasted so foul that he threw up again, this time over the steering wheel, his pants, and the floor.

Cracking the door, he pushed it open with one foot. The nausea was coming in waves now, the pain so intense that it doubled him over. He wasn't sure he could make it up to the house. As he was about to give it a shot, a familiar voice said, "Are you okay?"

He looked up, tried to clear his vision. "Help . . ." was all he could squeeze out.

"What's wrong? You don't look so hot."

"Help me," he rasped, easing back into the front seat. "Call 911."

"No, I don't think so."

His vision was blurred. Nothing made sense. "I'm sick."

"Glad you finally admit it."

When he looked to the side, the sight that met his eyes caused him to jerk away.

"Bye bye, Noah. Rot in hell."

2

Seven Days Earlier

On the flight home from Denver, Fi began to make a list of everything she had to do to catch up at work. Her return to the theater after a week away would undoubtedly be filled with all the problems she'd left behind when she and Annie had gone on a hiking trip to the Colorado Rockies. It was their one-year-anniversary present to each other. Marriage was a dream come true for both of them, the point in a romance novel where the girl gets the girl and they both walk off into the sunset together, happily ever after.

Living beyond that sunset was what they were about now. Fi had never been happier, and she felt she could say the same for Annie. Still, when the magical glow that erased all flaws and made everything seem possible began to fade, as it inevitably did, the negotiations that typified the day to day of relationships revealed a far more nuanced and often difficult reality.

A case in point: Annie never wanted to talk about her past. For three years, ever since they'd first begun to date, Fi would press a little whenever a conversation would stray in that direction, trying to assemble a clearer picture of the puzzle. All she got for her efforts were short comments about the death of Annie's mother, and her father not taking it well when Annie had come out to him. He was apparently politically conservative, though not particularly religious. When Fi broached the idea of getting in touch with him, just to see if his attitude had thawed, Annie shut the conversation down. She told Fi, with a sudden intensity and coldness Fi had never seen in the love of her life before, to mind her own business. And that was the end of that.

A group of Boy Scouts streamed down the jet bridge toward them as Fi and Annie made their way to the baggage area. Just before they reached the elevators toward the front of the terminal, Fi's cell phone pinged inside her backpack.

Annie heard it and smiled, shaking her head. "And so it begins," she said a little wistfully. "We're back."

"Can't live in the mountains forever."

"No, but sometimes I wish the Internet had never been invented."

"Would you really want that?"

"Probably not."

Fi had turned on her cell as they were waiting in line to get off the plane. She'd heard a seemingly endless series of barks and pings, alerting her that she had messages and voice mails. She hadn't checked any of them. One of the reasons she and Annie had decided to vacation at this particular lodge was because of its remoteness. Neither wanted any of their normal daily distractions. The point was to spend time with each other. As they'd driven down out of the mountains, they'd agreed to leave their phones off until they returned to the Twin Cities in an effort to prolong the quiet cocoon as long as possible.

5

Pressing the phone to her ear, Fi listened to the message from her friend, Roxy DeCastro, whose voice fairly bubbled with excitement.

"Where the hell are you? I've been calling
for hours. Look . . . umm, something's come up.
Talk to me before you go home. And
don't blow me off. This is important. You're
going to be . . . amazed. Stunned. Totally blown
away. I can't take all the credit, but I can
sure as hell take some. But you need a heads-up.
This is seriously awesome. Call me!"

"What?" asked Annie, pulling her rolling briefcase onto the escalator as they glided down to the lower level.

"Roxy."

Annie rolled her eyes. Roxy wasn't one of her favorite people.

"I have to call her. Something's up. She's hyperventilating."

"When isn't she hyperventilating?"

Roxy had worked with Fi as a production assistant on several plays, which was how they'd met. The reason they'd become friends had more to do with one theater rat recognizing and generally appreciating another. Roxy's theatrical pedigree wasn't quite as stellar as Fiona's, who'd graduated at the age of twenty-two with a major in theater arts from Barnard, and had worked behind-the-scenes theater jobs in New York until, at age twenty-seven, she'd left to come to Minnesota to take a position as an assistant stage manager at the Allen Grimby Repertory Theater in Saint Paul.

Annie would never entirely understand Fi and Roxy's devo-

6

tion—their obsession, really—with all things theatrical, and therefore she had a hard time understanding why the two of them remained close. Roxy was loud and aggressively heterosexual; a woman who, on more than one occasion, had been accused of failing to keep all her mental oars in the water. On the other hand, she was also fun, clever, and willing to push boundaries—all things Fi admired.

"Something's up," said Fiona, stopping next to a section of chairs and sitting down. "Would you mind getting our bags from the carousel? I need to call her back."

"Can't it wait?"

"She says it's important, that we need to connect before we go home."

"She probably burned the house down. Accidentally, of course. Or maybe she sublet it for the summer."

"Come on, Annie."

More eye rolling. "All right. Tell her we need to ease back into our normal lives, which means, if she's planning on coming over tonight to welcome us back with a bucket of greasy KFC and a twelve-pack, tell her thanks, but no thanks."

"Be nice."

Annie walked off, leaving her rolling briefcase next to Fi. Three rings later, Roxy's voice burst through the phone line.

"Thank God. Where are you?"

"At the airport. We're getting our bags. Where are you?"

"At your house."

"Why?"

"Look, Fi. I need to give you a heads-up. I wish I could see your face when I tell you this. I mean, it's such incredible news. See, when you and Annie get back, you're going to be met by a

7

few reporters. There's even a TV van out there. I invited the man from *The Advocate* to go sit by the pool. Figured we should act especially nice around him."

"*The Advocate*? As in the magazine?"

"Cool, right?"

"Roxy, tell me why there are reporters at my door."

"Because I told them you'd be back this afternoon."

"Why."

"Because of the video."

Fi's frustration was building. "What video?"

"Well, I mean, it's gone way beyond YouTube now. You have to understand, it might have been my idea to put the thing together, but I wasn't the one who created it, or posted it. But now that it's up, it's nothing short of awesome."

Fi glanced over to the carousel and saw Annie watching her. She smiled, gave a thumbs-up. "What's on this video, Roxy?"

"O-M-G, the guy from *The Advocate* nearly fell in the pool. I gotta get out there."

"Don't leave me hanging. Roxy? I mean it."

"I'll meet you when you get home. Honestly, this is so cool. Chill."

The phone disconnected. Fi immediately phoned back, but the call went through to voice mail. She glanced up as Annie came toward her with the bags.

"What's wrong?" asked Annie.

"I'm not sure." Since Fi didn't actually know anything, and because Roxy was at the center of whatever was going on, she decided to play it down. "We'll find out soon enough when we get back to the house."

"We still have a house?"

8

Fi stood and slipped her arm around Annie's waist. She could always find Annie in a crowd because of her platinum-blond boy crop and her height—almost five ten, four inches taller than Fi. At the moment, Annie's hair was covered by the baseball cap she'd bought in Boulder. "I love you."

"You're changing the subject."

"Let's go get our car."

"Another subject change."

"And on the way home, I think we should stop for ice cream."

"You must seriously not want to tell me what's going on to resort to ice cream."

Picking up one of the bags, Fi started for the exit. "I'm in the mood for chocolate-almond fudge. How about you?"

An hour later, Fiona turned her VW Beetle onto Birchwood Trail.

"Why are there strangers milling around on our front lawn?" asked Annie, finishing the last of her cone. "Hey, is that a WCCO van parked across the street? What the—"

Fi pulled into a wide, daylily-lined drive next to a midcentury modern home. All midcentury modern houses looked like boringly designed bank buildings to her. Since her father owned the place and had offered it to them free of charge, she had very little reason to grouse. As she cut the engine, Roxy, dressed in her usual bib overalls and clogs, was out the front door, rushing toward them. Her hair was covered by a navy-blue bandana. "You made it," she called, smiling almost maniacally, eyes darting to the side as two men advanced on the car. Roxy held up her hand and nodded for them to wait.

"Explain," said Annie, as Roxy slid into the backseat and shut the door.

Before she could respond, one of the men tapped on the driver's side window and said, "We're here to interview you two about the video."

Annie twisted around and nailed Roxy with her eyes. "What video? What's he talking about?"

Motioning aggressively for the guy to back off, Roxy lowered her voice and said, "Okay, look. This is so cool. It all started because I asked everyone who came to the Christmas party—those who took video of Fiona's marriage proposal on their cell phones—to give me what they had. Leo put it all together with some clips of the wedding, made it into this amazing anniversary gift. He sent it to a few of us to get our reactions and we all loved it. We were going to present it to you as an anniversary gift when you got back. I don't actually know who put it up on the Internet, but it's all good. Jeez, don't look so grim, Annie. You two are rock stars. I will say, it started kind of slow. But by last Wednesday, it was getting over a hundred thousand hits a day. Today, it hit a million. You've got your own hashtag on Twitter—#Fiona&AnnieLove. You're a huge presence on Instagram. The video is rocketing all over Facebook. I don't know what's considered viral these days, but it shows no sign of stopping. Coming on the heels of the supreme court decision, it's just what the LGBT community needs."

Fi had to admit, she thought it was exciting.

"Just talk to them," said Roxy. "The reporter from *The Advocate* is still back by the pool. FYI, your personal Facebook page, Fi—it's overflowing. I couldn't find yours, Annie."

"That's because I don't have a Facebook page."

"Well, then, your Twitter account—"

"I don't tweet."

10

"Whatever. You do have to admit that this is great news." Roxy's round face was flushed with excitement.

Annie continued to stare daggers at her. "How did they get our personal information? Who told them where we lived?"

"How does anybody get anything these days? You can find pretty much whatever you want on the Internet."

Turning just as the WCCO van's door slid open, Annie covered her face. "They've got video cameras. This can't be happening."

"Annie?" said Fi, touching her arm, not sure why she was having such a negative reaction. "I think we should talk to them."

Annie opened her door and took off, making straight for the house. Reporters rushed up to her, plying her with questions, but she never said a word as she entered the house and slammed the door behind her.

"That went well," said Roxy, her shoulders drooping. "Talk about a buzzkill."

The less people knew about you, the better. That had been Sharif Berry's guiding principle ever since the summer he turned fourteen, the year his life changed forever. Up until then, he'd been a trusting kid who'd hero-worshiped his older brother, Cleavon, and his older brother's friends. Trust was something that was hard to come by these days, which meant he wasn't exactly a master at maintaining intimate relationships.

Sharif had met his current girlfriend, Tamika Wilson, a couple months after he was hired as the new football coach at Whitney High, the largest high school in Hammond, Ohio. Tamika was on the school board, a young woman with a determined glint in her eyes and a desire to climb the administrative ladder. Sharif must have seemed like an intriguing addition to the teaching staff because of his recent NFL history. He'd managed to get drafted by the Minnesota Vikings right out of Boston College, though he'd only lasted a couple of years before being cut by the team. Still, the patina of athletic fame had attached to him and he wasn't above using it.

Sharif was a six foot five dark-skinned twenty-nine-year-old, in perfect physical shape and, according to his oldest and best friend, Annie Johnson, had a smile that could melt ice from a football field away. Sharif's father was African American, born and raised in Houston, and his mother was from Pakistan, a semi-devout Muslim, whose parents had moved to Berkeley, California, when she was eleven. Sharif had been raised a Muslim, though he didn't consider himself religious. He figured that at some point in his life, he might regret his spiritual ambivalence, but because he was so busy and his days were so full, he had no interest in making any changes.

The coaching position he'd accepted required him to teach tenth-grade civics first semester and social studies second, which meant he had to attend faculty meetings regularly. Tamika had been at the first meeting and raised her eyebrows ever so slightly when he walked into the room. He'd noticed her right back. By the end of the following week, they were dating. Sharif always figured he'd end up as a high school coach. He'd never been particularly driven. Unlike Tamika, there were no professional ladders he wanted to climb. All he asked was a quiet life in a quiet town—for bigots, racists, and small-minded assholes to leave him the hell alone and let him live in peace. Hammond, Ohio, seemed like as good a place as any to put down roots. The only problem was, the baggage he carried around inside him didn't always coexist well with the quiet he craved.

On a hot late June afternoon, with Tamika in his kitchen making lunch, Sharif dug through a shelf in the garage, looking for his leather suitcase. He was leaving the next day, taking his motorcycle up to the Twin Cities to spend a week or so with Annie and her wife of one year, Fiona McGuy. He'd asked Tamika if she wanted to come along, and was disappointed when she said she couldn't get away. It was possible he'd done something to upset her, but if he had, he didn't have a clue what it was.

What irked most of Sharif's girlfriends had been his "emotional unavailability." He refused to count the number of times those words had been hurled at him in the heat of an argument. The thing was, he'd been trying unusually hard with Tamika. Not that he was about to spew his guts for anyone—ever. If what he offered wasn't good enough, well . . . take it or leave it. It pissed him off when girlfriends made him feel like he wasn't living up to their standards.

As he spied his bag on the shelf behind a couple of boxes, Tamika opened the door from the kitchen and called his name.

"What?" he replied, noticing with some disgust that a crack in the ceiling had allowed water to leak onto a couple of the boxes. "Damn it all," he said under his breath. The reason he'd bought a newer home was so he wouldn't have to put up with this sort of crap.

"Come in here," said Tamika.

"Can't it wait?"

"No. It can't." She sounded upset.

He glanced over at the door, hoping to glean something from the look on her face, but she'd already gone inside.

Now what? he thought, climbing back down the ladder. When he entered the kitchen, he saw that she wasn't there. Two ham-and-cheese sandwiches sat on the cutting board, ready to eat. Next to the cutting board were a bag of potato chips and a freshly made pitcher of lemonade. The sight of the food made his stomach growl. "Where are you?" he called.

"In the bedroom."

Wiping cobwebs and dust off his hands with a wet paper towel, he crossed into the living room, then into a rear hallway. As he came into the bedroom, he saw that she was standing by his dresser, one of the lower drawers pulled all the way out. His immediate thought was, What the hell are you doing messing with my stuff? And then he realized what she'd found.

"Explain," she said, hands on her hips.

"You mean the handgun?"

"What's it doing in your drawer?"

What did she think it was doing? The question was stupid. "Sleeping," he said, cracking a smile. "Or maybe it's hibernating."

"You never told me you owned a gun."

"You never asked."

"Stop it, Sharif. This is serious. You're a teacher. A role model. You have no business with a gun in your house."

A wave of heat crept up his neck. "I disagree. In civics class, I teach my students that we have the right to keep and bear arms. In case you've forgotten, it's called the second amendment."

"I don't care if it's legal. It's wrong. You know how I feel about guns. My brother was shot to death in the street outside our house in Flint."

"What's that got to do with me owning a piece? I didn't shoot him. I don't belong to a gang."

She shoved the drawer shut with her foot. "I refuse to co-exist in a house with a gun."

"Tamika, come on."

"I mean it. They're ugly. Dangerous. Why do you need one? I don't get it."

It was none of her business. "Honey, please. Let's go have lunch. Those sandwiches you made look great."

15

She folded her arms over her chest and stood her ground. "You have to choose, Sharif. It's either me or that gun."

"Are you kidding me?" He looked around his bedroom, calculating all the changes she'd made in the last year. New pillows. A new down comforter. A series of photographs she'd taken on a trip they'd made to Boston. She'd framed and hung them above the bed—pictures he didn't even like. Then there were the matching lamps and nightstands. What the hell did he care about matching anything? He'd bought the stuff to make her happy, to help her feel welcome in his home—in his bed.

"Well?"

He ordered himself to speak calmly and softly. "I think you're being unreasonable."

"Whether I am or whether I'm not is beside the point. It's how I feel. It's not going to change."

Count to ten, he told himself, but before he mentally got to five, he blurted out, "I'm not choosing the gun, but I'm not getting rid of it either."

"Then I guess your decision is pretty clear." The fierceness in her eyes was immediately replaced by hurt.

"I care about you. We've got something good going here. I don't want you to leave."

"I thought we were soul mates," she said, wiping tears off her cheeks.

He didn't believe in soul mates. "No matter how much I care about you, it will never be enough, will it." It wasn't a question, just a statement of fact. "You'll always find something wrong with me, something I either can't or won't change. No matter how hard I try, you're eventually going to walk away. I thought you were different, but you're just like every other woman I've ever dated."

Tamika uncrossed her arms and lowered them to her sides. "Maybe I am, Sharif. Or maybe . . . just maybe, I'm not the problem. Maybe the problem's inside you."

After Tamika took off, Sharif poured himself a bourbon and water. Consuming alcohol on an empty stomach wasn't really his thing, but at the moment, it seemed like the right move. He sat down at the kitchen island and gazed around at all the modern amenities everyone said he should have: stainless-steel appliances, granite countertops, the most expensive coffeemaker. What the hell good was all this crap when he had nobody to share it with? He wondered if he should call Tamika, tell her he'd get rid of the revolver. But that seemed like giving in, like becoming his old man. No way was he going to repeat that pattern.

After downing both ham sandwiches and half a bag of chips, he returned to the garage. He climbed the ladder once again, but instead of reaching for his bag, he pulled the box that had received the most water damage off the shelf, lifting it down onto a workbench. Dragging over a stool, he sat down and opened the top, curious what might be inside. He'd hauled a ton of boxes around with him through his various moves—from Boston to Minneapolis to Chicago, and now to Hammond. If he'd been a more organized person, he would have gone through the contents and tossed out what he no longer wanted. Instead, he spent his free time pumping iron at the gym, or riding his motorcycle, which meant he was healthy but surrounded by organized chaos.

Inside the box he discovered a couple of old Boston College T-shirts stuffed down next to a second box. He removed one of the shirts and held it up, wondering if he could wash the moldy smell out of it. Opening the smaller box, he found more moldy clothing, this time a pair of women's sneakers and green mesh shorts. The contents had to belong to Annie. He must have somehow packed up some of her stuff while he was packing his own.

Under the shorts he found a wire-bound notebook. As he picked it up, a page slipped free and fell to the garage floor. Sharif scooped it up and was about to replace it when his name, written in Annie's feathery script, caught his eye. He read silently:

Just know this: If Sharif hadn't opened his door to me, I'm not sure what I would have done, where I would have gone. Boston is as good a place to hide as any. It's cold, which I hate, so I've stayed in the apartment and watched TV. For months, it was all I seemed to be good for. Right away I started playing with the idea of stepping out in front of a bus. But then I thought, What if I was maimed instead of killed? God, that would be the worst. I'd be at your mercy. Sharif would try to help, but you would surely step in and then my life would really be over.

His head snapped up. The idea that Annie had been considering suicide while she'd been staying at his apartment both surprised and appalled him. Sure, he knew she'd been in a bad place. Right before she knocked on his door that late September day, she'd been in Northern California, attending her sister's wedding. He'd invited her to move into his spare bedroom because to do anything else, especially when she seemed so depressed, even desperate—was unthinkable. All she would say was that her family hadn't taken it well when she'd come out to them. Sharif didn't press her about it. He figured that if she wanted to talk, she would. She told him she just needed a little time to regroup, but ended up staying in his spare bedroom for almost two years, until he moved to Minnesota. As it turned out, she moved right along with him.

Gazing down at the pages in his hand, a wave of guilt washed over him. This notebook was undoubtedly private. He had no business reading it. And yet he couldn't help himself. Even if he convinced himself to repack it in the box and put the box away, he'd eventually come back out to get it. Maybe not tonight, but another night. He figured he might as well give in and bring it inside. Thanks to Tamika, his dance card, for the foreseeable future, was entirely free.

4

A thunderstorm broke over Eden Prairie just after midnight. Fi and Annie sat on the shag rug in their darkened living room, backs propped against the couch, each reading e-mails on their laptops and occasionally looking out through the long glass wall as a flash of lightning illuminated the center atrium and part of the front yard.

"Maybe we should go to the basement," said Fi. "The storm's getting worse."

A crack of thunder rumbled overhead.

"Let's give it another few minutes," said Annie, glancing at Fi over her reading glasses.

This was their favorite spot from which to view storms moving through the Minnesota River Valley. They had a ritual. They would turn off all the lights. Fi would pour herself a glass of wine. Annie would crack a can of Diet Pepsi. Annie didn't drink anymore, mainly because she said it made her do stupid things. They weren't entirely heedless of the danger presented by the weather. If a tornado was in the area, they would retreat to the basement, but until the rafters started to shudder, they both enjoyed watching the storm.

The sound of heavy rain hitting the skylights formed a percussive backdrop to the otherwise silent house.

"It feels like a metaphor," said Annie.

"What does?"

"The storm."

Fi didn't understand Annie's level of hostility about the video. They'd watched it together after Roxy took off. Fi found herself crying at the end, deeply moved, while Annie sat next to her, rigid as a block of cement. Sure, the fallout might not all be positive. Fi had read some of the posts on her Facebook page. The majority had been expressions of love and support, though definitely not all. The comments below the video on YouTube were less favorable. Some were even outright abusive. And yet it was all in a good cause. They'd be okay. Interest in the video would blow over soon enough and they could go on with their normal lives. In the meantime, Fi had agreed to do a couple of interviews. What was the harm?

Even though she felt she had a more balanced perspective on the matter, she was still worried about Annie. She'd followed her inside after Roxy's revelation in the car, only to find that Annie had gone into their bedroom and locked the door. When Fi knocked, Annie shouted "Get rid of those people. Do it now. That includes Roxy."

Fiona talked briefly with the reporters, gave a few statements of surprise and made a couple of dates to discuss the video in more detail after she'd seen it. She'd walked everyone to their cars or vans and thanked them for their interest. She didn't invite Roxy inside. Standing in the driveway, she peppered her with questions.

Roxy was obviously distressed by Annie's negative reaction, but mostly she was annoyed. It was her opinion that the more interviews Fi and Annie gave, the better the outcome would be. She kept insisting that it was unbelievably perfect timing. All the news outlets were talking about the Supreme Court's decision on gay marriage. Fiona and Annie put a beautiful, young, sexy, romantic face on the issue. What could be bad about that?

At the moment, Fi felt like a ball ricocheting between Roxy's optimism and Annie's anger. "So," she said, taking a sip of wine as the wind blew hard against the tree branches outside the windows. "You think we're in for a bad storm in our lives."

"Like I said. The perfect metaphor."

Fiona thought about it. "I'm sorry," she said finally.

"Why? It's not your fault."

It was hard not to feel a little guilty. Fi had been the one who'd made the decision to propose to Annie at that Christmas party a year and a half ago in front of all their friends. Right around Thanksgiving that year, Fiona had begun to sense that Annie's feelings might be cooling toward her. The thought scared her so much that it caused her act on an idea she'd been toying with for months. She had no doubt that Annie was the one for her. Her plans came together in a matter of days. She had a good singing voice and a grand piano in her living room. And she had the perfect song. It was a gamble. She would be laying her feelings out there with no guarantee that Annie would reciprocate. She practiced the song over and over. Roxy suggested that half a dozen friends, all members of a local women's chorus—Calliope—could enter into the living room on the

22

second verse, holding candles and doing backup vocals. Fi wasn't sure, but after practicing it together just once, hearing the results, she was thrilled. She had no idea that Roxy had gone one step further. Behind the scenes, she'd encouraged everyone with a cell phone to record the proposal. Thank God Annie, in the end, had said yes.

"I know you're upset," continued Fiona, covering Annie's hand with her own. "Is there something you're not telling me?"

Annie gazed out the windows at the rain-swept darkness.

"We'll get through it. The interest in the video will eventually die down. That only stands to reason. People will move on to something else."

"Not if you give a bunch of interviews."

"I promise, I'll only give two."

Annie withdrew her hand. "If you give two interviews and then stop, it'll just mean they'll chase you harder. And next they'll want to talk to me."

"Would that be so terrible?"

"Yes."

"Then just say no."

"Thank you, Nancy Reagan. What if they track me to school—or to where I work? What do I do then?"

Annie was in her second year of law school at William Mitchell in Saint Paul. She worked as a part-time paralegal for Justice House Minnesota.

"I don't want strangers knowing my business," said Annie. "Digging into my past."

Ah, thought Fi. The light finally dawned. Here was the most likely reason for Annie's outsized reaction. She was afraid the video might encourage some eager reporter to delve into her personal life—perhaps into the family she never wanted to talk about. And, of course, that made Fi wonder all the more what she had to hide.

"We need to shut down our e-mail accounts," said Annie. "Set up new ones through a different service."

"Okay," said Fi, thinking it sounded like a lot of work. As always, she wanted to talk about Annie's family, but knew, with Annie's emotions rubbed so raw, that this wasn't the time. When was it ever the right time?

Annie set her laptop aside as another bolt of lightning lit up the night sky. "Hey, did you see that? I think someone's standing in our front yard."

Fi scrambled to her feet. When another streak of lightning burst across the sky, she spotted a tall, bulky figure wearing a dark hoodie standing by the lilac bushes. He appeared to be staring at the house.

"Who is that?" asked Annie, a quaver in her voice. "What's he doing out there?"

"I have no idea." But she was sure as hell going to find out.

"You're not going out to talk to him."

"If he doesn't mind getting wet, neither do I."

"But he could be dangerous."

Fi was fed up. Rushing to the front door, she charged out into the night. "Hey," she yelled, scraping rain from her eyes. She was instantly drenched. If anything, the storm seemed to be getting worse "You there. This is private property."

The man darted to his left, then raced toward a pine tree, gesturing wildly. Between cracks of thunder, she heard him shouting. "Baxter, come. Come here, boy! Baxter you little idiot, get over here right now."

"Phil?" she called. "Is that you?" Phil Banks owned the white colonial across the street. He was a fat basset hound of a man, a recently retired bank executive, and a friendly, generally quiet neighbor.

When he turned toward her, his face was filled with anguish. "Fi. Oh, God. I opened the front door and Baxter ran out."

Baxter was Phil's miniature schnauzer and, from what she could tell, the love of his life as well as the bane of his existence. Lately, the dog seemed to run away fairly frequently.

"I think he may have gone under the boughs of your pine tree," he said, pulling his hood more tightly around his face. "I'm going to skin him alive when I find him."

Feeling relieved that the man in the hoodie wasn't some shambling member of the Walking Dead, Fi joined him in his search. It took another few minutes, but they finally found the dog back at Phil's house, hiding under a wheelbarrow in the backyard. By then, the rain had begun to subside.

"Come here, you miserable little runt," said Phil, dropping to his knees and cradling the dog in his arms.

Fi turned as Annie came up and stood next to her.

"Everything okay?" asked Annie. She clicked on a flashlight. "When I realized it was you in our yard, Phil, I figured your pooch was on the loose again."

"I was terrified he'd get hit by lightning," said Phil. Still holding the dog, he struggled to his feet. Nervous energy poured off him in waves.

Fi had helped him find Baxter before, though she'd never seen him this unhinged.

"I better get the little guy inside and dry him off. Wouldn't want him to catch a cold."

"Call us if you need anything," said Fi.

"You two all right? I saw a bunch of people milling around your house this afternoon."

"We're fine," said Fi, slipping her hand through Annie's.

"That's good. I noticed that there was a van that had 'WCCO' printed on the side. Probably had to do with that video, yeah? Have to say, I really enjoyed it."

Fi squeezed Annie's hand. "Our fifteen minutes of fame," she said lightly, tugging Annie back toward their house.

"Well, thanks again. Night, ladies."

As they made their way back across the street, Fi heard Annie swear under her breath.

"I'm going to personally strangle Roxy with my bare hands," Annie muttered, adding more loudly, "and I'm going to enjoy every minute of it."

5

"So, Janey, not to pry, but are you still seeing that therapist?" A satisfied smile spread over Cordelia's face as she eased lower into the water and turned the jets up to high.

Jane glanced over at her friend, took in her black bathing suit, the pearl necklace and matching earrings. Cordelia believed one should dress for the spa.

"Comfortable?" asked Jane.

"Very."

"Can I get you anything else? More black cherry soda? Another Fudgsicle?"

"No, no. I'm good."

Last March, Jane had contracted with a local company to build a patio enclosure on top of a concrete slab attached to her garage. Once it was complete, she bought a hot tub and had it installed. She filled the remaining space with comfortably padded teak chairs, a chaise lounge, and a small wet bar. She'd been advised by her therapist that hot tubs were good ways to relax and unwind. Cordelia, her oldest and best friend, immediately began to take advantage of the tub—more often than Jane might have liked.

Jane owned a restaurant in south Minneapolis, the Lyme House. She was also a licensed PI—a part-time investigator who generally only took cases that interested her. On the surface, the two professions didn't seem like they'd mesh, and yet they represented two essential aspects of who she was—passions that made her want to get up in the morning. The problem had come last winter when she'd been in Wisconsin working a case. She'd been attacked in the woods and had come away with a concussion and bad case of posttraumatic amnesia. It marked the beginning of significant problems at the restaurant, mainly because she'd taken so much time off to recover. She was now paying the price.

"You know, Cordelia, you live in a mansion."

"I do. Actually, I've decided to call it Thorn Hall."

"How Downton Abby–esque. Why don't you put in your own hot tub?"

"Not to bring up unpleasantries, but it's my sister's house, not mine."

"Does Octavia have something against hot water?"

"No, of course not, but where would we put it? Our only real outdoor space is the rose garden."

"I'm sure the roses would be happy to make room."

Cordelia lifted her toes out of the water and wiggled them. "But Janey, that would mean I'd have to share."

What did Cordelia think Jane was doing? "Your sister's gone most of the time—jetting off to Monaco, Belize, or Beverly Hills, in search of her next husband. What number would he be?"

"Fourteen? Fifteen? You know, she said to me last week that, somewhere out there, there was a boy in grade school who will be just perfect for her when she hits her sixties."

Jane groaned, turning on the tub's blue lights.

"This is so peaceful. I love this tub."

A faint breeze tinkled the wind chimes on the back porch. Jane's dogs, Mouse and Gimlet, were asleep in the grass. Gimlet, a little black poodle, was hard of hearing, but Mouse, a large brown lab, was an excellent watchdog with a deep, menacing growl. Jane always made sure they were outside when she was in the tub.

"You didn't answer my question," said Cordelia, picking up her can of black cherry soda and languidly taking a sip. "About the therapist."

"Yes, I'm still seeing her."

"And?"

"I'm making progress."

"I should see a therapist. I'm terribly overworked these days."

Cordelia's newest venture was the development of a theater in downtown Minneapolis, the Thorn Lester Playhouse. She was part-owner and artistic director. The first show had completed its eight-week run last weekend.

"So you're sleeping better?" asked Cordelia. "No more nightmares?"

"Who doesn't have an occasional nightmare?"

Jane's memory had eventually returned after the beating she'd taken in Wisconsin, though the attack had left her with some difficult emotional repercussions. A low-grade depression had gripped her for months. Sometimes it seemed better, other times worse, but it had never entirely gone away. Jane's temper was much shorter these days. She easily lost patience with people and situations that wouldn't have caused even a slight rise in her blood pressure before the incident.

Hearing the back gate scrape open, Jane sat up. Mouse must have heard it, too, because he was instantly up and barking.

"Jane," came a tentative voice. "Are you out here? It's Fiona McGuy. Please don't eat me, Mouse. I thought we were buddies."

Gimlet began twirling, more excited than wary.

"Hi, doggies," came Fiona's voice.

Over the din, Cordelia called, "If it isn't my missing stage manager. Jane and I are lounging in the hot tub. Join us. The more the merrier."

Fi pushed her way through the screened door. "Don't you two look comfortable," she said, grinning. She was dressed in a red tank top and tan roll-up shorts. Her dark spiky hair looked spikier than normal. "I rang the front doorbell, but nobody answered. I saw Cordelia's convertible out front, so I figured you were out here." She carried a file folder.

"How was the vacation?" asked Cordelia.

"Good. Not long enough. I actually came to speak with you, Jane."

"Loved that video," said Cordelia. "Sent the link to friends all over the world."

"I have to say I watched it several times, too," said Jane. "There was something addictive about it. I'm curious why you chose that particular song?" Fiona had sung "You Must Love Me" from the movie version of the musical Evita. "It's so sad, so full of longing."

Fi perched at the edge of the chaise. "To be honest, right around that time, I was pretty desperate. It seemed to me that Annie might be pulling away. The song said what I needed her to hear."

"Gives me shivers," said Cordelia. "It's gone viral, right?"

"So I'm told."

"It's a triumph," she continued, adjusting her pearls over her impressive décolletage. "Probably did more good for the LGBTQ community than anything I can think of. Well, except for the actual Supreme Court ruling."

"Not sure I'd go that far," said Fiona, her gaze nervously roaming the backyard.

"Something wrong?" asked Jane.

"I'm just a little jumpy. We've received a lot of positive feedback since we got home, but it's not all good." Returning her attention to Jane, she said, "Do you think we could talk? I promise, I'll only take a few minutes of your time."

"Don't mind me," said Cordelia. "Having the hot tub all to myself is fine by me."

Me, too, thought Jane, rising out of the water. She grabbed her white terrycloth robe and slipped it on, then led the way back to the house, telling Mouse and Gimlet to lie back down. It was going on eleven, kind of late for a visit. Fi, like Cordelia, was a creature of the night and likely knew that Jane was, too.

Back in her study, Jane relaxed into a tired old leather desk chair as Fi set the file folder in front of her. "What am I looking at?" asked Jane, slipping on her reading glasses and opening the cover. "Something to do with the video?"

"Actually, no."

Cordelia chose that moment to appear in the doorway. She leaned her plus-sized figure, covered in a midnight-blue silk robe, against the door frame and delicately dipped a spoon into a pint of Ben & Jerry's Coffee Toffee Bar Crunch. "I got lonely out there." Her auburn tresses had been haphazardly piled on top of her head and secured with a couple of red lacquered chopsticks.

"What am I missing?" she asked, hiding her eager interest behind a studied nonchalance.

Fi seemed unsure whether or not to proceed with her employer listening in.

"Cordelia," said Jane, clearing her throat. "I think Fi may need some privacy on this one."

"No, it's all right," said Fi. Glancing up at Cordelia, taking in her significant girth and nearly six foot height, she added, "You might as well hear this. It might have some connection to the theater."

Cordelia raised an eyebrow, intoning a portentous, "Go on."

"A few months ago, I started receiving notes from someone who, I initially assumed, worked at the theater. They were all printed in black ink on a page torn from a yellow legal pad and sent through the mail in a nondescript white envelope with my name and the theater's address on the front. No return address. All postmarked Minneapolis. At first, I wasn't sure what to make of them. The words were flattering. Several said I was doing a great job as stage manager."

"How were the notes signed?" asked Jane.

"Take a look." Fi nodded to the folder.

Jane skimmed the first note and then read out loud, " 'XXX and a Full-Body O.' "

"Yuck," said Cordelia, her face puckering. "No name?"

"No," said Fi. "All the notes have been signed exactly that way. It took a few weeks for the content to become more personal. You can find those comments highlighted in blue."

Jane flipped to the third page. Halfway down, she read:

I HOPE YOU KNOW HOW BEAUTIFUL
YOU ARE. DROOLINGLY BEAUTIFUL, IF

THAT'S A WORD. LOL. I'M NOT
LAUGHING AT YOU, JUST THAT YOU MIGHT
NOT REALIZE.

Moving to the next highlighted section, Jane continued:

I WISH WE COULD GET TOGETHER
SOME NIGHT, HAVE A DRINK. YES, I
KNOW YOU'RE IN A RELATIONSHIP, BUT
WHAT THE HELL? JUST SEEING YOU MAKES
ME HAPPY. THE WAY YOU SMELL. IS
THAT PERFUME OR JUST YOUR NATURAL SCENT?

Another loud "yuck" from Cordelia.

Jane noted six more notes, all with blue highlights. She skimmed the contents until she came to this:

I THINK ABOUT YOU ALL THE TIME. YOUR
SEXY BODY, YOUR BREASTS, THE GRACEFUL
WAY YOU MOVE YOUR HANDS, YOUR DARK
GLOSSY HAIR. YOU'RE PERFECT TO ME.
PERFECT <u>FOR</u> ME. THE WAY YOU LOOK
INTO MY EYES, YOU MUST SEE THAT, TOO.
YOU'RE TOO GOOD FOR ANNIE. IF IT WEREN'T
FOR HER, I COULD COME OUT FROM THE SHADOWS
AND WE COULD BE TOGETHER. I SUPPOSE
I SHOULD STOP THINKING THIS WAY BECAUSE
YOU'RE MARRIED. ANNIE HAS NO IDEA HOW
LUCKY SHE IS. SOMETIMES IT MAKES ME
ANGRY.

33

"That's certainly an escalation," said Jane.

"The final note came to the house a few days before we left on vacation," said Fi. "It was dropped into our mail slot. No stamp this time."

The note was short, to the point.

WE HAVE TO TALK. I'VE HAD A REVELATION.
THIS WILL CHANGE EVERYTHING FOR YOU AND
ME!
XXX AND A FULL-BODY O

Moving into the room, Cordelia sat down on the love seat next to Fiona. "Here's a question," she said, raising a finger. "Are the notes written by a man or a woman? It doesn't really indicate, right? What's your gut say, Fi?"

"From the beginning I assumed it was a man. But . . . I mean, I guess it could be a woman."

"Nobody's been acting strangely around you?" asked Jane.

"That's the thing. I haven't noticed anything unusual. You'd think I would, because, apparently, this guy—or woman—is someone who is physically near me on occasion."

"If you worked with a stalker," said Jane, "yes, I would assume you would have noticed some odd behavior. That leads me to think you don't work with this person. Either that, or they're a very good actor."

"She spends her life in a theater, Janey," said Cordelia, bugging out her eyes. "Duh."

"I need to be more observant," said Fi. "I didn't think this was a big deal at first, but I'm beginning to think it might turn into a big deal if this person gets tired of worshiping me from afar and won't leave me alone."

"Next question," said Cordelia, licking the last hunk of ice cream off her spoon. "What's the intention here? The endgame? Is this nutcase planning to do something to make his or her dream come true?"

"Oh, God," said Fiona, wrapping her arms protectively around her stomach.

"Do you have a security system at your home?" asked Jane. "Security cameras outside?"

Fiona shook her head.

"Might be something you'd want to consider."

"My dad owns the house," said Fiona. "He bought it because he likes having a place away from New York where he can come and kick back and be totally invisible. He also thought it would be a good place for me to live cheaply while I'm working in the Twin Cities. He knows I don't make much as a stage manager."

In a tightly compressed voice, Cordelia said, "We pay industry standards."

"I'm not bitching about wages," said Fi. "It's just, it isn't a lot to live on. And Annie's in law school, so she only works part time. But I can talk to my dad about it. In the meantime, Jane, how do you think I should handle it if I receive more notes? What if he demands a response from me?"

Jane closed the folder and gave it some thought. "In situations like this, it's best not to engage in any way. That just fuels the fire. For the moment, I'd suggest giving it some time. If you ignore the letters, it's possible the writer will get bored and go away."

"I hope you're right."

"Beyond that, I'd be careful when I'm out and about. You need to be extra vigilant. Don't put yourself in a situation where you're alone, especially after dark. He hasn't threatened you. He's been inappropriate, but it doesn't seem like he has any intent to harm you. Save all the notes. You might want to report them to the police. If you have a question or a concern, call me. I'll do whatever I can to help." This was no small offer on Jane's part. She'd resolutely decided not to take on any new cases because of all the problems at her restaurant. If the Lyme House was going to thrive, it would need her full attention until certain issues could be resolved.

Fi rose and reached for Jane's hand. "Thanks so much. Just to know I'm not alone—"

"You're not," said Cordelia. "I'm here for you, too."

"I'll be at the theater first thing tomorrow," said Fiona, tucking the file folder under her arm. "Don't worry, I won't let this affect my work."

"See that it doesn't," said Cordelia, glowering, and then smiling.

ANNIE'S NOTEBOOK
Letter #1

I have to write about it. My sister's wedding. From the fog of memory, I want to draw out something concrete, a document I can hold in my hands and say, yes, that's it. That's what happened. It will not only be my truth, but the truth. Ultimately, I guess, I'm hoping that if I put my story down on paper, I'll be able to find some strategy, some approach, that will allow me to crawl away from the wreckage that night made of my life. The past is no place to live, but I can't move on until I examine what happened.

So, do I perform this exorcism backward or forward? Do I start with today, or with that night? Since I need a structure, I've decided to write a series of letters. If I sent them, they'd simply get tossed in the trash, right? Maybe I'll risk it. Maybe I won't.

Dear . . . no! To Whom It May Concern: (That's a warm way to begin.)

I'm sitting in a coffee shop on a busy street in Boston. No reason to tell you exactly where I am because you wouldn't be interested in that sort of detail. I happen to prefer this one particular table. It's way in the back, away from the din of conversations. I want to be with people and at the same time be alone. This is only the third time I've left Sharif's apartment since I've been here—and I've been in Boston for almost a year. If my special table is occupied, I leave. Crazy Annie, right? I can hear you saying the words. Another one of Annie's overreactions.

Just know this: If Sharif hadn't opened his door to me, I'm not sure what I would have done, where I would have gone. Boston is as good a place to hide as any. It's cold, which I hate, so I've stayed in the apartment and watched TV. For months, it was all I seemed to be good for. Right away I started playing with the idea of stepping out in front of a bus. But then I thought, what if I was maimed instead of killed? God, that would be the worst. I'd be at your mercy. Sharif would try to help, but you would surely step in and then my life would really be over.

How do I start? I guess with this: I hate you. There, I said it. More than anything else, you are why I left home—left school, left my job and my friends—the reason I was so emotionally devastated that I disappeared, fell off the earth. You have no idea that I'm living with Sharif—if "living" is the right word. That's the way I want it. I swore him to secrecy. Not that you've tried to find me. I don't want to talk to any of you, and yet I can't believe you'd just let me go. I trusted you, believed with all my heart that you'd understand—that you'd stand with me. Instead, like always, you put Bridget first. You didn't want me wrecking her big night—those were your exact words. You accused me of trying to sabotage her happiness. How could you misunderstand so totally? I wake in the middle of night now and realize I've been screaming at you in my dreams. I come to you for help and you tell me I've had too much to drink and to go sleep it off. You yell at me to grow the hell up. Well, I have grown the hell up in the last year. I hope that pleases you. Since I did what you asked, you're going to do what I ask. Every goddamn letter I write you're going to read. Don't think you can skim either.

You better study hard because there will be a test at the end of this exercise to determine your grasp of the essential elements. Anything less than an A will be considered a failing grade.

Good luck.

6

Fi spent the following day at the Thorn Lester Playhouse, work-ing overtime to catch up. The theater's second production, a social satire set during a symposium attended by world-famous psychics and mediums, would go up in early September and run through the end of October. Fiona had read the script multiple times, loved it, and had organized the initial audi-tions to take place two weeks before she left for Colorado. As with the first play, Cordelia had convinced two highly acclaimed actors, one American, one British, to play the lead roles.

Unfortunately, Fi had missed the first production meeting, where the set designer presented his initial sketches. Cordelia had apparently approved his ideas because, when Fi entered her cluttered office just after eight, she found blueprints with floor plans and elevations on her desk. She studied them with inter-est until she was interrupted by Charlotte Osborne, one of two PAs working on the new show.

Production assistants were considered the bottom rung of the theatrical ladder. They were generally young, full of energy, enthusiasm, and ambition, willing to do pretty much anything asked of them because they'd finally gotten their foot in the metaphorical door and wanted to make the most of it. Charlotte fit the description, although she was a talker and didn't seem to comprehend that she wasted a lot of time on pointless bullshit, or on sharing personal information that Fi had no interest in knowing. Stage management required superior interpersonal skills—the ability to listen, to show compassion and offer understanding, and yet Fi had learned early on that her job did not include caretaking or rescuing. Charlotte seemed to want both.

"Morning, boss," said Charlotte, slipping into one of the folding chairs in front of Fi's desk. "Whatcha looking at?"

"Have you made coffee yet?"

"Yup. Want a cup? I know just how you like it. One sugar, extra cream."

"Please."

On her way back into the room a few minutes later, Charlotte asked, "Did you and Annie have a nice vacation?" She set the mug in front of Fiona, then sat back down on the chair, tugging her too-tight blouse away from her ample breasts. Except for an overlarge upper lip, which made her look a little like Homer Simpson, she was reasonably attractive.

"It was too short."

"My mother hassled me every day while you were gone."

"Oh?"

"She wants grandchildren, can't understand why I'm not dating. I told her I don't have the time. That's when she started in on my wardrobe again. You know what she's like. How I need to dress better, spend more time exercising so I can lose weight. I mean, what do you think of a mother who's constantly telling

40

her daughter she's not good enough? I'd move out if I could. But then who'd take care of her? Did I mention she's in a wheel-chair?"

"Charlotte—"

"Is your mom like that with you? I bet you have really nice parents. Sometimes I wonder if I've got bad karma. But then I remember that I was chosen for my dream job with my dream boss, so it can't be all bad."

"I need to study these blueprints. You probably should get to work."

She went quiet, played with a button on her blouse. "It's great to have you back, you know. I missed you."

Fiona searched Charlotte's doll-like blue eyes. "You did?"

"You're a lot more organized than Roxy."

She didn't doubt that. Still, the statement left her wondering. Could Charlotte be her stalker? The idea struck her as ludicrous.

"You're my mentor," chirped Charlotte. "I admire you—probably more than anyone I've ever known."

"Are you buttering me up for some particular reason?"

"No, of course not." She seemed hurt.

"Have you finished making copies of the new script?"

"All done."

"The preproduction list I gave you?"

"I'm making good progress."

"So, better get busy." She returned her attention to the blue-prints. When Charlotte didn't leave, Fi asked, "Is there some-thing else?"

"Um, no. Well, I mean . . . yeah. I guess I just wanted to tell you how much I loved that video. Glen posted it on his Face-book page. That's where I saw it."

41

Glen Whittier was the other PA, a recent graduate from Minnesota State University, Mankato, with a BFA in theater. Fiona found him less overtly enthusiastic—and certainly less talkative—than Charlotte.

"Who knew you were so talented?" said Charlotte, her gaze roaming the room. "You should be on stage, not behind the scenes."

"Thanks. But no thanks."

"No, really. If you recorded a CD, I'd for sure buy it."

"I'm flattered."

"Okay," said Charlotte, tugging absently at the ends of her lank brown hair. "I guess I'll go. See you later." With a smirk, she added, "Alligator."

Fi covered her wince with a thin-lipped smile.

As assistant stage manager, Roxy had called the final few days of the first show while Fi had been out of town. From the note Cordelia had left next to Fi's phone, she'd done a good job. Roxy had also handled the last of the callbacks. Fiona now had a list of all the actors who would be offered a role in the next production. Thus, her morning was mapped out for her. She loved this part of her job—giving actors the news they'd been praying for. She wished she had the time to call back everyone who'd auditioned and offer a word of encouragement to those who hadn't made the cut, but she already felt like she was deep in the weeds. She had to prioritize.

A meeting with the production secretary went long that afternoon, and so Fiona didn't return home until close to seven. She'd stopped at the Lunds & Byerlys in Richfield to pick up an assortment of cheeses, crackers, and cold cuts. Every Monday

42

night, Annie's study group met at the house, even during the summer when they didn't have classes. They usually had lots of food around. Tonight, however, because neither of them had gone to the grocery store, the larder was bare.

While walking around the store, Fiona had the creepy sensation that other customers were sneaking looks at her. A few made eye contact for just a tad too long. Some had probably seen the video and recognized her. It was also likely that Fiona was seeing behavior that wasn't actually there. Whatever the case, she was relieved to return to her car and get back on the freeway.

After preparing a tray of munchies, Fi entered the living room, only to find that Annie and her two study companions had ordered a pizza.

"You're welcome to a slice," said Annie, glancing up from her notes.

Fi walked around the coffee table to give her a kiss on the cheek. "Anything new I should know about?" she asked, sotto voce.

Annie shrugged. "More e-mails and phone calls. Saw a few people driving by taking pictures of the house. Two older women were on the other side of the street, trying to see inside. Someone sent a bouquet of flowers. I opened the card, but it wasn't a name I recognized. Oh, and Phil's dog got out again. I'm not sure why he always makes a beeline for *our* front yard when Baxter goes AWOL."

"Did you talk to him?"

"No, just saw him standing by the pine tree, calling for the dog."

"I should leave you all in peace," said Fi, turning to smile at the burly young man and the rail-thin honey-haired young woman sitting in the matching Wassily chairs. Both had a kind of preoccupied intensity that Fi found attractive. "Study hard."

When she returned to the kitchen, the landline was ringing. Fi had considered calling her father to ask about installing a security system, but because he was in London at the moment, working with the creative staff at the Barbican on Benedict Cumberbatch's upcoming Hamlet, she decided not to bother him. She scooped the cordless off the island and checked the caller ID. It was a number she didn't recognize, which meant she probably shouldn't answer it. Sitting down on one of the stools, she tossed caution to the wind and said, "Hello?"

"Fi, is that you? It's Sharif."

"Hey, my man," she said, breathing out her relief. "Where are you? You're still coming, right?"

"Something's come up," said Sharif. "I won't be able to get out of here until late tomorrow."

"Just as long as you'll be here soon."

"Oh, you bet I will. I was planning to ride my Harley. Found out I needed a part that the store didn't stock. With luck, I'll be out of here in the morning. Will anybody be around on Wednesday afternoon?"

"I'll be at the theater," said Fi. "Not sure what Annie's day looks like. I'd ask her, but her study group is here. I've already interrupted her once. You know what she's like when she's interrupted."

"No problem. If nobody's at the house, I'll figure something out. Still got plenty of friends in the Twin Cities. You doing okay?"

"I've been better."

"Want to talk about it?"

She gave him a few of the details about the video and the dizzying number of vicious comments that seemed to be proliferating on YouTube. "A friend suggested we install a security system."

"Crap, I'll help. In case you've forgotten, I'm imposing as hell. I'd be happy to camp out by the front door, run any assholes that show up off your property. In fact, I'd enjoy it. I worked as a bouncer at an upscale bar in Boston when I was in college. People take one look at this awesome black brother and if they know what's good for them, they run like hell."

"I can't ask you to do that."

"You're not asking. I'm offering. I like hitting people. What can I say? So, is Annie okay?"

Annie was always his primary concern. The love between them was deep. Fi had to admit she was a bit jealous—not that she begrudged them any part of their relationship, just that she wished she had the same kind of unconditional love from an old friend in her life. "Annie's good. She's excited to see you."

"Give her a squeeze from me."

"Will do."

"Anyway, I'm about to head over to a local steakhouse. Don't want to deal with any leftovers if I actually get out of here tomorrow."

Fi wished him a good dinner and a safe ride. For the next few minutes, she busied herself putting the cheese and cold cuts away in the refrigerator. Once the kitchen was clean, she poured herself a shot of tequila. She was on her way to her study when she passed by the bathroom. Out came the thin young law student. Her first name was Deb. Fi couldn't remember her last.

45

Discovering Fiona in the hallway, Deb seemed startled. "Oh, it's you. Hi."

"Hi," responded Fiona.

"Um, I, ah . . . like your haircut." She twirled her finger. "Like that shaggy look."

"Thanks."

"Did I ever tell you how much I, like, enjoy being in this house? Midcentury modern is my favorite."

"We call it 'City Hall Moderne.'"

The woman didn't smile. "Makes my apartment seem pretty crummy."

"I've spent a lot of time living in crummy apartments."

"That's hard to believe."

"I was in college once, too."

Staring deep into Fi's eyes, Deb said, "Maybe you're not so different from me."

"Ah, right. Well, I better get going. Lots to do."

"Yeah." Deb's eyes dropped to the shot glass. "Time to kick back?"

"I've got enough work to keep me busy twenty-four-seven for the next month."

"Huh." She didn't move, just kept staring at Fi.

"You better get back to your study group."

"They won't care if I don't come back right away."

"But you might miss something important."

"Well, yeah, you make a good point. Hope I see you later."

Before Fi had talked to Jane, she hadn't noticed anyone acting strangely around her. Now everybody seemed suspicious.

Instead of going straight to her study, Fi decided to check the mail. If Annie had already brought in a bouquet of flowers, it was possible she'd taken the mail in as well. Sure enough, a half-filled box sat on the floor under the console table in the front foyer. Every day the mail seemed to be growing. Just to make sure nothing had been missed, Fi opened the closet door and checked the mail slot. Inside was a single envelope with Fiona's name printed on the front. No address. No stamp. No return address.

Fi downed the tequila shot to steady herself. She set the empty glass on the console table and walked back to her study, where she sat down behind her desk. This letter, clearly from the person she now thought of as "the stalker," seemed thicker than the others. Opening it, she found that it was three pages long. It appeared to have been written in an excited state, with some words or phrases underlined, others capitalized. She skimmed it, but read more slowly as she reached the final page.

I CAN'T HOLD MY FEELINGS IN ANY LONGER.
OH YOU ARE AN ANGEL. YOUR
VOICE ON THE VIDEO, YOUR BEAUTIFUL
VOICE AND PIANO PLAYING. I AM CERTAIN
YOU WERE <u>PLAYING JUST FOR ME</u>. HERE'S
WHAT I'VE COME TO SEE. ANNIE
GOT IT ALL WRONG, AND THEN YOU—OH SO
KIND AS ALWAYS—WENT THROUGH WITH
THE WEDDING. I KNOW YOU DON'T
WANT TO <u>HURT HER</u>. SHE DIDN'T UNDERSTAND
THAT YOU WERE SINGING TO ME!!!!!!!!!!!!
<u>THAT VIDEO HAS MOVED ME DEEPLY.</u>
FIONA, MY ONLY TRUE LOVE.
I'VE BEEN LONELY ALL MY LIFE. I'VE

HAD A FEW RELATIONSHIPS, BUT I WAS
BADLY TREATED. I WON'T GO INTO DETAILS.
<u>WOMEN CAN BE SO SELFISH, SO COLD
AND UNCARING!!!!!</u>. NOT YOU. NEVER
YOU!! YOU'VE SUFFERED. YOU'VE HURT.
IT WAS WRONG OF YOU TO MARRY ANNIE, BUT
I <u>FORGIVE YOU</u>. I KNOW YOU'RE DIFFERENT.
I CAN SEE INTO YOUR HEART.
WE ARE THE PERFECT COUPLE. <u>I KNOW
THAT NOW BEYOND ALL DOUBT!!!!!!!!!</u>
XXX AND A FULL-BODY O

"He's crazy," whispered Fi, closing her eyes, dropping the pages as if they were radioactive. She'd been counting on the guy getting tired of writing her, and yet the opposite seemed to be happening.

Fi hadn't mentioned any of these letters to Annie. She'd been hoping they'd go away and she wouldn't have to. The video had trained a spotlight on their lives, and yet these letters predated that and might turn out to be a more serious problem. What unsettled Fi the most was that she had no idea where the stalker was going with all this talk of undying devotion. Did he—or she—actually think Fi would leave Annie?

Opening her laptop, she tried hard to switch gears. She had so much work to do, and yet instead of getting down to business, she opened her Facebook page and discovered she had been "liked" by over 22,000 people. Could this be real? She ignored her main page and went directly to messages, where she clicked on "Filtered." These were people who weren't friends, but who had nevertheless left her a note. She scrolled through a seemingly endless array of new comments, all posted today, and all about the video.

While many of the comments were positive, even laudatory, she wasn't able to take the abuse for more than a couple minutes. She moved to YouTube to make sure the video had been taken down. Roxy had texted her around noon to say that Leo had removed it. But there it was. She typed in "Fiona Loves Annie"—the name that had somehow been given to it—and found over a dozen sites where she could view it. She even found a parody, which she watched in horrified silence. It was so mean, so crude and cruel, it made her nauseous. Is this what people were like when they could remain anonymous? Scrolling down, she began reading the comments under the parody, which ranged from disgusting to outright threats.

Social media, thought Fiona, that darling of the twenty-first century, was turning out to be nothing but a sinkhole. Whoever had first posted the video—and Fi had a sneaking suspicion that Roxy had pushed Leo to do it—had opened up a Pandora's box of hurt. The only way to get away from it was to shut down her computer—or toss it in the trash—and then return to that idyllic lodge in the Colorado Rockies, plug her ears, cover her eyes, and pray that the world would leave her alone.

Not exactly an option.

7

After a fine steak dinner at his favorite restaurant in Hammond, Sharif found himself in a philosophical mood. Watching a pretty waitress move from table to table, coffeepot in hand, his thoughts turned to Annie and what the next few days would bring. He'd read through her notebook and now understood what he never had before. Some journeys in life took you far from where you started. Some brought you closer to where you came from. He felt certain that his trip back to Minnesota was the latter kind of journey.

Sharif had first met Annie when they were sophomores together in an unfamiliar high school. The summer after Sharif's mother had divorced his father, he'd moved with her from Berkeley to Pasadena. That same summer, Annie and her family had moved down from Bakersfield. Their outsider status during those early fall days had somehow thrown them together. Not knowing where to sit in the lunchroom, they'd drifted to the same table. They talked haltingly at first, but quickly became not only friends, but confidants.

A big black kid with an angry chip on his shoulder, something he hid behind a cocky attitude and wide grin, two years older than everyone else at the school, and a tall, willowy, towheaded girl, a straight-A student with wire-rimmed glasses and a serious demeanor, on the face of it, didn't seem like a good match. But they were. They were like two halves of a coin. Athletics had always been Sharif's claim to fame. Football, basketball, baseball, track. He stood out from the pack in every one of them. Annie was a brain. Down to earth, and yet intellectual. They had vastly different personal styles and strengths, and yet what they held in common were the essentials: a dream they each wanted to pursue and a willingness to work hard to make that dream come true.

By senior year, Annie had decided on premed. Sharif, thanks to the encouragement and intervention of his high school football coach, had been offered an athletic scholarship to Boston College. What kept them close, however, had nothing to do with any of that. He understood it now in a way he hadn't before. The truth was, evil had come creeping into each of their lives, and nothing, not the air they breathed nor the world they thought they knew, had ever been the same again.

Back at his house, sitting propped against several pillows on the bed, his laptop open in front of him, Sharif brought up the YouTube video. He'd already watched it many times, though after talking to Fi, he wanted to see it again. He'd never imagined it would cause such a stir. Sure, he knew firsthand about bigotry. What black guy with an Islamic first name didn't? If he'd thought about the possibility of Fi's proposal going viral for more than a few seconds, he might have seen it coming.

The video opened with a single camera shot of Fiona's vibrant Irish-American face, her shiny black hair, her cheeks brushed with even more color than usual. The living room was darkened. Perhaps it was a Gaelic trait, but somehow Fi managed to smile, look worried, and appear sad all at the same time. As the camera backed away, the viewer saw that she was seated at a grand piano, several dozen people crowded around, all holding candles, a tall, fair-haired young woman standing directly to her left. The camera shots now cut in from a multitude of angles. Whoever had put the video together had linked different cell phone shots, creating a sometimes jumpy, sometimes lingering view of the scene.

Gazing up at Annie, Fiona began to play. The sound quality was amazingly good. It was an unusual song to pick for what turned out to be Fiona's proposal of marriage to Annie—that is, until you realized that the words captured perfectly the strain that had crept into their relationship. All had not been right with them for more than a month.

During the bridge, which Fiona played without singing, a group of women entered and stood behind her, humming the song, their voices swelling as Fi began the last verse. Sharif had listened to Madonna's video of the same song on YouTube. He liked her voice well enough, though he thought Fi's version totally hit the ball out of the park. Her tone was a bit lower, less breathy and more resonant. When she sang, "You *must* love me," as the song ended, there wasn't a dry eye in the room. Reaching for the tiny box she'd set next to her on the piano bench, Fiona looked up at Annie with uncertain eyes. "Will you marry me?" she asked.

She handed Annie the box.

Annie must have known something was up, though perhaps she never imagined that it was this. It was, after all, a Christmas party. Opening the box, she took out the ring. She didn't say anything for several seconds. It felt like hours to Sharif, so it must have felt like an eternity to Fiona.

Annie's eyes traveled around the room until they finally alighted on Fi. "Yes," she said simply, as if the issue had never been in doubt. They kissed, held each other. Everyone clapped.

At that point, the video cut to a clip of the wedding, to the vows they made to each other the following July. After they'd both said their piece, they held hands and, in unison said the words from a movie, words that meant so much to them, "Through life, past death, and into the hands of God."

Maybe he was a sap, but even after seeing it many times, tears streamed down his face. He wanted so desperately to believe that kind of love existed in the world. Others must have felt the same way. It was why the video had caught on so quickly. What compelled people to watch again and again was the love. It broke down barriers because it was real and raw and true.

Tomorrow, Sharif would head up to the Twin Cities to help his friends celebrate their first anniversary. Nothing and nobody was going to get in the way of that. It was a promise he made to himself. And to them.

8

Entangled in each other's arms, Fi and Annie woke the following morning to the sound of thumping on the roof of their house.

"What on earth is that?" groaned Annie, pulling away from Fi and sitting up.

"Sounds like someone's walking around up there."

"Doing what?" Still half asleep, she rubbed her eyes.

Fi threw on her bathrobe and went out into the living room. Her attention was immediately drawn to one of the skylights, where three unfamiliar young men were peering down at her, grinning and waving. "Good grief," she whispered. "Get the hell off of my roof," she yelled.

"What's going on?" asked Annie as she shuffled into the room. She hadn't bothered to put on a robe. She should have, because she always slept in the nude. "Oh, my God," she cried. Seeing the smiling faces, she rushed back to the bedroom. "Call the police."

Fiona stormed out the front door, ready to give the men a piece of her mind. She was stopped by the sight of a group of women who had assembled on the front lawn. Seeing Fi, they began singing, "Over the Rainbow." The woman who was more or less directing the makeshift choir, turned and smiled at Fi. "We love you," she called. "You and Annie are our heroes!"

Neighbors began coming out of their houses to see what was going on. Phil came out of his colonial with Baxter and walked to the curb.

The young men climbed down a ladder they'd propped against the side of the house. "Hey, Fiona," they called, still grinning and waving. "We are *such* fans." The tallest of the three, said, "I'm Gary. This is my partner, Michael." He nodded to the redheaded man standing next to him. "That's Joel. His partner got called in to work this morning, so he couldn't come."

"Really," was all Fi could manage.

"Yeah. Nearly broke his heart. He loves you and Annie so much. I told him we'd take pictures."

"You took pictures of us through the skylight?"

"No, but I was hoping we could all get photos with you two before we leave. We want to put them up on our Facebook pages."

The choir switched to another old highly esteemed gay spiritual: "True Colors" by Cyndi Lauper.

This is a zoo, thought Fi. These people are nuts.

Annie emerged from the front door, dressed in a black tank top and green combat fatigues, her short blond boy crop twisting in every direction. Making a shooing motion, she yelled, "Get the hell out of here. If you're not gone in one minute, I'm calling the police."

The choir members didn't seem to hear, but the three men did. Their faces registered shock. "No, see, you don't understand," said the redhead. "We're here because we're your friends. We support you."

"How can you be my friends if I've never laid eyes on you before?" shouted Annie. "Do you think we *like* people crawling around on our roof? Are you total morons?"

The tallest guy stepped in front of the redhead. "Look—"

"No, you look," said Fi. "Your intentions may be good, but this isn't the way to show support."

"Get out of here," shouted Annie. "All of you. *Now.*"

Phil and his dog strolled across the street. "Can I help in any way?" he called.

Annie went back into the house and slammed the door.

Fi walked over to the choir director. "You all need to leave. You're upsetting the neighbors."

"I wouldn't think you'd care about them," said the woman, readjusting her rainbow scarf. "They're not gay, are they?"

"What's that got to do with anything?"

"We're all lesbians—members of your tribe—and we're here because we're in awe of what you've done for us. We felt we needed to give something back."

Lowering her voice, Fi said, "I do care about my neighbors. This is where I live, do you get that? I appreciate the sentiment, but I need you to leave."

"But we have three more songs—"

"Please," said Fi.

Members of the choir began to surround her. Some reached out to touch her, one tried to give her a kiss on the cheek. Another threw a heavy arm over her shoulder and pulled her close.

"Group hug!" cried a forty-something woman wearing a rainbow tie-dyed T-shirt.

Fiona backed away and ran for the house. This wasn't a zoo, it was a nightmare. Standing on the steps, she called, "Thank you all. Loved the songs. But it's time for you to leave."

"Did we come too early?" called a woman in a yellow, broad-brimmed sun hat.

"Yeah," said Fi. "It's too early."

"We want pictures," called a woman in the back of the group. She held up her cell phone. Others chimed in, holding their phones above their heads. Some were already taking pictures.

"Another time," Fi called back. She escaped into the house and locked the door behind her. When she turned around, Annie stood glaring at her.

"Those people have left the planet," Annie said.

"They think they know us because they watched the video."

"This was an invasion."

"The irony is," said Fi, "they're on our side."

"I need caffeine," said Annie.

Fi felt more like a shot of tequila. Not the best way to start the day.

9

Cordelia had been more than generous in offering Nolan & Law-less Investigations a corner office in the theater annex, a wing of the Thorn Lester Playhouse. Jane usually stopped in once a week to check the mail and finish writing any outstanding reports. Since she hadn't come by in over a month, and because Nolan was off on a road trip with his neighbor and girlfriend and wouldn't be back until the middle of August, she felt she needed to make a quick visit.

Jane was so immersed in reading a thank-you note from a married couple she'd helped last summer that she failed to notice Cordelia standing in her doorway. That is, until Cordelia snapped her gum.

"I thought I saw your Mini out in the back lot," Cordelia said.

Looking up, Jane found her friend, dressed in an ankle-length vest over a print tunic and black leggings, a gold chain belt hanging just below her waist, with a curious piece of white fluff on her head. "What's that? A new hat?"

"It's Wally," said Cordelia, moving carefully and stiffly into the room, looking like a child with a book on her head being taught correct posture. "Our new theater cat. He's Iranian."

"You mean Persian." When Wally raised his head, Jane could see that his eyes were as bright as copper pennies. "Does he always sit on your head?"

"You don't think it's a good look for me?"

"He's cute. But . . . I mean, what's he doing?" The cat was licking Cordelia's head, occasionally running his paw over her hair.

"He's grooming me." She patted him, then intoned in her deepest voice, "Oh, Wally. Wally."

"Doesn't he get your hair wet?"

"Yeah, it's kind of gross. I can only stand it for a few minutes. But, you know, it gives him a purpose in life."

"That's good. All cats need a purpose."

"FYI, he doesn't get along with our ghost cat."

Jane was amazed that Cordelia continued to maintain that the theater was home to a feline spook. Cordelia also believed that one-time owners of the theater, Gilbert and Hilda King, still walked the halls, arguing with each other. But that was how Cordelia's mind worked. She often quoted Shakespeare, " 'There are more things in heaven and earth, Horatio, than are dreamt of in your philosophy.' " Jane could hardly disagree with Cordelia *and* Hamlet.

"Have you heard anything more from Fiona?" asked Cordelia, disentangling the cat from her hair. She tried to cradle him in her arms, but he wiggled free and jumped to the floor, zipping out the door just as Fiona was coming in.

"Did I hear someone mention my name?" she asked. "Am I interrupting anything important?"

"Of course not," said Jane.

Cordelia spent a moment fluffing the part of her hair that Wally had flattened with his spit.

"Anything new from the stalker?" asked Jane.

Fi took the chair next to Cordelia. "He thinks that video is really about him—not Annie. That Annie misunderstood and, because I'm unquestionably kind, I married her out of pity."

"Goodness," said Cordelia, fanning air into her face.

"But he forgives me. It was wrong of me to marry Annie when I was really in love with him."

"Or her," said Cordelia. "All pronouns are not equal."

"Actually," said Fiona. "I'm not here because of those notes. It's the video. I mean, it's all getting so tangled. In addition to the vile Internet comments, we're starting to receive threatening e-mails. I thought we could take the air out of the tire by removing the video from YouTube. Leo took it down, but there are copies popping up all over the place. It's everywhere. The Supreme Court ruling is the generality and we're the specifics."

"I'm so very sorry that this is happening to you and Annie," said Jane.

Fi explained about the young gay men on the roof of their house and the lesbian choir serenading them from their front lawn. "These people identified themselves as friends—fans. Fans! I know they didn't mean to upset us, but they did. Annie and I feel like we're living in an alternate universe. We just want it to stop."

Tapping a finger against her chin, Cordelia asked, "What kind of threats?"

"Oh, God," said Fi, crossing her arms. "Well, a bunch of different men said they wanted to screw our brains out. Sex with a real man was the only thing that would straighten us out. Several guys threatened outright rape, mainly as payback for being perverts. One said that we might not know when, but he's going to get to both of us. Just a matter of time. Another said he had a cell in his basement just waiting for *me*. Once he got done carving up my face, nobody—not even Annie—would want anything to do with me ever again."

"Lord," said Jane under her breath.

"Some preached at us, said that if we repented, gave our lives over to God, married a good Christian man and had his children, that we would be forgiven. If we didn't forsake our depravity, we'd find out the true meaning of pain. One guy said he wanted to take Annie out into the woods near his farm and use her for target practice. That's all she was good for. Another asked me if I'd ever considered what it would feel like for a rope to slowly tighten around my neck. He wanted to hang me from a tree. Said he'd really enjoy watching me choke. I mean, what part of lower hell did these people crawl out of?"

Jane had always known that within some human hearts beat a deep core of malevolence. The trick in life was to keep clear of those people. That was no longer an option for Fi and Annie. "What can I do to help?" she asked, trying to push away the panicked voice shrieking at her that she didn't have the time, that she couldn't take on anything new.

"I was late for work this morning because I printed out a few of the worst e-mail threats and took them to the police. I was told I could file a report, which I did. The cop I talked to said that the report would put the e-mails on record. If anything bad happened, it would help them with the case." Fi's hand trembled as she touched her chin. "Did you get that? *If* anything happened? I couldn't believe it was all the cop could offer. I may not understand all the legalities involved, but I can sure recognize an intent to do harm when I see it. The cop just sat there and kept saying there was nothing more he could do. Based on his general demeanor, I'd say he's not a big supporter of gay rights."

Jane removed her reading glasses, pinched the bridge of her nose. "Doesn't surprise me."

"So, here's my question. Is there anything you can think of that Annie and I should do about the e-mails? A way to handle them? My hope is that they're all hot air. It's easy to be vicious when you can remain anonymous—or in another part of the world. If the man writing the note is in Iowa with a full tank of gas, well, that's something else."

Sitting back, Jane opened her laptop and tapped few keys. "I made friends with a hacker a while ago. She might be able to figure out who sent one or more of those e-mails. Yeah, here she is. I'll contact her, see if she'd be willing to help."

"That would be incredible," said Fi. "I can get you—or her—the e-mail addresses later today."

"That works. As much as you may not want to hear this, you need to take those threats seriously."

Fi lowered her eyes.

"Better to be safe than sorry," said Cordelia. "When the shoe fits . . . sorry." She winced. "This isn't a time for clichés."

"Next," said Jane, "it would be helpful if you printed out all the e-mails threats. You'll likely get more before this is over. Set up individual files for each person, each e-mail address. Print out future e-mails messages as you receive them and put them in the dedicated file. Don't delete any of the e-mails from your computer. They're evidence."

In response, Fi groaned.

"Finally, once again, don't respond to any of them, no matter how much you might want to. Don't threaten these people back."

"Yeah," said Fiona. "I get that. I mean, what exactly would I say to a man who wants to rape or hang me?"

Jane pressed a fist to her mouth, feeling strangely faint. The room grew suddenly airless as everything around her began to spin. It took a few seconds, but she finally realized what was happening. "Will you excuse me for a minute?"

"Sure," said Fiona.

"Something wrong?" asked Cordelia.

"No, no. Be back in a sec."

On the way to the restroom, Jane felt like her brain was flipping through a million TV channels all at once. Pushing through the door, she stood leaning on the sink, her heart pounding so hard she was afraid it might burst through her chest. She struggled to catch her breath. And then, she started to cry. It was always better if she cried. It was over faster. Wiping the tears from her cheeks, she flipped open a prescription bottle and took a pill.

Cordelia chose that moment to rush into the room. "What's wrong? Janey, you're crying."

Jane turned away. "I'm okay."

"No you're not. Did Fiona upset you?"

"Of course not," she said, still trying to catch her breath. "I'm a criminal investigator. I deal with things like this all the time."

"Then . . . what?"

Go away, thought Jane. Please, just give me a minute alone. She squeezed her eyes shut, clenched her teeth and worked to regain control, to slow the world down. "Just go back and sit with Fi. I'll be there in a second."

"I'm not leaving you alone, not when you're like this."

"I'm not like anything. I just need a freakin' minute."

"Well, pardon me for caring."

Jane held up her hand. "Wait," she said. Another few seconds went by. Then a full minute. She was beginning to feel a little better. "Maybe it's a touch of stomach flu."

"Right," said Cordelia, narrowing her eyes as Jane turned toward her. "The stomach flu always makes me cry."

Splashing water into her face, Jane asked Cordelia to hand her a paper towel. Her heart rate was still faster than normal, but it was no longer the out-of-control metronome it had been before.

"If you need to lie down, you can use my office," said Cordelia.

"I'd like to finish up with Fi."

"If you say so."

Jane placed her hand on Cordelia's shoulder. "Thank you."

"You need to see a doctor."

"I'm already seeing multiple doctors."

"I trust you don't include Julia Martinsen in that number. She doesn't count, Janey. And, by the way, if I thought you were actually 'seeing' her instead of just being casual—and I underscore the word 'casual'—friends, I'd lock you in a trunk and throw away the key."

"Your constant trunk threat lacks meaning because you never follow through."

"Next time you're over at Thorn Hall, we should go downstairs, pull out the trunk in question and make sure you fit."

"I'm not seeing Julia, Cordelia. I ended that relationship years ago."

"But she keeps sniffing around. You might have moved on, but I doubt she has. I don't trust her."

"Neither do I. There's nothing to worry about on that front."

As they walked back down the hall, Roxy and a deeply tanned man in a wrinkled gray linen business suit and dark aviator sunglasses came around the corner.

"Cordelia," said Roxy, stopping abruptly. "Ah, hi. I'm looking for Fiona."

"She's in my office," said Jane.

"Hello," said the man, taking off the shades. An expensive-looking digital camera hung from his neck. "I'm Gideon Bell." He removed a couple of business cards from his inner pocket and handed them over. "I'm a reporter for *People* magazine."

Cordelia's eyes fairly glittered as she took his hand in both of hers and shook it warmly, acting as if she'd just met her long-lost brother. "Lovely to meet you. I'm Cordelia Thorn, the creative director of the theater—and the owner."

Roxy seemed equally excited. "Gideon has a layover in the Twin Cities and wants to interview Fiona and Annie."

"Well, come right this way," said Cordelia, leading the parade back to Jane's office.

Jane was relieved that Cordelia's attention had been hijacked by something new and shiny. Once back in her office, she stood by the window and continued to monitor her breathing. Too many deep breaths and she'd begin to feel dizzy. This panic attack had been about as intense as she'd ever experienced. She

65

never entirely understood what sent her down the rabbit hole. Lately, she'd begun to think she was getting better. She hadn't experienced one in almost a month.

Sitting down next to Fi, the *People* reporter delivered his pitch. "I saw your video yesterday," he said. "I knew I had this layover today, so I called the theater from LAX this morning. Roxy was kind enough to phone me back."

Roxy beamed proudly.

"I don't know what to say?" said Fi, clearly at a loss.

"Look, you have to understand, this wouldn't be a feature, just a sidebar. I talked to my editor yesterday afternoon. He's as keen to cover your story as I am. I wish we could offer you more, but we need to jump on this. Maybe down the line, depending—"

"Annie won't agree to any sort of interview," said Fi.

Gideon looked crestfallen. "Okay. I guess I can live with that. As long as you'll talk to me, let me take a few photos."

"You want to do it here?" asked Fi.

"What if you photographed her on stage?" offered Cordelia. "This is, after all, where she works."

"Right," said Gideon. "You're . . . a set designer?"

"Stage manager," said Fi.

"Right. Right. Your father is Brendon McGuy, the Broadway producer. I read all about him on the flight here. Sure, I think doing the interview on stage is a great idea."

"And while we're heading over from the annex, I can give you a little background on the playhouse." Cordelia waited for him to get up, then put her arm around his shoulder and led him out of the room.

"Thanks, Jane," said Fiona. "You've been a big help."

"Keep me posted," said Jane. "And send me those e-mail addresses ASAP so I can pass them along to my friend."

ANNIE'S NOTEBOOK
Letter #2

Dearest Dirtbag:

A new year. A new letter. Lots to celebrate, right? I'm sure Bridget and Noah are still the golden couple, and you still think I'm despicable. You're glad I had the good sense to disappear. Which means the new year changes nothing.

Wanna know a secret? Bridget flew to Boston right after New Year's. I wondered when one of you would figure out where I was and come calling. She came to Sharif's apartment yesterday while I was here at the coffee shop, demanded to know where I was. Like a good soldier, he lied for me, said he had no idea what she was talking about. But Bridget spotted my leather jacket tossed over one of the chairs in the living room, so he was busted and had to come clean.

You're probably not interested, but I'll give you the blow by blow.

Bridget found me sitting at "my" table in the coffeehouse. At first, I couldn't believe she was right there in front of me. I was so excited I burst out of my chair and hugged her. We held each other for a long time. But then, she didn't know I'm a homewrecker. She sat down, took off her gloves. The weather was frigid and her clothes were way too Pasadena to keep her warm. I offered to get her something hot to drink. She seemed kind of

67

nervous, so she got right to the point, like she always does. (I'll do this like I'm writing a novel. Just so you know, it's the complete truth.)

"Why did you leave school?" Bridget asked. "Leave home? Why did you run away and not tell anyone where you'd gone? You never even said good-bye the night of the wedding. I didn't know you'd left until Noah and I got back from our honeymoon."

I sidestepped the question. "Did you have a wonderful time? Santorini, right? Are the sunsets as spectacular as they say? Did you stay in one of those pristine, whitewashed villas?"

Reluctantly, for it wasn't what she'd come to discuss, she did give me a few details. I could see she still glowed when she talked about her husband, her new life. Eventually, she came back to her questions.

"I kind of got into it with Mom and Dad," I said as an explanation.

"I figured as much. But they wouldn't tell me what it was about."

"No?"

"And anyway, what's that got to do with me? I didn't do anything to upset you, did I? Why wouldn't you let me know where you were?"

I gave her that tried-and-true cliché: "It's complicated."

She took my hand. "Please, Annie. Tell me what's wrong."

It was such a broad question I almost laughed. "I'm gay," I said. Her reaction was about what I had expected—like watching a rock hit a windshield in slow motion.

"Are you . . . sure?" she asked.

"Yup," I said. "I like to have sex with women, not men. That's pretty much the definition."

Her lips formed an O, as if she might say something more, but she remained silent. She began to fidget, releasing my hand and taking my napkin, wiping a coffee spill off the table.

"Are you surprised?" I asked.

"Well, yeah," she said. "You'd think I'd know if my sister was gay."

"Not necessarily. You have no idea how blind straight people can be."

That caused a frown, a moment of deep indignation. "You don't look like a lesbian."

"What's a lesbian look like?"

"You know. I don't have to spell it out."

"Ugly? Mannish? Sad? Hostile? I can think of a lot of straight people who fit that definition."

"Don't be obnoxious."

We were off on a tangent that had nothing to do with why I'd actually left. I felt sorry for her because she was so completely in the dark. That's when I wondered if I should tell her the truth. But no, you'll be relieved to hear that I didn't. I couldn't.

At some point in the conversation, Bridget covered her stomach with her hand.

Realizing what the gesture might mean, I asked, "Are you pregnant?"

"Three months. I'm not showing yet."

"Are you . . . happy about it? Is Noah?"

Her eyes shimmered. "Over the moon. Both of us."

As far as I was concerned, that was the end of the conversation. But she wasn't done.

"Do you have . . . a girlfriend?" Saying the last word seemed to cause her physical pain.

"Several." I wasn't seeing anyone. I sure wasn't going to tell her that it had taken me a year to work up the nerve to leave the apartment and walk to a coffeehouse a block away.

"Nobody special?"

"I like to keep my options open." Such a load of bull.

"You know, Annie, there are people who can help you . . . change . . . who you think you are."

"I'm perfectly happy with who I am."

"Then why leave home? Why change your life so radically?"

"Because nobody in my family shares that opinion. I choose to be around people who support me. Think about it: Would you want to spend your life with people who hate your husband, who say he's the scum of the earth and you were a fool for marrying him?"

"Now you're being ridiculous," she said. She asked about school.

I told her I was rethinking my decision to become a doctor. That's true. I've got another profession in mind. And no, I'm not planning on taking up stripping.

Oddly, after a few more minutes, we didn't seem to have much to say to each other.

I told her to go home. To have a safe journey. She asked if she could tell you where I was living. I told her no. If I wanted to get in touch, I would. By the end of the conversation, I was shivering inside. I don't think she saw it, or if she did, she didn't say anything. There was no way she could understand and no way for me to explain it. Certainly not that day. Probably never.

And so she left.

Are you happy? Do you consider me a grown-up now? Did I pass your test?

Fuck you.

10

In late May, Jane had hired an independent stock auditor to do weekly inventories, product by product, and report his findings directly to her. She was beginning to get a picture of where the thefts were occurring. Under normal circumstances, she did her own inventory. She'd structured the restaurant a little differently than most, doing much of the job of general manager herself. She'd created a front-and-back-of-the-house manager position to fit her needs. Because of her health, and the time she'd spent away from the restaurant, she'd been leaving product inventory to this manager. Everything had been fine as long as Brad Young had been in charge. Brad had been personally trained by Jane and had done a fine job for many years. But in early April, he'd left to start his own restaurant in Duluth's Canal Park, and Jane was forced to hire someone quickly to fill the job. Wayne Fossen had looked good on paper, and he talked a good game, but Jane was beginning to see that he was the main reason her bottom line was suffering.

If a restaurant's food and labor costs inched up past 70 percent of gross sales, that restaurant was in deep trouble. Jane had always maintained costs of around 62 percent. She performed random spot checks, especially in the bar, which helped to tighten up stock losses and put employees on notice. Since she'd missed so much time at work, she'd asked Wayne to do the spot checks. He'd also been put in charge, temporarily, of reviewing the weekly profit-and-loss statements. He'd even begun to do some of the ordering. She blamed herself for his lack of training and her lack of monitoring. But before she called him in to talk about the range of problems besetting the restaurant, she had to have a better idea of what those problems were and what, specifically, had caused them in the first place.

Shorty after three, Jane received an e-mail from Fiona with the e-mail addresses and the threatening comments that went with each. She forwarded them to her hacker friend to see what she might be able to figure out. During the dinner rush, the hacker called and left her a message, saying she'd Skype Jane around nine. Feeling exhausted after dealing with a line-cook's temper tantrum, Jane left the restaurant and walked up the hill to her house. She poured herself a glass of iced tea and sat down behind her desk, waiting for the call.

Jane had met Gemini Jorgensen for the first time at the Lake Harriet Band Shell at exactly ten minutes after one in morning. Because her restaurant sat directly across the lake from the park, after a long day, she would often head out along the lake path to get some air. If she had a lot on her mind, she might circle the entire lake, as she had that night.

Gem, as she called herself, had been sitting on the edge of the band shell. When Jane came past, she'd stopped Jane to ask her if she knew the time, which was why Jane remembered exactly when they'd first met. Gem asked another question before she could move on.

"Do you think human beings are actually some kind of virus?"

Jane figured the young woman was either insane, drunk, or a budding philosopher. Or all three.

"I mean, because of the way we live and what we do, do you think we'll destroy the earth?"

Jane sat down on one of the benches.

Gem went on to say that she'd just turned seventeen, was a junior at Washburn High School, though she doubted she'd graduate. Not because of her grades, which were good, but because she saw little point in higher education, so why go to the trouble of graduating.

Jane asked her what she did see a point in.

"Technology."

Gem considered herself a hacker, which she viewed as a necessary and noble profession. There weren't many female hackers, so Gem said she was one "the few, the proud, et cetera." Jane wasn't sure she agreed with the definition. When she said as much, Gem told her that *she* was part of the problem. Jane asked her what the problem was, to which she responded, "People your age. You don't get what's happening. The world's moved on and you didn't even notice." She said governments didn't get it either. Politicians were bought and paid for, useless as change agents. What the world needed was Internet guerrillas—hacktivists—like her. "We're at war and you don't have a clue."

There was something about Gemini that Jane found likable. Maybe it was her extreme friendliness. She had a soft voice and a quick smile. Even her most belligerent pronouncements were delivered with a kind of innocent sweetness. When Gem found out that Jane owned the restaurant across the lake, she started stopping by after school. Jane always made time for her, invited her up to the dining room for something to eat. She enjoyed talking to Gem because she wasn't like anyone Jane had ever met before. Gem always ordered the same thing: ginger cake with a dollop of cream cheese and extra lemon sauce. And a Coke. She never seemed to want any real food. Her attire rarely varied from the standard black jeans, immaculate white cross trainers, and a black hoodie over a pink, blue, or yellow T-shirt.

Now, at eighteen, she'd shaved her brown hair, added some tattoos and a nose ring. She continued to live at home, still refused to wear a watch, even though she had a job at an electronics store by day. By night, she hacked. Gem recently mentioned to Jane—over her usual cake and Coke—that a weird-looking dude in a black business suit had come to her parents' house. The dude professed to be from a covert government agency. He'd given Gem a card with his phone number on it, but nothing else. The agency wanted to hire her to hack for them. Since Jane had never caught Gem in a lie, she tended to believe that this had actually happened. Gem turned the offer down. She didn't think it was ethical to work for a government she otherwise despised. Since they'd become friends, Gem always made a point of telling Jane that if she ever had a problem she could help with, not to hesitate to ask.

As soon as Gem's face burst onto Jane's computer screen, she grinned. "This is totally chill. I'm glad I can do something for you for a change."

Jane smiled back. "Can you see me okay?"

"Yes, Jane," she said, with exaggerated patience. "And I can hear you."

Jane didn't Skype all that often. Maybe Gem was right. She *was* a technological Luddite. "So what did you find out?"

"That your friend's heard from all the usual suspects."

"You know these people?"

"No, but I know the type. If you want actual names and locations, just let me know."

"You found info on all of them?"

"You only sent me thirty-seven addresses."

"I thought that was a lot."

"They're morons. They hide their tracks behind a Yahoo address or the equivalent, like they think that gives them complete anonymity. They've probably never even heard of a proxy server or the deep web. Maybe half a dozen were a little more cagey, but that's not saying much. These people spread their poison all over the net. They're equal opportunity hate-fuckers. They don't like gays, blacks, Latinos, Muslims, Jews, atheists, feminists, socialists, intellectuals, people on welfare, people who believe in evolution, global warming, vegans. The list goes on and on and on. Your friend Fiona should consider herself in good company."

"Who *are* these people?" asked Jane.

"Your next-door neighbor. The guy who waits on you at the convenience store. The woman who cuts your hair. You want specifics?"

"Yes, I guess I do."

"Okay." She stroked her chin and looked to the left. "Muscle Man@bingo.com is a seventy-one-year-old grandmother from Meridian, Nebraska. She's the one who said Annie should be taken out into the woods and used for target practice because that's all she was good for. Then there's Dude55224@gogo.com. He's a fifteen-year-old boy from Mullin, Texas. He was the one who wanted to hang Fiona from a tree and watch her choke. FYI, that kid really hates fat people. He reserves his worst judgments for them."

"Worse than wanting to watch someone choke to death?"

"Oh, yeah. Far worse."

Jane was beginning to feel sick.

"Want more?"

"No, that should do it."

"Here's the deal," said Gem, lifting a can of Coke to her lips and taking a sip. "There are ways to hide if you really mean business. It's ridiculously easy to acquire someone's identity. You can go high tech or low. For instance, you can buy the identity, or steal it yourself. The idea that anything is totally secure is fiction. When I was fifteen, I used to go over to a friend's house after school to play video games. One afternoon, I walked by the kitchen table and right on top of a stack of papers, for anyone to see, was a page with his dad's Social Security number on it, and under that was a bank statement. I could have taken over that guy's life and he would never have seen it coming. That's low tech. Anybody can do it."

"But you didn't."

"I'm just telling you it's simple. Lots of people buy burner phones. Then they go get themselves a prepaid credit card and use the burner phone number and a fake address. Once you have that, you can get yourself an e-mail account that's fairly blind. Someone like me could still find out who the asswipe is, but it's a little more work. Thankfully, none of these people went to that kind of trouble. I guess I figure when someone does, you know they mean business."

Gem was right. This was a new world that Jane didn't understand and didn't really want to. When her front doorbell chimed, Mouse jumped up and began barking. Gimlet started to spin. "Someone's here," said Jane.

"Yeah," said Gem. "I heard the bell."

"Thank you so much."

"Anytime. You be chill, yo. I'll be in touch." Her face disappeared from her screen.

With the dogs racing ahead, Jane went into the foyer and opened the door. Julia Martinsen stood outside, her head down, attending to important business on her cell phone. There were times, when Jane hadn't seen Julia for a while, that she was still struck by how lovely she was—eyebrows tweezed to precise arches, shiny, sleek blond hair and perfect makeup, expensive gray suit that accentuated all her curves. The body remembers, thought Jane, what the brain might like to forget.

Lifting her eyes, Julia said, "I got another ten Ativan for you." Taking one last glance at her phone, she switched it off and slipped it into her pocket. Removing a small plastic bottle from her purse, she handed it over. "If you want, I can get you more by the end of the week."

"Thanks, but this should do it. I don't take them very often. Would you like to come in?"

"I've had a shitty day, Jane. One of the worst ever. I'm not interested in our usual playtime ritual."

"Excuse me?"

"I make a pass, you reject me. I take it in stride. You reject me some more."

"Do you want to talk about your shitty day?"

"Why would I? It's not like you care."

Was this a new tactic? wondered Jane. Julia seemed upset, and at the same time, preoccupied.

"To top it all off, I got stung by a bee as I was leaving the hospital." She examined her index finger, then shook it. "Anyway, that's all I came for. Night." She turned and walked back down the steps.

"Julia?"

She kept going. "What?"

"Thank you."

"Don't mention it." She lifted her hand, waved.

Stepping out onto the front steps, Jane called, "Wait."

Julia stopped.

"Come on. Come inside for a few minutes. We don't have to play games, do we? Seems like you could use a glass of wine. My day hasn't been that great either."

Turning around slowly, Julia said, "Well, I guess one glass with you wouldn't be the end of the world."

"Gee, you'll turn my head with such compliments."

Once they were settled at the kitchen table, wineglasses in hand, Jane again asked Julia if she wanted to talk about her shitty day.

"Not really. You want to talk about yours?"

"Problems at the restaurant."

"Fixable problems?"

"I hope so."

"Care to be more specific?"

"I don't have the steam."

Julie swirled the wine in her glass. "Okay, since we have nothing else to talk about, let me ask you a question: Do you feel indestructible?"

"Me? Hardly."

"I do. I've had my share of physical illnesses, but I've always bounced back, stronger and more determined than ever."

"I admire that about you."

"I doubt you admire anything about me, Jane."

"That's not true."

"Just forget it. I shouldn't have brought the subject up."

Jane wondered what "the subject" was. "Are you saying you no longer feel indestructible?"

"I'm saying . . . things change. We get older."

"Forty-six isn't old."

"It isn't young," said Julia.

"Why are we talking about age?"

"We're not."

"Then what are we talking about?" asked Jane, feeling completely confused.

"Imperfection." She paused, draining half her glass. "Illness."

"Are you sick?"

"Do I look sick?"

Not once in the years they'd been together had Jane ever felt she entirely understood Julia. For one thing, she liked to keep secrets. She also liked to tell lies. Maybe it was a power thing. Or maybe it hurt too much to tell the truth. "You look good. Healthy. Fit."

"Then that's what I am," said Julia, her gaze drifting to some indeterminate point in space. Once again, her thoughts seemed to be somewhere else. "How you look is what you are."

"That's ridiculous."

She smiled, drained the rest of her glass. "Thanks for the drink."

"Are you leaving? So soon?"

"Honestly, Jane, I can feel a pass—or at the very least some indecent remark—about to cross my lips. And then you'd be forced to reject me yet again. That would be the cherry on an already hideous day."

The comment was simply an easy out. And yet, since Julia seemed determined to go, Jane walked her to the door, resisting the urge to give her a friendly hug. "Again, thanks."

Julia paused for a few seconds, studying Jane, a question in her eyes, something that hadn't quite formed itself yet, and then she leaned in and kissed her. "It's easier to ask forgiveness than permission."

"I guess," said Jane, moving back.

"By the way, that wine was awful." She brushed a lock of Jane's hair away from her face. "Bring home something better next time."

11

Jane arrived late to work on Wednesday morning because of a doctor's appointment, which put her behind once again. She'd always believed that she juggled her life pretty well, keeping all the balls in the air—at least most of the time. At the moment, the balls seemed to be flying in every direction, bonking her on the head on their way to the floor.

Last week, her therapist had recommended a holistic doctor, suggesting that this particular man might be able to help Jane regain some of her energy. Thus, shortly after eight, she'd met with him for an hour and a half. She'd come away with a large bill, one her medical insurance wouldn't cover, and a long list of supplements she needed to buy and start taking. He urged her to exercise more, possibly take up yoga or tai chi, consider getting a weekly massage, and of course, get more sleep and begin a daily meditation regimen. He'd also offered her a complimentary list of foods she needed to eat and those she should avoid.

Sitting down behind her desk with a cup of coffee and a slice of buttered Irish soda bread, she noticed that coffee was high on the list of banned substances. So were sugar, wheat, corn, beef and pork, alcohol, all dairy foods, all animal fats, non-organic vegetables and fruits, and anything from the nightshade family—potatoes, tomatoes, peppers. In essence, pretty much everything that made life worth living. As someone who had spent her entire adult life working with food, creating new dishes, loved to eat, the list felt like telling an artist that she could certainly go ahead and continue to paint, but she would, from now on, be restricted to only two colors. What was the point?

Jane pushed the lists away. As she did, she found a Post-it note she'd stuck to her desktop earlier in the week. On it, she'd written: "An independent woman is someone who is in control of her life." Leaning back in her chair and nibbling the soda bread with grim abandon, she contemplated the message. By that yardstick, she was an utter failure. She hated failing—at anything—and yet the harder she concentrated on her health, the closer her business came to going broke. Sure, when everything was in balance, juggling was easy. When the ground kept shifting beneath you, it was an entirely different matter. And that made her think of Fiona and Annie and the stress they were under.

As Jane was finishing up an e-mail to Fi, passing along the information Gem had given her last night, Jane heard a knock on her office door. "It's open," she called.

Tom Riggs, her headwaiter, poked his head into the room. "We still on for the staff meeting tomorrow afternoon?"

"Absolutely."

"Should I set up the small banquet room?"

"Perfect."

He nodded. "Thanks. See you then."

Jane hadn't met with her waitstaff in in a couple of months, assuming that Wayne had it covered. She assumed he had it covered because she'd directed him to freakin' cover it. Again, her failure. She should never assume anything where Wayne was involved. The meetings were vital, a way to keep a finger on the pulse of the restaurant and an opportunity for her staff to vent frustrations and offer suggestions. She'd asked Wayne about it yesterday. He'd snapped his fingers and acted like the monthly meetings had simply slipped his mind.

A Come-to-Jesus Meeting was definitely in Wayne's future. Jane needed to begin looking for another manager ASAP. If she lost her temper and fired him, which was a definite possibility given her current inability to keep her cool, she'd have to take over all his responsibilities for the foreseeable future. She had an assistant manager, but he wasn't up to the task. She wasn't quite sure where, in all her copious free time, she was going to fit in the tai chi, the massage, and the meditation, let alone shopping for all those organic vegetables. Something more to fail at, she figured.

Slipping on her reading glasses, Jane was about to open an e-mail from her accountant when she heard another knock. "Come in," she called, lowering her glasses. When Sharon Stein appeared, Jane stood up and offered the woman a welcoming smile.

"Do you have a minute? I should have called and made an appointment, but I was in the area so I thought I'd take a chance."

"Come in," said Jane. "It's great to see you."

Sharon was a feature writer for *Twin Cities Monthly*, one of the major local magazines. She was a round-faced, middle-aged woman with curly brown hair and a gift for making people feel appreciated and understood. She'd done an extensive article on Jane and the Lyme House for last year's December edition.

"I have a couple of reasons for coming," said Sharon, taking a seat in front of the desk. "First, I'm wondering if I could interest you in judging our 'Young Chef Minnesota' contest. I've already got Jim Metcaff from the Metropolitan Grill and Raif Sallis from Sweet Cheeks on board. We need one more. It would be a great way to promote your restaurant, lots of coverage in the magazine and in the local papers."

Jane could hardly say no. "How much of my time are we talking about?"

"Oh, probably a few interviews, and then the day of the contest. It will have a similar format to *Iron Chef,* only with four chefs working per round. Three rounds. And then a final round to pick the winner."

"Sounds like fun. When would this happen?"

"We're writing the rules right now, but the actual event won't be until September."

"Then count me in."

Sharon seemed pleased. "Wonderful. I'll get more information to you as we develop it. The second reason I wanted to talk to you is because I'm hoping to do a feature article on Fiona Mc-Guy and Annie Johnson, but I can't get either of them to return my calls."

"Doesn't surprise me," said Jane.

"I know Fi works for the Thorn Lester Playhouse and that you and Cordelia are close. I could contact her, but since I'm here, I thought I'd ask if you knew Fiona and Annie."

"I do."

"Is there any way you would feel comfortable contacting them on my behalf? The video of their engagement has made such a huge impact at the magazine."

"That's great to hear," said Jane. "It hasn't been an entirely good experience for them."

Sharon sighed. "I wondered about that. Maybe an extremely positive article would help. I mean, it couldn't hurt."

Jane wished she shared Sharon's sentiments. "Please don't take this the wrong way, but sometimes media attention can feel like being mugged."

"I get it. I do. But . . . would you try to talk to them on my behalf?"

"Of course."

"Tell them I have no desire to be intrusive, or to ask difficult questions, although I would like them to talk about the court's recent ruling, the impact it's had on their lives. That sort of thing. Anyway . . ." She stood, hooking the strap of her purse over her shoulder. "I should let you get back to work. Give Cordelia a hug from me. Love that woman. That new theater of hers is the best thing to happen to downtown Minneapolis in a long time."

"I'm sure she agrees."

"I'll just bet she does," said Sharon, giving Jane a broad wink.

12

Rolling into Eden Prairie that afternoon, Sharif thought back to the time in his life when football had been king, the hunger for fame had been queen, and sex had been his own personal "tree of the knowledge of good and evil."

And now, here he was, an old man of twenty-nine. There were days when he truly did feel old—as his grandfather used to say, "Rode hard and put away wet." He'd only been part of the NFL for two years, part of the time on the practice squad, and yet that didn't mean he'd escaped injury. When you spent your high school years, college days, and then even more time in the NFL slamming yourself into other hard bodies at full speed, nobody came out a winner. Money helped ease the pain, but at Sharif's level, there wasn't even much of that. The experience had at once toughened him up and broken him down. In his opinion, that was the fundamental irony of life.

Sharif was glad to see that Annie's dinged and rusted puke-green Legacy was in the driveway. He wouldn't need to figure out something to do until Annie or Fi got home. Before he reached the sidewalk up to the house, Annie was out the front door, rushing toward him and into his arms.

"God, it's great to see you, girl," he whispered into her ear.

"I missed you," she said, squeezing him hard. "How come you always smell so good?"

"Because I'm full of the sweetness of life. And . . . I've got superb taste in men's cologne."

She backed up, took hold of his hands. "Why do we have to live so far apart?"

"You wanna move to Hammond, Ohio?"

"No. But you could move back here."

Putting his arm around her shoulder, he walked her toward the house. "I'll think about it."

"Seriously?"

"I'm not married to any one place. You know me. I always like a little adventure."

Annie invited him to sit in the living room while she went to the kitchen.

Breathing in the familiar scent of sandalwood incense, he dropped down on the couch. "You still burn that stuff?" he asked as she returned with a longneck beer for him, a can of Diet Pepsi for her, and a bag of his favorite munchies, Snyder's of Hanover Honey Mustard & Onion Pretzel Pieces.

"I'm sure I would have been a flower child if I'd lived in the sixties."

"And I would have had an afro and a hair pick in the back pocket of my bright purple bellbottoms."

The image made Annie laugh. "We would have looked ridiculous."

"I don't know," said Sharif. "I think I'd look great with an afro."

"You think you'd look good with an upturned bowl of spaghetti on your head."

She had a point. He ran a hand over his shaved head.

"The goatee is new. Very badass." Ripping open the bag of pretzels, Annie grabbed a couple and then set the bag down on the coffee table between them.

"All the comforts of home," said Sharif, scooping it up. "Fiona here?"

"She's at the theater." Annie tucked her slender frame into the corner of the couch, legs drawn up next to her.

"You look tired, babe. Fiona told me a little about what's been happening. You wanna talk about it?"

She pressed the palm of her hand to her forehead. "It's like . . . this unbelievably bad movie. I don't even want to go outside the house for fear some reporter will pop out of the bushes and take a picture of me. The last thing I need is to become some sort of poster child for the gay community. All I've ever wanted was privacy."

"It's not like your face isn't already out there."

"Yeah, but I doubt my family spends much time on YouTube."

"Ah. I get it."

She fastened her pale blue eyes on him. "I don't want them to find me. Ever."

Now that he'd read her journal, he understood. Back in Boston, she'd lied to him about what had happened at the wedding. If he'd given it any real thought, if he hadn't been so completely absorbed by his own life, he might have realized that what she'd told him wasn't enough to motivate such an extreme reaction.

"Bridget was able to track you to Boston," he said.

"But you know what happened. When I told her I was a dyke, she almost left skid-marks on my face trying to get away from me."

He took a long, slow pull on his beer. "Have you explained any of this to Fiona?"

"No, and I don't intend to."

The question for Sharif was: Did he tell Annie he'd read those journal letters and knew the whole truth, or did he withhold that information and wait until another time? He wanted to tell her. He thought it would be healthy to get everything out on the table so that she could talk, could finally process with another human being what had happened. Still, an inner voice stopped him. Maybe it was partly the skittish, wary look in her eyes. Seeing her biting her nails, squirming to get comfortable, which never seemed to happen, he could tell she wasn't doing so well. Sharif had seen her on the edge of a very dark precipice once before and he couldn't stand the idea that he might be the one to put her there again.

"Can I tell you something?" she said, finally remembering she had a soda. She picked the can up off the end table and took a sip, then held it, rolling it between her palms.

"Anything."

"When Fi and I got back from our vacation and found a gazillion emails waiting for us, we deleted our addresses and opened up new accounts. I updated the security on both of our laptops. Honestly, I did everything I knew how to do. I thought we'd be safe." She set the soda down, pulling her legs up close to her chest. "This is so hard."

"I'm here for you, Annie."

Her eyes seemed to lose focus. "I got an e-mail around noon today from a man named Kyle. Kyle888666@yahoo.com. I did a reverse e-mail search on him. Even paid for the search. I think the results I received are bogus."

"Because?"

"It said Kyle was a fifty-one-year-old woman living in East Walpole, Massachusetts. The real Kyle, if that's his name, sent me some screen shots he'd taken of me in the last couple of days—taken through my own laptop camera. *God*." She sucked in a breath. "I never thought to put tape over it. Like I said, I assumed we had the security issue handled."

"There are lot of hacker creeps out there."

She swallowed, then swallowed again. "Yeah. I know. A couple of the photos showed me undressing, ready to go into the bathroom to take a shower."

He closed his eyes.

"He went on and on about how pretty I was. Said he wanted to meet me. Apparently, he knows where we live." Another hard swallow. "And then . . . do you know what he said?"

Sharif shook his head.

"He said, 'Why do you cry so much, Annie?' " She burst into tears.

Sharif got up from his chair and sat down next to her. Cradling her in his arms, he said, "It's okay. We'll cover the camera. And then we'll buy you the best security system that's available."

"You think security is the answer? When Hollywood studios,

multinational corporations, and the U.S. government get hacked all the time? There is no such thing as Internet security. If I didn't realize that before, I do now. I refuse to be connected to the Internet anymore. If I need it for work or for school, I'll use the one at the office. If I need to contact someone, I'll call or text them. So far, nobody has hacked my phone."

Surely she understood that it was only a matter of time before someone did. A burner phone might be a temporary solution, but they could talk about that later.

"I'm not falling apart," she said, straightening up. "I'm not. Sure, I'm upset, but I'm *not* a weakling."

"I know you're not."

"Then . . . why do I feel like one?" she asked, her eyes concentrating on him with a terrible fierceness. "I know what you're going to say. I may not be weak, but I've been acting that way."

"I would never say that."

Looking down, Annie went on. "Fiona has given a couple of interviews, but she said she'd stop. And now I find out she gave an interview to a reporter from *People* magazine yesterday. When I heard that, I wanted to hurl something at a wall. She knows I want us to keep a low profile until this all blows over."

"Are you angry?"

"We had a fight this morning before she left for work. I texted her a while later and apologized. I mean, I started thinking: What am I afraid of? What's the worst that can happen?"

He figured it was a good question. "What *are* you afraid of?"

She pressed her lips together, looked down at the soda can. "That my family will find out where I am and try to contact me." She let the statement hang in the air for a few seconds, then added, "But maybe it's time to forget about them. Maybe I'm

92

hiding for no reason. It's not like they couldn't find me if they wanted to. Might take some effort, but I haven't changed my name or anything. And if they did contact me, it doesn't mean I'd have to respond. I'm an adult. I'm happily married and busy getting on with my life. They have no power over me anymore."

"The only power they have is the power you give them."

The comment stopped her. She appeared to think it over, but still seemed agitated. Finally, she turned to him and said, "I'm glad you're here."

"Me, too."

"I have some serious thinking to do."

"I'm here for you, Annie." He reached for her hand.

"Just . . . don't let go."

13

Fiona felt surprisingly upbeat when she returned home late that afternoon. Annie had forgiven her for going back on her word. She was making good progress on the new play and was still riding high from yesterday's interview. The reporter had peppered her with thoughtful questions that drew out equally thoughtful responses. He wasn't gay himself, but he was supportive of the Supreme Court's decision on marriage, thought it was about time, or even past time, that same-sex couples were granted the legal right to marry. Before the interview had even begun, he mentioned that he'd been raised by two fathers who'd been in a committed relationship for thirty-seven years. The world was changing, at least in some quarters.

There wasn't much Fi could do to alter the popularity of the video. Even if she did have that kind of power, her choice would be to let it run its course and hope for the best. She truly wanted to embrace the platform she'd been given for as long as the spotlight was trained on her. The only problem was Annie.

When Fi walked into the kitchen and saw Sharif standing at the stove, she cried, "Our chef has returned." He wore a red apron over his T-shirt and jeans and stirred something in a large yellow pot.

Turning and grinning, he said, "Consider me your personal Julia Child."

Annie sat at the center island, nursing a glass of iced tea. She looked happy for a change, even contented.

Fi gave her a quick kiss and then moved up to the stove see what was in the pot. "Smells wonderful." She gave Sharif a hug.

Pouring Fiona a glass of wine, Annie said, "This bottle is a gift from Sharif."

"Your tastes have matured," said Fi, examining the label.

"Not really. Still like beer best. But when I want to impress, I follow the advice of the guy who owns the wineshop near my house."

"So, what time did you get here?" asked Fi, sitting down next to Annie.

Before he could answer, the doorbell chimed. "Why don't I get that?"

"If it's some creep . . ." said Fiona, not sure how to finish her sentence.

"I know what to do with creeps," said Sharif. "Leave it to me."

"I'm so glad he's here," said Annie, moving her stool closer to Fi.

"That makes two of us."

Annie gave Fi a long, slow, greedy kiss, the kind that always made Fi feel like she'd been zapped by an electric wire.

Coming up for air, Fi said, "Maybe one of us should stir the pot."

"I thought that's what I was doing," said Annie.

Sharif trudged back into the room a few moments later,

looking disgusted. "It was some guy wearing a clerical collar and holding a Bible. He said he'd seen the video. He asked to speak with you two, that he had a special message from God."

"Fabulous," said Fiona.

"I told them you were out back sacrificing a goat to Zeus— like you do every evening."

"You *didn't*," said Annie, looking horrified.

"Nah. Told them you weren't interested. I pointed to a house across the street and suggested he deliver his message there." He returned to the stove.

Fiona poured herself more wine. She was going to need it.

During dinner, they stuck to neutral topics. Sharif talked about Hammond, Ohio, his coaching job. Annie asked him if he was still dating Tamika and seemed sad to learn that they'd broken up. They were on their last bites of spicy coconut, peanut, and chicken stew when the doorbell chimed again.

"You people sure do get a lot of visitors."

"Aren't we lucky?" asked Annie, reaching for a piece of French bread.

"Good thing you've got an in-house bouncer." Without being asked, Sharif pushed back from the table. "I like that idea of the goat sacrifice. Think I'll use it for real this time."

"Don't you dare," called Fi to his retreating back.

"No smart-ass bullshit," added Annie. "*Smart-ass.*"

He was gone a little longer this time. When he came back, he seemed troubled. Slipping his hands into the back pockets of his jeans, he fixed his gaze on Annie. "What?" asked Fiona.

He hesitated a moment longer and then said, "Annie, your dad . . . your whole damn family are in the living room."

Annie opened her mouth, but nothing came out.

Fiona stood.

"What should I do?" asked Sharif. "It didn't seem right just to send them packing."

"Of course not," said Fi. "If they came all the way from California, the least we can do is talk to them."

"I feel sick," said Annie, staring down at the half-empty bowl in front of her.

"Should I get rid of them?" asked Sharif.

This had to be a positive sign, thought Fi. If they were here, it likely meant they'd come looking for Annie's forgiveness. "I know this is difficult, sweetheart, but if you're ever going to repair your relationship with them, this might be the time."

"God," said Annie, covering her face with her hands.

Fiona was dying to meet Annie's family. It was all she could do keep from running into the living room.

Annie glanced up at Sharif. "What do you think?"

"That . . . Fiona's right. If they're here because they want to make amends, you have to give them a chance. Family's family."

"What if they're not here for that?"

"Then, I guess you listen politely to what they have to say and if you're not interested, I'll tell them they either get lost, or I'll drag them out back to watch you do your nightly goat sacrifice."

Annie didn't seem to find his comment the least bit funny.

"You're ganging up on me," she said.

Fi placed a gentle hand on Annie's arm. "Why don't I go welcome them? You can take a minute to think about what you might want to say."

Annie didn't look up. "This won't end well," she whispered.

Hurrying out of the kitchen, Fi slowed her pace as she approached the living room. When she entered, she found two men, two women, and one small child standing at the windows facing the backyard pool. "Hello," she said, waiting as they turned around. "I'm Fiona McGuy."

"Of course you are," said the older man, crossing the room to her. He was stocky, with a heavy, craggy face, graying blond hair, a beard starting to turn white, and silver wire-rimmed glasses. Fi searched for any resemblance to Annie, but other than the fair hair, she couldn't find any. The black T-shirt he wore had the words U.S. Marines emblazoned across the front in bold red letters. "It's wonderful to meet you. I'm Ted. Ted Johnson."

"I'm Noah Foster," said the younger man. When he smiled, he revealed dazzlingly white teeth.

A woman with dark blond hair and the same sky blue eyes as Annie's held the little boy's hand. She moved hesitantly away from the windows. "I'm Bridget. Annie's sister."

The child was an adorable sandy-haired boy, dressed in blue-and-white-striped shorts, white athletic shoes, white knee-high socks, and a red Spider-Man T-shirt. He was fidgeting, and attempting, with no luck, to drag Bridget out of the room.

"And this is my son," said Bridget. "Say hello, Tyrion."

The little boy slipped behind his mother's legs and refused to speak.

"Tyrion, as in Tyrion Lannister?" asked Fiona.

"You know Game of Thrones?" asked Noah, clearly delighted. "I'm a huge fan. Tyrion's my favorite character."

"Don't get him started," said Bridget.

"Is Annie here?" asked Ted.

Fiona noted that no one had introduced the sharp-faced young woman who remained by the windows. Nodding toward her, Fiona smiled and asked, "And you are?"

"Willow. Tyrion's nanny." Her voice was barely audible.

"Nice to meet you. So," she continued, cupping her hands in front of her. "Did you fly? Drive?"

"We drove," said Noah. "It was—" He stopped midsentence as Annie and Sharif entered the room.

All eyes turned to Annie.

"Hi," she said, keeping her distance, backing up as her father moved toward her.

"Annie, please," he said, coming to a full stop. "Just listen for a second. We had to come. I'm not the same man I was six years ago. I'm ashamed of the way I reacted when you told your mom and me that you were gay. If I could take it all back, I would."

Fiona narrowed her eyes. What had he just said about Annie's mother? Moira Johnson had died giving birth to Annie— at least, that's what Annie had told her.

"Mom didn't come with you," said Annie. "Why doesn't that surprise me."

"She died last year," said Bridget. "She was diagnosed with cancer two years ago."

Annie stared straight ahead, taking in the information without reaction.

"We're here—I'm here—because I need your forgiveness," continued Ted. "I suppose, if you refuse to give it, I'll have to live with that. I behaved badly. I was wrong. You know I'm not the kind of man to admit that easily. When Bridget saw that video on YouTube last week, she showed it to Noah, and then brought it to me and asked me to watch it. I'm an old curmudgeon, a man who can be harsh in his judgments, inflexible even, but it touched me. Deeply. Bridget found an article online that mentioned you lived in the Twin Cities. I finally realized I couldn't let this estrangement go on. A phone call or a letter wasn't enough. I needed to look you in the eyes when I asked you to forgive me. I want to be part of your life again, Annie, for whatever years I have left. Will you let me?"

Annie stood very still as he moved ever so slowly toward her. "Oh, Daddy," she said at last, stepping into his embrace.

Tyrion raced across the room and grabbed Ted's legs. "Don't cry, Grampa."

Bridget wiped tears from her eyes.

Holding his daughter, Ted kissed her hair. "I've missed you so much." When he backed up, he shook Sharif's hand. "Thanks for being such a good friend to my daughter."

"We brought a case of superb California wine with us," announced Noah. "It's out in the van. Why don't I go get a couple bottles and we can celebrate our reunion?"

Annie eyed him warily.

"Or," said Bridget, apparently noticing Annie's reticence, "maybe we should give you some time to process all this. We need to find a hotel for the night. We're hoping we can spend some time with you and Fiona tomorrow. We'll only be here for a few days."

Fi didn't want them to leave—not yet. These were the people Annie had tried so hard to hide from her. Fi had so many questions, not the least of which had to do with Annie's mother. "Look," she said, warmed by the sight of Ted with his arm around Annie's shoulders. "We've got room here if you'd like to stay. It might be a little tight, but if you're only here for a few days, it would give us the most time together."

Sharif stiffened, gave his head an imperceptible shake as he looked straight at Fi.

"Well, sure," said Noah. "That would be great."

"We didn't expect you to put us up," said Ted.

"Annie?" asked Bridget, appearing uncertain. "Is that okay with you?"

"Um," said Annie, her eyes traveling from face to face, finally lingering on her father. "Okay."

Fi understood instantly that she'd made a mistake. She'd been making a lot of them lately. And yet now that it had been decided, she could hardly rescind the invitation without creating bad feelings. For good or ill, they'd simply have to get through this unexpected family reunion.

For the next couple of hours, everyone gathered in the kitchen to talk. While the comments were initially stiff, Noah brought in three bottles of wine, opened them and passed around glasses, which seemed to help ease the tension in the room. Noah kept refilling his glass. In fact, if Fi had to guess, she figured he'd polished off the better part of two bottles all by himself. Ticking off boxes in her head about her new brother-in-law, she concluded that Noah drank too much. He'd also stood at the stove and finished off the last of Sharif's stew, much to Sharif's amazement and silent disapproval, which Noah either wasn't sensitive enough to notice, or more likely, didn't care.

The conversation eventually turned to Bridget and Annie's childhood memories—common ground without any obvious land mines to trip over. Some of the stories were hilarious and served to get everyone laughing. Nothing of importance was discussed and that was probably good.

A while later, as Annie and Bridget and their dad continued their conversation at the kitchen table, and Willow gave Tyrion a bath, Fiona and Noah made up the bed in the smaller of the three bedrooms. Willow and Tyrion would stay in that room. Ted agreed to sleep on the couch in Fiona's study, and Noah and Bridget would sleep in the larger spare bedroom. Sharif, of course, had commandeered the basement, as he always did. He liked space to spread out.

"What do you do for a living?" asked Fi.

"I'm a psychiatrist," said Noah, fluffing one of the pillows before slipping it into the pillowcase. "I have a private practice, and I also work at a local hospital. What about you?"

"I'm a stage manager at a local theater."

"Must pay well," he said. "This house is amazing."

Taking in his rose-gold Apple watch with its midnight-blue band—one she'd looked at online and knew cost around fifteen thousand dollars—and large diamond ring, she decided not to tell him that her father owned it. "Thanks. We like it."

"Did Annie ever finish medical school?"

Fi cocked her head. "She's in law school."

"Really. She was premed at USC the last time I saw her. She always said she wanted to become a doctor like me."

"Were you two close?"

"Very close. I always thought of her as my little sister."

Fiona tossed a light cotton blanket over the bed and began to tuck it in. "I'm curious about Annie's mom. I'm not sure why, but I was under the impression that she'd died shortly after giving birth to Annie."

"Nope. Well, Moira always said it was a difficult birth, but both mother and daughter came through just fine."

"What was she like?"

"Moira?" repeated Noah, picking up a second pillow. "She was hardworking. Generous. She could also be demanding. Hard-headed. And, at times, I saw her as impulsive. But she was a good wife and mother. My parents died when I was pretty young. My aunt raised me. She was a wonderful woman, but she had to work hard to keep a roof over our heads. There wasn't much time left for me. Moira became like a second mother to me. She believed in me. I can't tell you what that meant. Ted took her death very hard. So did I."

Fiona sat down on the edge of the bed. "I'm sorry."

"Thanks."

"Ted seems like a nice guy. Couldn't help but notice his Marine T-shirt."

"Yeah, he's proud of his service. He's a tough old geezer, but the last couple of years have been hard on him. I hope reuniting with Annie will help."

"The grieving process. For his wife."

"Yes, that and . . . other problems I probably shouldn't get into." He staggered slightly as he moved around to the other side of the bed, the results, thought Fi, of too much wine. He held it well, but he was obviously buzzed. "Perhaps I shouldn't say anything," he continued, steadying himself on the bedpost, "but I feel I can trust you. You're family now. I'm sure Ted will tell Annie. Maybe he's even telling her right now. He tried to take his life four months ago. He didn't succeed, thanks to Bridget. He's seeing a therapist and is on some medication, which seems to be helping. It's been one blow after another for him. He wanted this reunion with Annie so badly. Like I said, I hope it helps." Yanking on the pillowcase, he added, "I don't understand why Annie left the way she did. She never told me she was gay. I wouldn't have had any problem with it."

Noah had curly black hair that was beginning to recede. His eyes might be spaced too close together, his nose too big, but he had beautiful lips that gave the impression of sensitivity, even delicacy. The one sour note, other than his drinking, was a certain lack of interpersonal skills. During the conversation in the kitchen, he never seemed to pick up on any of Annie or Bridget's unspoken cues, especially when they wanted to shut a topic down or when one or both of them became uneasy. Noah just forged ahead, heedless of the emotional wind change. For most people, it might not be a huge issue, but for a psychiatrist, someone who worked with people on such an intimate basis, it seemed like a strange flaw.

"I better go check on Willow and Tyrion," said Noah, rolling up the sleeves of his blue oxford cloth shirt. "I'm looking forward to the next few days, to getting to know you better."

"Me, too," said Fi.

"Good." He gave her a quick kiss on the cheek as he passed by her on the way to the door. "Hey, hope you don't mind, but I gotta say one thing before I go: Annie's sure got great taste in women."

Fi's smile froze on her face.

"See you in the morning, pretty lady."

14

When Fiona awoke the next morning, she turned over and found Annie, elbow propped against several pillows, head resting on one hand, watching her.

"What's going on?" asked Fi, raking a hand through her hair.

"I was just marveling at how lucky I am." She smiled down at Fiona, lightly tracing the curve of her cheekbone with a finger.

"You don't know how happy I am to hear that. I shouldn't have invited your family to stay without talking to you about it first."

"No, you shouldn't have."

"I fell asleep before you came to bed last night. How did your conversation with your father and sister go?"

Stretching out next to Fiona, Annie sighed. "Honestly? It was everything I ever hoped for."

Outside their room came the rapid thud of feet, and then a child's squeal of delight. "Noah seems nice."

"Do you think so?"

"What does Bridget do?"

"She trained to be a nurse. Apparently, she quit to help Dad out with his business a couple of years ago. Ever since I was a kid, he's owned garden stores—one in South Pasadena and one out in the Valley. He used to have one up in Bakersfield, but he closed that before we moved to Pasadena."

"Your brother-in-law drinks too much."

"I know. He must have polished off two bottles last night."

"He's rather of full of himself."

"You think?"

"Annie?"

"Hmm?"

Fi knew that if she brought up the lie Annie had told about her mother, that it would ruin the moment—and perhaps the entire day. She decided to wait. "Jane phoned me yesterday. She said that a reporter from *Twin Cities Monthly* wants to do a feature article on us. Is that totally out of the question?"

"I don't know. I guess . . . maybe I'd do it. If you feel strongly about it."

Fi was elated at her change of heart. "Do you know how much I love you?" She nuzzled closer. "I wish I didn't have to be at work by nine."

Annie kissed Fi's nose. "I need to shower. I'm hoping to take the next couple days off from work." As she swung her legs out of bed, she added, "We better get our asses out of this bedroom before that little boy takes our house apart, one piece of furniture at a time."

While Annie sang in the shower, Fiona dressed. Standing in front of the mirror over the chest of drawers, she tried on several pairs of earrings, finally deciding on simple gold hoops. She was about to leave when she heard a familiar voice in the hallway outside the bedroom. Then a knock.

"Fi, I have to talk to you."

It was Roxy.

Fi glanced over her shoulder to make sure Annie was still in the shower. "What's up?" she asked, opening the door. "Couldn't this wait until we get to the theater?"

"Can't talk about it there," said Roxy, setting her briefcase next to the bed and then sitting down. She nodded for Fi to sit next to her. "Didn't realize you were in the midst of a family reunion. I just met Annie's sister and brother-in-law." She lowered her voice. "You need to know about this."

"About what?"

She removed an iPad from the briefcase. "It's a porn site."

"Why would I want to see a porn site?" And then it dawned on her. "You're not saying——"

"Afraid so. You and Annie are the stars. I figured you needed to know it's out there. I didn't want you to be blindsided if someone mentioned it to you. See, it's pictures of women in various positions with your face and Annie's superimposed over them. You can find it by Googling *Doing the Dyke Duo*."

By now, Fiona was assuming things like this would appear in the Internet sewer. Recreation for pervs. "Annie's in a good mood today. I refuse to ruin it."

"Okay. Don't say I didn't warn you." Roxy returned the tablet to her briefcase.

"Who tipped you off about the site?"

"Leo. He feels pretty bad about what he did——putting that

video up on the web in the first place. That's why he's been checking around to monitor what's happening. Anyway, that's why I came. I guess I'll see you at work. Oh, hey, before I forget, let me ask you something. Maybe I'm wrong, but do you think Charlotte's been acting weird lately?"

"Weird?"

"You know how talkative she is. But yesterday afternoon, when she stopped by my cubical to drop something off, she didn't say more than two words to me. She looked dreadful. Like she hadn't combed her hair or changed her clothes in days."

"I'll talk to her when I get in."

"Yeah, she really thinks you walk on water. If anyone can figure out what's going on with her, you can."

Once Roxy had left, Fi headed to the kitchen. She needed coffee. She found Sharif sitting at the table, eating a bagel. Sniffing the air, she asked, "Did something burn?"

Sharif lifted his eyes and nodded to the stove. "Annie's dad tried to make himself some oatmeal the old-fashioned way. He forgot it on the stove. I'd say that pot of yours is toast. I'd also say we're lucky I came back when I did, otherwise he could have burned the house down."

"Yikes," said Fi, stepping over to examine the blackened piece of Le Creuset. "Where'd you go?"

"I got up early and drove over to that grocery store off Anderson Lakes Parkway. Thought it might be nice to make breakfast for everyone. Ted must have started his oatmeal while I was out."

The kitchen island was loaded with food—the remnants of

scrambled eggs, bacon, sausage, pastries, bagels, cream cheese, and orange juice. "You're a sweetheart for doing all this."

Stepping over to the window overlooking the backyard pool, Fi watched little Tyrion splashing around in the water inside an inflatable turtle. Ted was in the water right next to him, pushing him and pulling him, both of them laughing. Willow, the nanny, was lying on one of the chaises, reading a magazine.

"Looks like everyone has settled in," said Fi.

Bridget picked that moment to sail into the kitchen. "Has anyone seen my iPhone? Tyrion thinks they're all toys. He's always walking off with them."

"It could be anywhere," said Noah, brushing past her on the way to the island. "Wow, blueberry bagels." He picked out the largest one and began slathering it with butter. "Hate cream cheese," he said, looking up and grinning.

"Do you have your phone on you?" asked Bridget.

"Unless Tyrion made off with it when I wasn't looking."

"Call my number." As an explanation, she added, "Sometimes it's the only way to find them."

Willow came through the kitchen, her face looking sunburned. "Hot out there. I need something cold to drink."

"Plenty of soft drinks in the fridge," said Sharif. "Help yourself."

A moment later, Ted walked in, towel drying his hair. "That is one great pool."

Noah licked his fingers before clicking on his phone. He hit a couple of presets. "Hear anything?"

Bridget lowered her head and listened. She was about to leave the kitchen, when she glanced outside. "Willow!" she cried. "You left Tyrion out there all by himself."

"Ted said he'd stay while I came inside." As soon as she said it, she realized that Ted was standing right next to her.

"You can't trust *him*," cried Bridget, rushing for the door. "What have I told you? Tyrion is your responsibility."

Noah set his phone on the counter and rushed past his wife.

Everyone gathered by the pool as Noah waded into the shallow end toward his son, trying his best not to scare him. "Hey, buddy, are you having a good time?"

Tyrion gave an eager nod. Joy didn't get much brighter than a five-year-old playing in the water.

Ted kneaded his hands together as he stood next to Fiona. His agitated gaze skittered from person to person. "I'm sorry," he said over and over. "I forgot. I didn't mean . . . I would never—"

Now that Tyrion was safely in the hands of his dad, Bridget's expression softened. "It's okay. All that matters is that Tyrion is safe."

"Right," said Ted.

"Right," whispered Fiona. It seemed that one of the issues Noah hadn't wanted to talk about last night was Ted's memory. She wondered what else Noah had failed to mention.

Fi was getting ready to leave for the theater when Sharif appeared at the door of her study.

"You've got to come see this," he said, his forehead glistening with sweat.

"Can't it wait? I'm already late for work."

"No, it can't wait," he said ominously.

On her way through the living room, Fiona noticed that Noah was pacing in front of the windows, talking on his cell phone and rubbing the back of his neck.

"Not possible today," he said. "You're what?" His gaze roamed the room. When he saw Fiona, he mouthed the word "work." "This is one helluva surprise," he continued, listening for a few seconds. "Okay. All *right*. I got it." He clicked the phone off. "Some people have no sense of timing," he said, trying to make light of his obvious annoyance. "Hey, Fiona, will you do me a favor? Will you tell Bridget I had to go out. I won't be gone long. Why don't I take everyone out to dinner tonight? Pick some-place really nice and make reservations." He felt the back pocket of his jeans for his wallet. Assured that it was there, he dug in his front pocket for his keys. He nodded to Sharif on the way to the front door.

"Come *on*, Fi," urged Sharif.

Annie was already outside. With her hands in the back pock-ets of her cargo shorts and an irritable expression on her face, she watched Noah get into his van and drive off.

"You okay?" asked Fi.

"I've been better."

"You don't like him, do you?"

"Nope."

They stood on the sidewalk under the sweltering morning sun. Sharif pointed at a backpack lying in the grass about ten feet from the south side of the house. "Either of you recognize that?"

"Not me," said Annie.

"Me either," said Fi. "Some kid probably left it. If we look in-side, I'm sure we'll find an ID."

Sharif held Fiona's arm, refusing to let her go. "I'm not so sure. That thing worries me. When I was playing with the Vikes, we had an incident. A backpack was left by the door of our locker room. The offensive line coach was the one who found it. The police were called. Turns out, it was some sort of explosive device. I never got all the details, but it sure made an impression."

"You think that backpack's a bomb?" asked Annie.

"I may be overly cautious, but hey, it's better to be safe than sorry. I'm calling 911."

Sirens blaring, the Bloomington Bomb Squad arrived a short while later. They came in a large truck, maybe twenty feet long. Six men jumped out, all wearing khaki cargo pants and black polo shirts. Two police cruisers pulled up and parked along the street. In short order, a perimeter was set up and men began evacuating all the houses close enough to be in harm's way. Residents were asked to move to the park at the end of the street.

Fi wanted to stay and watch. If her home was about to be blown up, she felt she needed to be there when it happened. The cop in charge, a muscular dark-haired sergeant, Bill Larson, refused to allow it. He drew Fiona and Annie behind the truck, wrote down their contact information, then peppered them with questions. Did they have any reason to believe it might be a bomb? Could they think of a reason why someone might target the house? Fi explained about the video, the e-mails, the threats, and that she'd already filed a report with the Eden Prairie police.

"Good," said the sergeant, making a few final scratches in his notebook. "You did the right thing." He seemed far friendlier than the Eden Prairie officer.

On the way down the winding street to the park, Fi asked the officer assigned to the family, "Is it like *The Hurt Locker*? Do you send someone in dressed in a protective suit?"

"It depends on the situation," said the young man. He had a

military haircut and his arms were covered in tattoos. "In this case, we'll probably use a robot. Honestly, ma'am, we know what we're doing. I can't guarantee a good outcome, but I can say that ninety-nine percent of the time, it's not an explosive."

"What a job," muttered Annie, striding along beside Sharif.

"But what if it is a bomb and it goes off?" asked Bridget, attempting to spread sunscreen on her son's face with little cooperation from Tyrion.

"Let's hope some kid forgot his backpack on your lawn and there's nothing inside except books and candy bars."

"I like candy," said Tyrion.

"So do I," said the cop. Glancing back at Sharif, he added, "Your name is familiar. Sharif Berry. Should I know you?"

"I used to play for the Vikings."

The officer stopped and turned all the way around. "Sure. I remember you. You were a defensive back." He stuck out his hand.

Sharif shook it. "Strong safety. That was me."

"How come you're not playing for them anymore?"

"Got cut. It happens. I'm coaching high school now—in Ohio."

"That's cool."

"Are there any concessions in the park?" asked Ted, hoisting Tyrion onto his back.

"Afraid not," said Fi.

They continued on down the hill.

"Noah should be here," grumbled Bridget, looking around impatiently. "Where did he say he was going?"

"He didn't," said Fi. "He got a phone call, something work related. And then he left. Said he wouldn't be gone long."

113

" 'Work,' " repeated Bridget, scanning the parking lot. "Makes no sense."

After reaching a picnic table, everyone settled in while Fi stepped away and called the theater. She explained to Roxy what was happening, that there was no way she would make it in today.

"Gosh, I'm sorry. I'll tell Cordelia."

"You do that," said Fi, making no attempt at Minnesota Nice.

"Will you call me, tell me what the police find?"

"If you don't hear the explosion first."

Fiona recognized some of the neighbors milling anxiously around the park. A few were on cell phones, while others clustered next to picnic tables. Cars began arriving, pulling into the lot to pick people up. Most seemed determined to wait it out. Nobody said anything to Fi or Annie, but there were lots of accusing looks. It was clear that she and Annie, not the person who left the backpack, were being blamed for this potential disaster.

The neighborhood was a friendly place, so by now, everyone had to know about the video. Many had undoubtedly witnessed the enthusiastic choir on the front lawn as well as the men on the roof on Tuesday morning. Fi figured their lives provided the neighbors with lots of juicy gossip. "It's good to be of use," she said under her breath.

Phil Banks and his dog, Baxter, eventually ambled over to their picnic table. "Pretty scary, huh?" he said, cheerful as ever.

"Sure is," said Annie, reaching down to give the dog a scratch.

Tyrion jumped off the table and nearly landed on Baxter.

The dog growled.

"Is he friendly with kids?" asked Bridget.

"Kids who know how to be gentle with dogs," said Phil, yanking Baxter away.

Ted grabbed Tyrion's hand and said, "Let's you and me go take a walk."

"No," said Tyrion, struggling to get away. "I want to play with the doggie."

"We've never had a dog," said Bridget, "so he's not really familiar with them."

"Uh-huh," said Phil, unimpressed. Seeing that Ted had the kid corralled, he eyed Sharif for a second, then turned his attention to Fi. "How are you holding up?"

"How do you think? I'm scared to death."

"People can be pretty crazy. Reminds me of a friend of mine. This guy, he lives in New Jersey. His neighbor didn't like his bamboo fence, so he took him to court. The neighbor lost, so the next morning the guy's out there with a chainsaw hacking pieces out of the fence and screaming obscenities. My friend had to call the cops. The guy belonged in a loony bin."

Fi wasn't particularly interested in hearing stories about crazy neighbors. She wished Phil would go away.

"I can't believe anybody would want to hurt you," continued Phil. As an afterthought, he added, "Or Annie. Or any of you." They talked for a few more minutes, until Baxter tugged him toward the walking path.

Several hours passed. Ted spent a great part of the time sitting in the grass, playing mumblety-peg with Tyrion. A hush settled over the crowd as the muscular bomb squad sergeant strode at last into the clearing.

"Okay, listen up," he called, coming to a stop next their picnic table. "We've examined the backpack and I'm happy to report that it no longer represents a threat."

"Was it a bomb?" asked Sharif.

"Yes, sir, it was."

Annie pressed a fist to her mouth.

Fiona wanted to put her arm around Annie and help her through it, but Sharif already had his arm around her. There had never been a time in Fi's life when she wanted to be six foot five and built like a military Humvee, but she did at this moment. She needed to protect Annie, make her feel safe, and yet everything just kept getting worse. She was useless—*felt* useless.

"We ask your patience as we canvass the neighborhood," continued the sergeant. "We need to make sure there are no other devices that might pose a threat."

"Can't we go home?" asked a shirtless, middle-aged man in shorts and flip-flops.

"Until we're able to give the all clear, no. We'll let you know when it's safe."

"Any idea who left the backpack?" asked Fiona.

"The pipe bomb remains intact. It was never operational. Whoever made it didn't know what they were doing. We're in the process of examining it."

Fi let out a breath. "Thank you so much."

"Glad we had a good outcome." He added, lowering his voice, "You did the right thing to call the police. But just a word of caution: For the next couple of nights, you might want to stay somewhere else. Better safe than sorry. My hope is that we can find the guy who did this sooner rather than later, but I can't promise anything. We'll check out the police report you filed with the EPPD."

Fi thanked him again.

"You stay safe," he said, nodding and then heading back up the hill.

Fi's cell phone rang. Once again, she walked away from the picnic table and said hello.

"Oh, dearheart, I'm so so *so* sorry to hear about that monstrous bomb." It was Cordelia. Her voice was almost an octave higher than normal. "I trust nothing blew up?"

"It was a dud," said Fi. "It didn't go off."

"Really? That's . . . good news." Now she sounded disappointed. "No splintered rubble, then. No . . . crashing chandeliers or clouds of dust."

"Everything's fine."

"Ah, well, life isn't an action movie, is it. I guess that means you won't need my help. I was going to offer to let you and Annie stay at Thorn Hall until you could get back on your feet."

Thorn Hall? This was the first time Fi had ever heard Cordelia's mansion called by that name. It made her think of Toad Hall from *The Wind in the Willows*. For just an instant, she could almost see Cordelia as the Amazing Mr. Toad, wearing his Harris Tweed suit as he lifted off in an air balloon. Falling back to earth, Fi said, "Invite us to your house?"

"Of course, dearheart. We theater people must stick together."

"The police don't want us going back to our place until they can figure out who left the bomb."

"Really." Her voice brightened. "Well, then, it's settled. You and Annie will pack a bag and come right on over."

"There's one small problem."

"Nothing I can't solve, I'm sure."

"Annie's family—she hasn't seen them in many years—just arrived for a short visit. Bad timing, I know. It might be better if we rented hotel rooms for a few days. That way we'd get to see more of them."

"Heavens. I won't hear of it. You've been to my digs. I've got enough bedrooms to house the entire grand duchy of Tuscany, if it still existed. Bring them along."

"Seriously? Counting Annie and me, it would be eight people."

"My niece just left with her stepfather for a couple months in Australia. He's filming a movie down under. The place is quiet as a tomb, which I hate. You know me. I love an audience." She explained where she hid the front door key, just in case they couldn't rouse her ancient butler. The man had rooms on the third floor—an ex-actor who loved playing the part but was rarely around, unless he was too sick to go out.

"Cordelia, I could kiss you."

"Hold that thought. I'll see you tonight."

There was, as Fi well knew, method in this madness. Because Fi's father was a successful Broadway producer, and because nonprofit theaters like the Thorn Lester Playhouse occasionally signed up with commercial partners to help shoulder the risk of staging essentially unknown works by little known play-wrights, Cordelia was undoubtedly hoping to leverage their friendship in order to engage the famous Brendan McGuy in a mutually beneficial coalition. It might not be the only reason Cordelia had offered Fi the stage manager position last year, but it wasn't an insignificant part of the deal.

If Cordelia needed Fiona to be in her debt, inviting everyone to stay at her house for several days would be more arrows in her quiver. Annie's safety was Fi's primary concern. Feeling that she finally had something tangible to offer Annie, she made her way back to the picnic table to give everyone the good news.

15

"This is what happens when you go off your meds," Mimi's husband bellowed through the phone line.

"Why are you getting so worked up?" she asked. And people thought *she* had a screw loose.

"I'm as calm as any husband can be after learning that his wife just bought a twelve-thousand-dollar couch."

"Our old one was disgusting."

"That's what leather cleaner is for."

"I refuse to talk to you when you get like this."

"Mimi, this is insane."

"You mean *I'm* insane."

"I never said that. But you're ill, you know you are. You're not supposed to leave the house unless you let me know where you're going. We had a deal."

She was pretty sure she could hear his teeth grinding.

"Where were you last night?"

"Flying. Soaring. I'm a billion miles away on the other side of the moon."

"Right. You stayed with one of your girlfriends again, didn't you? When will you be home?"

"None of your business."

Mimi and Ethan Chandler lived in the tony North of Montana section of Santa Monica, in a three-million-dollar house—low end in their neck of the woods. They'd been married for eight years. Ethan owned a software engineering company and she . . . well, she'd given up a lot to marry him. She figured he owed her a little fun every now and then.

"I want you home for dinner. We need a serious meeting about finances."

"It's unlikely I'll be home tonight, Ethan." As it happened, Mimi had checked herself into the luxurious thousand-square-foot penthouse suite at the Maxfield West in downtown Minneapolis. She especially liked the wraparound balcony with its panoramic views of the city. It made her feel like a queen surveying her kingdom, which, as it happened, was exactly what she was.

"Are you at Lola's? Piper's?"

"Why would I spend time with them? You think they're my friends? Lola's a snake. And Piper's a witch. I know you don't believe in the supernatural. I do. My mother was a witch. Well, metaphorically. Makes me think I should go buy a broom, jump off a roof and see if I can fly."

"Slow down. You're talking so fast I can't understand you."

"You are *lame*." She exaggerated each word. "I'm. Hanging. Up. Now."

"Mimi, don't you—"

She clicked off her cell phone and tossed it on the king-sized bed. She hadn't expected to find such a nice hotel in Fly-Over Land when she arrived yesterday morning. Not that she'd ever been in Minneapolis before—or ever wanted to come. But Noah was here, so that made it a destination.

Her first order of business had been to rent a car. A special car. Nothing run-of-the-mill. Next, she'd studied her laptop, noting with some delight that Minnesota offered just what she needed. She entered the destination into the GPS and, in a little over an hour, she found herself in Saint Cloud. The whole thing was a dark whim, but then Mimi wasn't the kind of person to deny herself anything that truly captured her imagination.

Now, almost noon, Mimi was sure Noah would be arriving any minute. She wished it was dark out so she could light candles all over the suite, as she had the night they'd stayed at a private cottage on the grounds of the Langham Huntington in Pasadena. She snatched up the hotel phone and pressed 0, ordering the front desk clerk to send up three bottles of chilled Veuve Clicquot and four ham, strawberry jam, and blue cheese flatbreads. Noah liked to drink before sex, and eat after. She was too wired to eat. There was too much to do. Too many plans to make.

Mimi had graduated from UCLA with a bachelor's degree in organic chemistry and a master's in analytical chemistry. She'd been looking for a job in research when she'd met Ethan. She'd been in and out of mental health facilities for years, diagnosed with a number of problems, most prominently bipolar disorder. Her meds, as usual, had been giving her fits when Ethan waltzed into her life. He told her up front that he was an old-fashioned kind of guy. He wanted his wife to stay home and take care of him. At the time it seemed like a perfect solution.

On the day she said, "I do," four months after they'd first met, she knew it wouldn't last. For one thing, she was smarter than he was. He was reasonably bright, for a software engineer and budding business tycoon, but had a dull, plodding personality. On the other hand, he was cute and offered her a safe harbor, so she played his game. Now that she'd found Noah, everything had changed.

Mimi spent the next few minutes in the bathroom, freshening her makeup and making sure her new black lace strappy chemise looked perfect. She loved the color black. She'd dyed her chin-length hair black. Dyed her mousy brown eyelashes black. And she wore oversized black glasses. She might be six years older than Noah, but that didn't mean her body had gone to seed. If anything, she'd recently lost a few unwanted pounds due to a nasty bout with depression. She was trim and sleek, and even without a broom, was pretty certain she could fly.

When the knock came, Mimi felt an overpowering rush of passion. It happened almost every time she saw Noah, even if it was only a med check at his office. She opened the door, ready to fall into his arms.

Instead of being happy to see her, he snarled his way into the room.

"What the hell are you doing?" he demanded. He paused for a moment to study the modern painting hanging over the leather couch, and then whirled around to face her.

She felt a rush of power. "God, you're a beautiful man. Don't worry. I have everything planned. I don't really like what you're wearing though. We might have to go out and buy you a new suit. As it happens, I know just the place. I've been out walking the streets, examining the shops on offer in downtown Minneapolis.

Lots to choose from. While we're out, let's get some fresh flowers for the suite. I'm thinking lilies. My mom always loved lilies. She was an evil woman. Did I ever tell you about her? Noah, why are you glowering? Your face looks so piggy when you glower."

"It's *Dr. Foster*. Remember?"

"Of course, but I can call you Noah when it's just you and me."

"No, Mimi. Always. I'm your psychiatrist. I'm not your boyfriend."

"Sure you are." She cuddled up to him, draped her arms around his neck.

He removed them and backed away. "You have to *stop* this."

"You're here, aren't you? Don't you like what I'm wearing? I bought it just for you."

"You're married, Mimi. So am I."

"That never stopped you before. I even remember what you said the first time. You said, 'Mimi, you need to learn to trust men again. You've lost that trust and I can help you regain it.' Remember? Oh, Noah, you have such perfect skin. How do men get such perfect skin without even trying?"

He turned his back on her and strode angrily over to the windows. "I made a mistake."

"You made lots of them," she said, her voice growing low and seductive. "Remember when you took me to the Langham Huntington?"

He lowered his head. "You went to the hotel with your husband, Mimi, not me."

She sat down on the couch and crossed her legs, trying with all her might to contain the electric energy buzzing through her body. "Don't be insulting. I think I'd know who I was with. I even remember the wallpaper in the bedroom at that cottage, and the drinks *you* ordered. Two extra-dry martinis."

"I hate martinis."

"Noah?"

"What?"

"Look at me."

He blew out a breath and turned around.

"You don't want to cross me. I don't get angry, I get even."

"Meaning what?"

She shrugged.

"Mimi? What are you saying?"

"Seems to me that there's some medical board out there somewhere in the great beyond that might be interested in learning about your behavior toward me."

"You have no proof that we ever slept together."

"Don't I?" she said coyly.

He sat down, making sure to keep a ridiculously vast distance between them. "We've talked about this so many times. You know—"

"Yeah, yeah. I'm bipolar. Doesn't make me a crazy or stupid."

"You also happen to be a deeply disturbed narcissist. I'm not the first doctor to tell you that."

"Right. The world is all about *me*. What's wrong with that? What should it be about? So I love myself. Isn't that what all the self-help books tell you to do? Since I was born with that skill, I think it puts me way ahead."

"You're spinning," said Noah. "Talking too fast. Look, as long as you stay on your medication, you can lead a reasonably normal life. Are you taking your meds, Mimi?"

"Sure." She bounced up when she heard another knock on the door. "That should be our champagne."

"I'm not staying."

"But you have to stay. Everything's all set. I talked to the concierge and he gave me the name of this incredible restaurant. I've already made reservations for dinner."

"Mimi—"

"You said you loved me, that you wanted to be with me forever."

"What I said was—"

"You think I take things out of context."

"If you're not on your medication."

"I'm so sick of hearing about medication, like it's some sort of god. That junk you put me on makes me feel like a zombie. I hate it. I refuse to take it. You and Ethan think you know everything. Well, you don't." Frustrated by the continued knocking, Mimi opened the door. "You can take all that crap and dump it in the garbage," she said to the bewildered waiter standing in the hallway. "No wait." She grabbed a bottle of champagne. Slamming the door, she whirled on Noah. Seeing him sitting there on the couch, looking so sad, her heart nearly broke. He was perfect, if only he'd be a little more cooperative. But just like her, he had his moods. She'd been looking at honeymoon destinations online. It was all she could do not to tell him about the possibilities. She'd already sent away for a bunch of brochures.

"Okay," she said, peeling the foil off the top of the bottle. "If you force me to drink this by myself, I will. Go ahead. Leave. No wait." She shimmied out of her chemise, kicking it across the room. "Just so you remember *this*." She pointed to her body. "It's what you're going to miss."

Noah stood. "Promise me you'll get on the next flight back to LAX."

"Sure."

"Should I call and make reservations for you?"

"I know how to make reservations." She popped the cork on the champagne, sending a spray of the fizzy liquid all across her breasts. Smiling seductively, she said, "Are you sure you don't want to lick it off?"

"I'm your doctor. I want to help you, if you'll let me. I do care about you."

She lifted the bottle to her lips and took a few sips, delighted as always by the taste. "You are no fun at all."

"Will you call me when you land in L.A.?"

Moving back to the door, she opened it as wide as it would go.

"Mimi, you're naked."

"So?"

"Get away from there."

"I promise I'll make those plane reservations as soon as you leave." She had every intention of doing just that. She would get on a plane in the morning—maybe even this evening—though she wouldn't be returning to L.A.

"Put some clothes on," he said. He paused for a few seconds to take her in, then, giving her one of his meaningful nods, he left.

She stood in the hallway and watched him walk down the hall to the elevators. Before the doors closed in front of him, she stuck out her tongue.

Enough preamble. Let's go back in time to the night in question. Bridget and Noah's wedding, the dinner and the dance at the beautiful Casa del Sol motel up near San Rafael. What a perfect setting. Marin County, how gorgeous. The entire motel rented just for the occasion. All the rooms spread in a circle around the inner court, with its turquoise pool surrounded by a red-brick patio, areas to lounge and talk. And of course, the open bar. Bees to honey, I remember thinking. Always a swarm around that bar.

The wedding late that afternoon was the beginning—or, perhaps you would say it was the culmination—of months of hard work and planning. I remember standing next to Bridget, her maid of honor, forcing back tears because it was all so beautiful, so meaningful, so perfect. Not only did I love my sister, but I adored the man she was marrying. My family was everything to me. I was proud to be part of something so incredibly special.

We all walked back from the church and gathered in the open court to take photos. That endless picture taking. What a drag. The photographer was an ass with a grating sense of humor, but I guess nobody cared. Everyone was too happy, too focused on the joy they were feeling. Dinner followed. I have no memory of what I ate, but I do remember the toasts. Again, such high spirits. Such a promising future. Everyone was well oiled by then. People milled around the edges. The weather was too good to be true—warm, but not hot. Clouds floating like huge cotton balls against a cobalt sky. And then, as the evening wore on, I remember the dancing. It was Bridget's idea to hire that DJ, right? He was great. I'm not sure who selected the songs. Except for the Duran Duran moments, when I walked around plugging my ears, it all flowed. I danced with everyone. I was, needless to say, one of the bees swarming the bar. I started with rum and Cokes, and ended up with tequila shots. Probably a bad mix. No, definitely.

Bridget and I danced one song together, that is, until Noah broke in and danced with his arms around both of us. It all felt so right—the bosom of my beloved family and . . . well, all that.

Eventually, I wandered away from the crowd and stood at the edge, under the overhang from the second-floor balcony. I realized for the first time that the light had faded and it was now full night. In fact, it was going on midnight. The lanterns strung up over the patio glowed almost as brightly as the faces. Bridget was standing with her bridesmaids, talking, laughing. It was at that moment that I was attacked—yes, attacked is the perfect word—by a thought. Sure, I was filled with pride at what I was seeing, but I was also suffused with a crushing melancholy. As much as I tried to push the thought out of my mind, I couldn't. I would never have a moment like this. Never. And it wasn't fair.

Feeling dejected, I downed another couple of tequila shots and then went back to my room. I didn't want anyone to see me crying. How would I explain?

As I was fitting my key into the lock, feeling dizzy and a little nauseous from all the booze, I sensed someone come up behind me. Turning, I saw that it was Noah.

"Why are you crying?" he asked, his expression so full of concern that it made me cry even harder.

I told him I couldn't talk about it, that he should go back to the party. I was surprised when he followed me inside. I reached to turn on a light, but before I could, he put his hands on my waist and said, "No, tell me. I want to know." I figured he was as drunk as I was, and yet I couldn't ruin his night by dumping my problems on him.

"I'll tell you, I promise, but not now."

"Annie," he said, "you're so much like your sister."

"I'm not. Not really."

"It kind of feels like I'm marrying both of you."

Even in my disoriented state, I thought that was a deeply weird comment. He said some other stuff, too, but I don't re-member it now. What I do remember was that he was getting worked up. Very emotional, very . . . "I'll take care of you. You can trust me." He held me against him, then began kissing me. He kicked the door shut and forced me farther into the room. I tried to shove him away, to break his grip. I told him to stop.

He raped me. There. I said it. Noah raped me.

He pushed me down on the bed, pulled his pants down and forced himself on me. I was so stunned, I didn't even scream. I mean, can you believe that? There were a hundred people outside who could have come to my rescue if I'd screamed loudly enough. I let him do it to me. I just . . . let him. I can't believe I was that person—that passive—but I was. It hurt like hell because, you know what? I was a virgin. Mercifully, it was fast. And then he was gone.

Do you know what he said as he was leaving? Even today, it makes me sick to think about it. He said, "Thanks, Annie. That was great."

God. I mean, what?

I lay there in the dark for a long time, shivering. At some point, I must have gotten up because I remember standing in the shower with my dress on. Eventually, I peeled all my clothes off and tossed the sodden mess on the bathroom floor. I used almost an entire bottle of liquid soap, but the smell of him still stunk on me no matter how much I tried to wash him away. I'm sure I had all kinds of thoughts, probably about Bridget, about what would happen when she found out, how it would destroy her—though I have to admit that I don't remember any of them now. I just remember the hate. It was like a fever. A fever in the darkness that would never go away.

I turned on the bathroom light and stared at myself in the mirror for a long time, struggling to understand what had changed. My face had an ugly flush and there was a bruise under my chin where his wedding ring dug into me while he was holding me down.

How do I explain what the aftermath of rape feels like? I was moving in slow motion. I felt like my body weighed a thousand pounds. There was the present and then there was the moment it happened and the two got all confused. I was terrified he'd come back. I looked around for a weapon. If I'd had a baseball bat and he had come back, I would have killed him, no doubt about it.

I dressed in soft jeans and a sweatshirt. The normal clothing—my clothing, not the frilly bridesmaid dress—somehow comforted me, made me feel stronger. I don't think I combed my hair. It was still wet when I left the room and walked two doors down to yours. You know what happened next because you were there. What you can't know is what the next few minutes were like for me.

I can't write any more. Going back to that night, even in my mind, feels like it's happening to me all over again.

Next time, we'll talk about the second time I was violated that night.

16

"Um, hello?" said a soft voice. "This is Charlotte Osborne."

Jane didn't recognize the name. She'd come down to her office after working the dinner rush to go over the notes she'd made during the afternoon staff meeting. She was irritated by the interruption and almost didn't answer her cell. "Yes?" she said, only half listening.

"I'm a production assistant at the Thorn Lester Playhouse? I work with Fiona McGuy?" The woman appeared to phrase all her comments as questions. "I know you and Fiona are friends because I saw her in your office a few days ago? You're a PI right?"

"I am," said Jane, dropping her pen. "What's this about?"

"Well," said the woman, sounding unsure. "See, um, the thing is, I need to get in touch with Fiona, but she generally doesn't answer my calls when she's not at work? I have something she needs to see right away?"

"What is it?"

"She received a letter this morning. On the outside, someone printed the word 'URGENT' in all caps. So, well, I figure it's . . . urgent. Since she never came to work today, I tried to get in touch with her by phone, but, like I said, she never answered. I left a couple voice mails, but she hasn't called me back."

"Is there a return address on the envelope?"

"No?"

"What kind of envelope?"

"It's just, you know . . . white? Pretty standard."

Jane glanced at her watch. It was going on eight. "You're at the theater kind of late."

"There's so much to do for the next production that Roxy asked me to take care of a bunch of extra stuff?"

"How much longer will you be there?"

"Oh, well, I'd say . . . maybe half an hour? I need to get home to feed my cat. My mother says he's my responsibility. She doesn't like cats, thinks they're dirty. He's kind of a mean cat. Just my luck, you know? But I love him anyway. If you want to swing by and pick it up, I could meet you down by the stage door? There's a bench where I could sit outside and wait for you."

"Do you know why Fiona wasn't at work today?"

"Sorry. I don't."

Jane had been at work since just after six. She was tired and overwhelmed by everything she'd heard from her waitstaff at the afternoon meeting. She'd made sure that Wayne didn't attend so that everyone could speak freely. She'd received more than an earful, problems she needed to deal with immediately. Still, if this letter was from Fiona's stalker, Jane figured it might be important. "Okay, I'm leaving right now. Shouldn't take me more than fifteen minutes to get downtown."

"Great. I appreciate it. I never like to disappoint Fiona, and if this is truly urgent . . . well, I mean, it says it is so it must be . . . she needs to see it right away. Anyway, I'll be waiting."

Heading out to her Mini a few minutes later, Jane saw that the sky was filled with dark, threatening clouds. Thunder rumbled in ominously from the southwest. As she sailed down Lyndale, it began to rain. By the time she reached the stage door, the storm was directly over the city. A bolt of lightning lit up the empty bench. Jane assumed that Charlotte was inside, escaping the weather.

Dashing through the wind and rain, a newspaper held over her head, Jane rushed up to the door. She was about to knock when she noticed a rain-soaked white envelope on the ground under her boot. She scooped it up, finding a piece of transparent office tape still attached to one end. Concluding that Charlotte had decided to leave and had taped the envelope to the door, Jane raced back to her car.

As thunder rumbled overhead, she examined the ink on the outside of the envelope and saw that it had smeared, though she could still read the word "URGENT." She began to worry that the rainwater had seeped inside and damaged the letter. She opened it. Inside was another yellow sheet of legal paper, just as sodden as the envelope, but readable. As she scanned the message, she couldn't imagine why someone would think this drivel was urgent.

It was a poem. Sir William McGonagall was hardly a household name in the U.S. Jane happened to know him because of the years she'd spent living in England. He was considered one of the worst poets that had ever put pen to paper. "The Bonnie Lassie o' Dundee," the entire poem written out in the note, did not prove an exception. Jane read through a couple of the stanzas and that was about all she could take:

> I see her in my night dreams,
> Wi' her bonnie blue e'e,
> And her face it is the fairest,
> That ever I did see;
> And aboon a' the lassies e'er I eaw,
> There's nane like her to me,
> For she makes my heart feel lichtsome,
> And I'm aye richt glad to see
> The bonnie broon-hair'd lassie o' Bonnie Dundee.

> Her eyes, they beam with innocence,
> Mostly lovely for to see,
> And her heart it is as free from guile,
> As a child on its mother's knee;
> And aboon a' the lasses e'er I saw,
> There's nane like her to me,
> For she aye seems so happy,
> And has a blythe bhnk in her e'e
> The bonnie broon hair'd lassie o' Bonnie Dundee.

At the bottom of the poem, someone had written, "YOU are the Bonnie Lassie of Dundee!!!!!" Hardly a threatening message. Feeling more than mystified, Jane put her car in gear and drove off.

The rain was finally beginning to let up. Turning off the air-conditioning, Jane rolled down her window, glad that the storm had blown in some cooler air. It felt so delicious that she didn't want to return immediately to the restaurant. Instead, she decided to drop by Cordelia's house. She doubted she'd ever get used to calling it Thorn Hall.

Pulling to a stop in the dark, leafy circular drive, she cut the motor and got out. She stood for a moment breathing in the night air and was surprised when she caught a slight whiff of cigarette smoke. As she approached, she realized that Fiona was sitting on the ledge under the stone portico.

"I didn't know you smoked," said Jane, refastening an earring.

"I don't," said Fiona. She looked up and smiled as she cupped her hand around the lit cigarette to hide the glowing tip. "I quit years ago."

"How come you're here?"

"Cordelia didn't tell you?"

"Tell me what?" She sat down on the ledge and listened as Fi explained about the bomb, and that Cordelia had invited her, Annie, and Annie's family to stay with her until the bomb squad figured out who was responsible.

"Boy," said Jane. "You and Annie just can't catch a break." She watched Fiona flick ash into the dirt next to a tall arborvitae hedge, a noticeable strain in her eyes. "How come Annie's family is in town?"

"It's a surprise visit," said Fi. "She hasn't seen or talked to any of them in almost six years. They didn't take it well when she came out to them so she disappeared from their lives. When her sister happened across the video and then showed it to their dad, he wanted to make amends."

"How did they know where she was living?"

"Found out on the Internet, of course." Fi studied the tip of the cigarette. "They're not exactly the Brady Bunch. Even so,

Annie was feeling really positive this morning. She agreed to do that interview with the woman from *Twin Cities Monthly*. Now, after we found the bomb, all she wants is to hide inside Cordelia's mansion and never come out."

Jane fell silent. She had no idea what to say. "You probably don't want to hear this," she said eventually, "but you received another letter from your stalker."

"Oh. Fabulous."

Jane explained that Charlotte Osborne had called her, and that she had stopped by the theater to pick it up. She apologized for reading it, but said she was afraid, because it was soaking wet, that the letter might be ruined. She said it was nothing but a silly poem written by a dreadful Scottish poet. "It's in my car, if you want to see it."

Fi shook her head.

"Have you mentioned the letters to Annie?"

"I let her read them earlier tonight. She was already in such a wretched mood that I figured more bad news would just blend in with the rest."

"How did she take it?"

"How do you think?" She stubbed out the cigarette next to one of Cordelia's garden gnomes.

"I wish I could do something to help you. To make this all go away."

"There's nothing to be done. Hey, you want to come in and meet the anti-Brady Bunch?"

It was the last thing Jane wanted. "Sure. But just so you know, I can't stay very long. I need to get back to the restaurant."

"I wish I had somewhere I needed to be."

"Does that mean you don't like Annie's relatives?"

"I haven't decided yet," said Fi, unwrapping a peppermint candy. "What I do know is that ever since I met Annie, she hasn't wanted to talk about her past. Now I learn that she actually lied to me about her mother. Everybody has a few secrets, but I'm beginning to think Annie has more than her share."

17

Before Fi headed up to her bedroom later that night, she checked the kitchen to make sure it was cleaned and ready for the morning. She found Sharif loading the dishwasher. "How did you get to be such a great guy?"

"I enjoy the entire process of cooking," he said. "It's like meditating. I need that in my life. You calling it a night?"

"Think so."

"Hey, I've got one of those four-poster beds. So does Ted. What's yours like?"

"Just a regular bed, but with a velvet bedspread and this huge snowdrift of satin pillows. Cordelia's really into opulence."

"Tell me about it. I've been wandering around, checking the place out. Never seen so much marble, mahogany, and brass in my life. And that Tiffany glass and all the fringed lamps. Feels like we're in some kind of time warp."

Hearing a burst of laughter coming from the living room, Fi asked, "Who's that?"

"Apparently Bridget plays Scrabble with Ted every night.

Usually they get together for a game after dinner. We were late eating tonight, and then that woman came in for a while."

"Jane."

"Right. Jane. Anyway, Ted still wanted to play. Cordelia decided to join them. She claims she's the Scrabble champion of North America. So does Ted. Should be quite a match up."

Fi lowered her voice. "Have you noticed that Ted seems to have memory problems?"

"I asked Bridget about it. He has Alzheimer's."

"Oh, no, I'm so sorry. Is it a secret?"

"Not sure. Bridget doesn't like to talk about it, especially around him. He's on some kind of drug therapy that's supposed to slow the progression. It's the main reason she quit her nursing job to take over his business. She even moved him into her house last winter. I get the impression that Noah doesn't make all that much money. What he does make, he likes to spend. Between you and me, I think Bridget's pretty disgusted with him."

"Do you know if Bridget's mentioned the Alzheimer's diagnosis to Annie?"

Sharif pulled a stool over and sat down behind the island. "I saw them talking before dinner tonight. It looked intense, so I left them alone. All I can say is, I hope she told her."

"I don't think Annie likes Noah."

He flicked his eyes to her, then back down at the counter. "No."

"Do you know why?"

"You should ask her."

"So you *do* know."

"Like I said—"

"Okay. I get it. You don't think it's your place to talk about it."

"Pretty much."

Fi looked in on the Scrabble game before returning to her bedroom. Ted and Bridget were seated on either side of an ornately carved library table, the board spread out in between them. Cordelia, dressed in a fringed flapper dress and a black headband with a peacock feather stuck through the front, stood at a wooden lectern on the other side of the room, peering intently through a magnifying glass at a massive book.

"It *is* a word," she declared. "If my compact version of the O.E.D records it, it's valid."

"Define it," demanded Ted.

Cordelia raised a finger. "Zoeal. An adjective relating to 'zoeae,' the larvae of crustaceans such as crabs."

"Ridiculous," grunted Ted.

"That means forty-eight more points for *moi*." Cordelia did a few *Saturday Night Fever* moves on her way back to the table.

"Well then," said Ted, "if you can do that, I'm going to use your Z. 'Lazo.' It's an alternate spelling for 'lasso.' Go ahead, check it out. By the way, that's twenty-three points for me."

Ted seemed to be having a wonderful time, and the love in Bridget's eyes for her father touched Fi. She desperately wanted Annie to find her way back to both her sister and her dad. Noah, well, that was another question.

Because Fi didn't want to intrude, she tiptoed away, climbing the broad central stairs up to the second floor. She was about to head down the hallway to her room when she heard the sound of a door creak open. Ahead of her, ducking out of Bridget and

Noah's bedroom, came Willow, the nanny. She stopped for a second to finish buttoning her blouse, then walked across the hall and disappeared into the room she was sharing with Tyrion. The verdict seemed pretty inescapable.

Entering her own bedroom, she found Annie standing at a mullioned window overlooking the back garden. "Dad and I are going to start playing poker together tomorrow afternoon," she said, lightly touching the curtains. "Until he returns to California. Bridget said it's important to keep him active, his daily activities regulated." She turned to Fi and said, "He has Alzheimer's."

Fi slipped her arms around Annie's waist and nuzzled her neck. "I'm so sorry."

"Seems par for the course. I just get him back only to find that I'm going to lose him again. Bridget says it's like fog. It rolls in and out. She never knows from one moment to the next how present he'll be."

"I don't know how much this helps, but I love you."

Annie leaned back against Fi. "Sometimes, that's the only thing that keeps me going."

Fi longed to feel Annie's hands on her, the softness and the weight. But there was something she wanted even more. Secrets could derail a relationship. Fi couldn't stand the thought that Annie's secrets might split them apart. "I need to ask you something."

"Mmm."

"Why don't you like Noah?"

Annie stiffened and pulled away. "I don't want to talk about him."

"I just saw Willow come out of his bedroom. She was

buttoning her blouse. He was apparently having sex with her while your sister and your dad are downstairs playing Scrabble."

"That freakin' sack of shit," said Annie, her eyes registering anger.

"Is that why you hate him? You knew he cheats on your sister."

"No, I didn't know, but it doesn't surprise me."

"Do you think Bridget knows?"

She shut her eyes. "God, that man poisons everything he touches."

Fi sat down on the bed. When Annie came and sat down beside her, she was trembling. "What is it?" asked Fi. "There's more, isn't there. Please, Annie. I need to know."

"I . . . can't."

"There's got to be a reason you hate Noah so much."

She turned her face away.

"Don't you trust me?"

"Of course I trust you."

"Then?"

She sank back against the mattress and drew herself into a fetal position.

"Oh, sweetheart," said Fi, lying down facing her. "If it hurts that much to talk about it—"

"It's just . . . there was no reason to tell you before because I never intended to see him again. I never would have if it hadn't been for that wretched video."

Fi waited a few seconds and, unable to stop herself, she asked again. "What did he do?"

In a voice so distant, so muffled and hollow that it could have come from another universe, she said, "He raped me."

"Oh . . . oh, God." She sat up.

"It was the night he and Bridget got married."

Fiona felt something inexpressible tighten inside her stomach.

"You have to understand, I spent years blaming myself for what happened. I eventually figured it out. *He* was to blame, not me."

"Annie—"

"He was my friend. I loved him like a brother. If it hadn't been for Sharif, my whole world would have collapsed."

Fi had to ask. "Did you tell your parents?"

Wiping tears off her cheeks, Annie sat up and swung her legs off the bed. "Mom knew. Dad and Bridget didn't. Don't."

Fi waited a heartbeat. "Why did you tell me your mother was dead?"

"Because she *was* dead. To me. I couldn't talk about her. Just thinking about her felt like a being cut by a razor. I hated her. Okay, so she's dead and gone now and I should forgive her, but I can't."

It explained so much. Turning back to look at Annie, she said, "Is that why you backed away from me when you thought I was getting too serious about you? That whole month before I asked you to marry me?"

Annie's gaze drifted off to some indeterminate point in space. "After the rape . . . it was hard to trust anyone. It's like . . . if you never open yourself up to someone, you'll never have to experience the pain that comes when your love is betrayed."

"But I'd never do that."

Looking down, Annie said, "What I didn't know, what you taught me, is that we heal by letting love in. We move forward by being loved and loving others."

Fiona reached for Annie's hand.

"Can this be enough for now?" asked Annie. "I've worked so hard these last few years not to let that rape define me. I thought I'd made progress, until . . . Noah reappeared."

"How can you even be around him now?"

"I didn't exactly invite him back into our lives, did I?"

For the first time, Fiona understood what she'd done by inviting Annie's family to stay with them.

"So, I guess being around Noah again is the price I pay for trying to repair my relationship with Bridget and Dad. I need them in my life," said Annie. "I want that more than I can say."

In that moment, Fi also understood something else. Once she got over the shock of Annie's revelation, her own temper would kick in. Noah needed to pay for what he'd done.

If she did nothing else with the rest of her life, she needed to make that happen.

18

Friday morning dawned sunny and hot, with jungle-wet air a gift from last night's thunderstorm. Jane dropped a box of fresh-baked pastries from her restaurant at Cordelia's house just after seven. She'd stayed at Chez Thorn much longer than she'd anticipated last night. Noah had opened a couple of bottles of wine. Everyone seemed to be in a talkative mood—everyone, that is, except for Annie. Jane had never seen her so quiet.

The only person she was able to rouse at such an early hour was Sharif, who seemed delighted by the offering and lifted the box from her arms, saying that he'd start the coffee brewing. He held the door open for her, assuming that she would come in, but she begged off. She had somewhere else she needed to be.

Driving through rush-hour traffic on her way to Blooming-ton, Jane had a lot of time to think about how she should approach Sergeant Bill Larson, an old buddy of her partner in investigations, A. J. Nolan. Bill and Nolan had first become friends when they worked together as part of the MPD's Special Operations Division. Nolan had brought Bill and his wife, Alyssa, to the Lyme House for dinner a few years back, though

Jane doubted he would remember her. It was well before she and Nolan had formed their partnership, so Bill knew her only as a restaurateur. She hoped that dropping Nolan's name would be the magic bullet to get her inside his office door.

And indeed, half an hour later, she was sitting in front of his desk, explaining her current relationship with Nolan, handing across a card that said, NOLAN & LAWLESS INVESTIGATIONS.

"I knew he'd gone private since he retired from homicide," said Bill, examining the card. "I didn't realize he'd taken a partner. You any relationship to Ray Lawless?"

"He's my father." She waited to see what his reaction might be. Cops and defense attorneys didn't always mix well.

"I know him," said Bill, leaning back in his chair. "I even voted for him when he ran for governor."

That seemed like ancient history to Jane now, though some people still remembered it. "That's great to hear."

"So what can I do for you?"

She explained that she was a friend of Fiona McGuy and Annie Johnson.

"And I suppose you're here to see if you can shake any information loose about our investigation into the pipe bomb on their property."

"I know it's an ongoing investigation, so you probably can't comment on it."

He smiled at her with lifted eyebrows. "But you're still hoping for a few crumbs, friend to friend."

She returned his smile. "Pretty much, yeah."

He picked up a pen and began to play with it. "Well," he said, thinking it over. "I suppose it would be okay for you to tell Ms. McGuy and Ms. Johnson that we're about to make an arrest."

"That was fast."

He shrugged. "We got lucky. Found a sales receipt in the backpack. I would imagine the bomb maker either forgot about it or figured it would be destroyed when the bomb detonated. Either way, we knew we weren't dealing with a criminal Einstein. Once we had the receipt, we were able to subpoena the store video and the credit card number that was used and the name on that card."

"Man or woman?"

He shook his head.

"Do you have any idea about motive?"

"Yeah, we think we do, but I can't speak to that, at least not right now."

"Okay. I'm very grateful for your time."

"Ms. McGuy and Ms. Johnson can rest easy. We've got this one under control."

Jane stood and shook his hand. "That will mean a lot."

"Tell your friends that when I'm able to give them the full story, I will. And next time you see that old reprobate, Nolan, tell him hey from me."

Sharif returned to Cordelia's mansion just after eleven, sweating and dirty. He'd left because he needed to clear his head, to get away from all the family drama. He'd gone for a motorcycle ride out in the country. The sight of farms and fields always calmed him down. Then again, he'd forgotten how hot Minnesota could be in the summer. Might as well live in a South American jungle or set up housekeeping in equatorial Africa.

Climbing the stairs, hoping he wouldn't run into anyone until he'd had a chance to shower and change his clothes, he ducked into his room only to find Ted sitting on the bed with his back to the door.

"Hey, man, I think you're in the wrong place. Your bedroom's across the hall."

When Ted didn't move or make any response, Sharif noticed that the revolver he'd brought with him from Ohio was lying on the bed. And then it hit him. Ted was reading Annie's letter diary. "Oh, God, man, no. That's not for you." He leapt for the gun, stuffed it back in his case, then grabbed for the notebook.

"Back off," said Ted, yanking the notebook against his chest.

Both the gun and the notebook had been packed in Sharif's suitcase. Ted must have come in, thinking it was his room, and found both. "Come on, man. You shouldn't be reading that." When he reached for it this time, Ted let go without a fight.

"Doesn't matter," said Ted. "I finished it." He stared straight ahead. His eyes looked dull, confused. "My daughter was—" He swallowed.

"Yeah. I know."

"Did . . . did I know? Did I forget?" With pleading eyes, he searched Sharif's face.

"Oh, man, no. Annie never told anyone, not even me. I learned about it the same way you did—from reading those letters."

"Letters she wrote to—" Here, he swallowed again. "Moira."

"Yeah. I thought Annie was upset with her mom because of the way she was treated when she came out to her."

"We were awful," said Ted. "Both of us."

"She forgives you. I know she does."

"Raped," he whispered. He seemed to be trying to comprehend what it all meant. "Noah raped her on his wedding night."

"Every time I see him, I want to beat the living crap out of him. I will one day. That's a promise."

The dullness returned to Ted eyes. "How? How could I have loved a man like that all these years?" Looking up sharply, he asked, "Does . . . Annie's sister—" He glanced down, searching for the name. "Does Bridget know?"

"I don't think so."

"Annie needs to press charges."

"Yeah, I guess. Except, it would be hard to prove so many years after the fact. I'm not even sure she could press charges now. It might be too late."

"If she'd only come to me."

"Look, Ted—"

"No," he said, rising from the bed. "This has gone on long enough. Bridget needs to know the truth."

"I agree. But maybe we should talk to Annie first. You know, see how she wants to handle it."

"I want to kill that bastard," said Ted, balling his hands into fists.

"You'll have to stand in line."

Moving around Sharif, Ted made straight for the door.

"What are you going to do?"

"What I should have done a long time ago."

19

Mimi lived for the unexpected. When she'd flown to Minneapolis to be with Noah, she couldn't believe she was still dithering about whether or not to accept Noah's marriage proposal—when he finally made it. But of course she would accept. He was perfect for her. The more she thought about the few minutes she'd spent with him yesterday, the clearer it became. He was fighting his feelings, for sure, but it was only a matter of time before he realized how much he loved her, that he couldn't go on living without her. That was why she'd boarded a plane last night, landing in New York just after ten. She'd taken a taxi to the theater district and booked a room overlooking Times Square at her favorite hotel, the Marriott Marquis. She stayed up all night watching the lights outside her window. She was too amped to sleep.

This morning, after downing an entire pot of coffee, she'd taken a cab to Bergdorf's. Who knew the store didn't open until eleven? What sort of business practice was that? Forced to walk the streets, she eventually found herself talking to a cruise ship agent at a tiny storefront several blocks away. The moment the man began explaining about an opportunity to book a last-minute thirty-five-day Mediterranean adventure cruise, she knew it was just what she and Noah wanted. Thirty-five glorious days all to themselves. She bought tickets right there, on the spot.

By the time she returned to Bergdorf Goodman, the doors were mercifully open. She hurried up to the bridal department and, after some deliberating, purchased a couture Marchesa gown. She asked for it to be overnighted to her hotel in Minneapolis, just in case Noah popped the question before they returned to California. In fact, she saw no reason to return home at all.

Landing back at Minneapolis–Saint Paul International shortly before three, the cruise tickets tucked safely in her purse, Mimi was riding high. A whirlwind trip to New York was just what the doctor ordered. She hated puns, but laughed anyway. What Mimi craved more than anything was excitement. Warp speed was pure joy, the solution to her problems. Drugs couldn't make a woman healthy and happy, they just made her numb.

Returning to the Maxfield West, Mimi ran herself a bath. While it was filling, she stripped off her clothes and stood in front of the mirror. She'd left last night without a suitcase or even an overnight bag. She was a woman on a mission and couldn't be bothered with silly preparations, like bringing a toothbrush or even makeup. But now that she was back, she needed to groom herself for a night of lovemaking. She called Noah, left him a message, and then sank down into the hot water, allowing it to ease the tension in her muscles.

The only problem was, the longer she spent soaking in the tub, the more she began to grow sluggish and dull. She felt like a balloon with a slow leak.

"No," she said, pressing her fists to her eyes. "Not now. Leave me the hell alone." The black hole was out there, she could feel it. It was hovering just outside her field of vision, close enough to breathe its hot, foul breath against her neck. "I hate you," she screamed. "My life is good for once. You have no right to ruin it! Please, God, don't let the dark take it away."

20

"You got another one of your fan letters," said Roxy, swaggering into Fiona's office and dropping the envelope in front of her. "That makes two this week."

"Lovely," said Fi, looking up from her laptop.

Plunking down on the chair opposite the desk, Roxy chewed her fingernail. "Are they from a secret admirer?"

"It's a long story," said Fi, wishing the letter would quietly crawl away and burn to a crisp. So far, her day had felt endless, and this little gift just made it worse. She was behind on everything, yet her thoughts were still on what she'd found out last night about Annie. And Noah. It was impossible to concentrate on anything else.

"You don't want to talk about it, do you?" said Roxy.

"Huh? Oh, the letters? No, not really."

Roxy folded her arms across her chest. "I was thinking about that pipe bomb. If you don't feel safe at your place, you could always come live with me for a while."

"Cordelia invited us to move into to her house for a few days."

"Wow. Staying with the boss. That's cool."

Fi rested her chin on her hand and gazed across the desk at Roxy, wondering why she looked so disappointed. "Besides, you and Burton don't have room for us in that small apartment."

"I'm not living there anymore."

"What?"

"We split, must be two months ago. I'm renting the lower half of a duplex near the university. Got lots of room."

"Wait, wait. You and Burton split? Why didn't you tell me?" She shrugged.

"Are you okay?"

"Me? I'm great. It was my idea."

This was all news to Fi. "I thought you two were so happy."

"He was. I wasn't. I'm not the same person I was when I first started dating him."

"You're not?"

Yanking on the front of her bib overalls, Roxy flashed Fi a smile pregnant with meaning.

"I don't understand. Is there someone else?"

"Yeah. I mean, I know how I feel."

"But you're not sure if he feels the same way."

"Well," said Roxy, raising an eyebrow, "let's talk about it over a drink one night soon."

"Sure."

On her way out the door, Roxy stopped. Turning around, she said, "I love you, babe."

"I love you, too."

"Thought so. Later."

Fi worked quietly at her desk for the next few minutes until she was interrupted by Charlotte poking her head into the room and clearing her throat.

"You busy?" asked Charlotte.

She kept her eyes on the report in front of her. "Yup, pretty busy."

"Could I have . . . just a minute?"

Looking up, she saw that Charlotte was gnawing at her lower lip. "Of course," said Fi, taking pity on the poor girl. It was probably her mother again. Charlotte needed a therapist, not a coworker.

Moving hesitantly into the room, Charlotte settled into a chair. She fidgeted, yanking at her hair, pulling on her denim jumper.

"I should thank you for calling Jane last night," said Fi.

"Oh, God, does that mean she found the letter? I said I'd wait for her outside the stage door, but then it started raining. Felt kind of creepy out there all alone, you know? So I taped it to the door. Then I got to thinking that, if she didn't see me sitting on the bench, she might have driven away, but when I looked this morning, I didn't see the letter anywhere. I was so worried that it had blown away?"

"It's all good," said Fi.

"I mean, you weren't here yesterday and I thought you'd want to see it?" With her eyes cast down, she added, "I heard all about the bomb at your house."

"It didn't go off," said Fi. "We're all safe. What was it you wanted to talk to me about?"

"Oh, well." Now she seemed flustered. "I . . . I'm so ashamed. I hardly slept at all last night."

"Why?"

"Well, I mean, you know that cat? The white Persian? The one who likes to sit on Cordelia's head?"

"Wally."

"Yeah. Him. When I went out the stage door last night he . . . he slipped out. I didn't even know he was there. I never meant for it to happen. Cordelia's going to be furious at me when she finds out. She'll fire my ass, I just know she will."

Fi held up her hand. "I saw the cat this morning in Cordelia's office."

Her eyes widened. "You did?"

"If he got out, someone must have let him back in."

"For real? He's back?"

"He's here and he's safe."

"Oh, boy. I dodged a bullet on that one."

"Nobody's going to fire you for inadvertently letting a cat out a door."

She squirmed some more. "My mom thinks it's only a matter of time before I lose my job. She said all I'm good for is lying on the couch and watching TV."

"Well, you tell your mother from me that she's wrong," said Fi. "Now, if that's it, I really need to get back to work."

"Absolutely," said Charlotte, regarding Fi with almost religious awe as she stood up, running her hands over the wrinkles on her jumper. "Anyway, I'm glad you're back at work today. Like I said, I always miss you when you're gone. Um, I'll go." She backed toward the door. "Thanks. You're the best."

Once Fi was alone, she picked up the letter Roxy had delivered. The last one sounded so inane, she figured this one would be more of same. But when she ripped the top open and removed the piece of paper, she found one short paragraph that nearly took her breath away.

I'M BEGINNING TO THINK YOU DON'T
GET IT!! WHY HAVEN'T YOU DUMPED
ANNIE? DO I NEED TO PROVIDE A
LITTLE PUSH?

21

Sharif sprawled across a fainting couch in Cordelia's living room, otherwise known as the great hall. Annie and Ted sat across from him on the main couch, with Bridget on the oriental rug between them, playing with Tyrion. Spread in front of the little boy was a brightly colored set of plastic, interconnecting gears. Tyrion appeared rapt, forcing the gears into different configurations and laughing at the results. "Look, Mama," he kept saying. "Look!"

While Annie and Ted's attention was on the little boy, Sharif studied Bridget. She seemed pretty calm for a woman who'd just found out her husband had raped her sister. Without consulting Annie, Ted had broken the news to her shortly after leaving Sharif's bedroom. And now, they were all gathered together, waiting for the big explosion.

It was going on five. Noah had been out most the afternoon, but had returned a few minutes ago. Bridget said she'd left him a note on the bed, telling him to come down to the hall right away.

"What's this about?" demanded Noah, striding into the room

a few minutes later. "I don't appreciate being summoned." He studied his cell phone, then looked up. When nobody responded, he asked, "Where's Willow?"

"I fired her," said Bridget.

"Fired her," he said, shock replacing his indignation. "Why on earth would you do that?"

"Because she was sleeping with my husband." Her eyes were so fierce, it stopped him cold.

He glanced around, perhaps comprehending for the first time how much hate was directed his way, or maybe he was as clueless as usual. Sharif really couldn't tell. What he could see was that Bridget's comment had knocked him off his game.

Noah forced a smile. "That's . . . ridiculous. Where did you get an idea like that?"

"Do you deny it?" demanded Ted.

"Well, yeah, absolutely."

"Oh, cut the crap," muttered Bridget. She drew Tyrion into her arms and kissed his head.

Annie glared at him. "You are . . . filth. Why don't you go stick your head in a blender?"

"Excuse me? A dyke tells me *I'm* filth?"

Sharif shot to his feet. With a straight-arm to Noah's face, he knocked him back against the wall, feeling a satisfying crunch when his knuckles connected with Noah's nose. He lunged at him a second time, but Noah ducked and dodged away, knocking over a standing lamp.

"You people are *insane*," he shouted, seemingly aghast when he touched his upper lip and realized he was bleeding. "I should call the police and press assault charges. You attacked me, totally unprovoked."

"You wanna talk about provocation?" said Sharif through clenched teeth. "Go ahead. Call the cops. Let's talk about what you've done."

"Stop it," said Bridget. "Sharif, leave him alone. This is between me and Noah."

"I don't know what's wrong with you people," said Noah. "But I'm not going to stand here and listen to this bullshit."

It took every ounce of willpower Sharif possessed not to beat the slick bastard to a bloody pulp.

As Bridget stood, she lifted Tyrion into Annie's arms. "Noah? We need to talk. Alone." Her face was flushed a deep red.

Noah's gaze bounced from person to person. "I don't think so," he said. "No, this is some kind of trap." He turned away, then stopped and swiveled back around. He set his jaw and said, "I'm not a perfect human being. Okay, so I've made mistakes. But remember, there are two sides to every story. I'm the same man I've always been—the man you say you love. I've been an integral part of this family for a long, long time. I don't deserve to be treated like an outlaw."

Sharif couldn't help himself. He came at him with a cocked fist.

This time, Noah took off and didn't look back.

Jane was on her way up the walk to Cordelia's front door when Noah burst out, his face flushed and his nose bleeding. "Are you okay?" she asked.

"Those people in that house are lunatics," he said, using his remote to open the door to his van. "Enter at your own risk."

She stood on the pavement and watched him roar out of the

circular drive, unsure what was going on. After ringing the bell, she waited until Ted Johnson opened the door.

"Can I help you?" he asked, peering at her as if he had no idea who she was.

"I'm Jane," she said. "Jane Lawless. We met last night. I'm Cordelia's friend."

"Oh, of course." Tapping his head, he said, "Senior moment. Come in."

She had the sense that he still had no idea who she was.

"I don't think Cordelia's here, though I could be wrong. Let's ask."

He led her into the hall.

"Something wrong with Noah?" asked Jane, pausing under the arch.

"Is he still here or did he leave?" asked Sharif, examining his right knuckle. He stood next to an overturned floor lamp.

"He took off in his van."

"Good."

"If we're lucky, he'll never come back," muttered Ted, dropping into one of the wingback chairs.

Annie was sitting on the couch. Tyrion played on the floor in front of her. Bridget stood facing the stained-glass window, looking up. When she turned back to the room, her lips pressed together and trembling, she wiped tears from her eyes.

Jane wondered what she'd missed. When nobody offered an explanation, she slid her sunglasses up on her head and forged on. "I come bearing good news."

"That would be novel," said Annie,

Jane could easily have called after visiting the Bloomington Bomb Squad this morning, but she wanted to deliver the news in person. Meetings had kept her from stopping by until now. "The Bloomington police are about to make an arrest. They found the person who left the bomb on your front lawn."

Annie's eyes widened and blinked. "That's incredible. How did you find out?"

"I talked to Sergeant Bill Larson this morning. He happens to be a friend of a friend. I don't have any details, but I figured you could use some positive news. The police will call when the person is finally in custody. Shouldn't be long."

Annie relaxed into the couch cushions. "That is incredible news. Maybe we can go home soon."

"I kind of like it here," said Sharif, sitting down next to her and spreading his arms wide across the back of the cushions.

"I prefer a house with a pool," said Ted. "Rose gardens don't do it for me."

"I prefer a house without Noah in it." Annie looked down at her hands. "Scratch that. Make it a *world* without him in it."

"We can work on that," said Sharif. "In the meantime, when he gets back, let's tell him to take a hike. Go check into a motel. Or better yet, let's pack his bags and tell him to mosey on back to California. If he wants to argue the point, he might just run into another one of my fists."

Jane had apparently missed a major family fight. "Well," she said, "I should let you get back to—" She wasn't sure how to finish the sentence.

"Thanks so much, Jane," said Annie.

"You're welcome to stay for dinner," offered Sharif. "Without Noah, we've got one extra rib eye."

"Better get back to the restaurant."

"Big green salad? French bread slathered with garlic butter?

Homemade peach ice cream for dessert. I'm just about to start the coals in the Weber."

"Wow," said Jane. "If you ever decide to give up coaching football, you've got a job waiting for you at my restaurant."

"Something to consider," he replied, capturing Annie's neck in the crook of his arm and kissing her cheek.

22

Mimi sat hunched over her laptop, checking her husband's Facebook page to see if he'd mentioned her absence. He hadn't. He'd left her a good twenty messages in the last couple of days, voice mails and texts, none of which she'd answered. He'd spent a lot of time taking her for granted. A little worry on his part might snap him out of it.

After her bath, she'd done a couple lines of coke and felt much better. She'd dressed in a sexy georgette chemise, with an open front and a matching thong. She wanted to be ready for Noah if he decided to stop by, though the longer she waited, the more churlish she became. She'd ordered a club sandwich from room service not five minutes before, so when the knock came so soon, she was surprised.

"Boy, that was quick," she said, opening the door. Instead of a waiter, Noah stood outside. She cocked her head. "What happened to your face?"

"A muscle-bound thug happened," he said. "I need to use your bathroom. And I need some disinfectant, and some ice."

"Okay," she said, watching him stomp into the bedroom. She

curled up on the couch, wondering why she wasn't happier to see him. He didn't seem to be in a very good mood, so there was that. Well, as it happened, neither was she. She switched channels on the flat screen, looking for something more interesting than CNN.

When the sandwich arrived, Noah ate the entire thing, hardly even looking up. He was pissed that she didn't have any disinfectant and that he'd been forced to get his own ice. "I'm still hungry."

"You know," said Mimi. "I didn't order that for you. I didn't even know you were coming."

He examined the plate. "There's a piece of kale left."

"Oh, yummy."

He tried a sheepish grin. "This hasn't been one of my better days. I got your message, so I knew you were still in town."

"Yup, still here."

"So," he said, wiping his mouth on a napkin, "tell me what's going on. Some new drama, no doubt."

"Oh, just this and that. Nothing special." She didn't feel this was the best time to tell him about the wedding gown. When she remembered the cruise tickets in her purse, she wondered why on earth she'd bought them. It would take time for both of them to negotiate their divorces. Months—perhaps more. The cruise ship left Rome in less than a week. She hoped she could get her deposit back. Well, to be more accurate, Noah's deposit. Poor guy. There were times when she thought he was the most brilliant, gifted man she'd ever met. At the moment, he just seemed dense. She didn't like dense, stupid people. In fact, they repulsed her.

Gingerly touching his swollen nose, he said, "I think I'm going to call it quits with my wife. Her entire family is ganging up on me."

"For what?"

"Let's just say that, on occasion, I can be a bad boy."

"Tell me something I don't know."

"You like bad boys, don't you Mimi?"

"What if I do?" She didn't really feel like talking. "I've got an idea. Let's have sex. I promise, I won't come near your nose."

He raised an eyebrow.

"Oh, hell. You're in a funk. So am I. Maybe it will help."

He appeared to think about it. "If we do sleep together, I don't want you to think it's more than it is."

"I know you love me."

"Mimi?"

"As much as you're able. Sometimes I think you're the one who has a problem. With real love and commitment. I don't think you're very good at it."

"What a hurtful thing to say."

"Yeah, well. *Physician, heal thyself.*"

Now he was angry. "What would you know about real love?"

"I know how I feel about you."

"Oh, Mimi, what do I do with you?"

They spent the next hour going at it like rabbits, at least that's how Mimi thought about it while it was happening. They became nibbling, flopping, single-minded bunnies. She knew the image wasn't the least bit romantic, which was unlike her. Eventually, sweaty and breathing hard, they broke apart and lay on top of the sheets. Twilight was falling over downtown Minneapolis and the room was growing dim. Mimi had always hated twilight—the in-between time. All afternoon she'd been feeling her mood grow more and more sour. It was her internal twilight that worried her most, the hours between euphoria and a deep, viselike depression. Why on earth had she bought that wedding dress? Noah was never going to marry her. He'd lied to her over and over. All he did was use her for sex. Though . . . to be fair, he deserved one last chance.

"Noah?"

"Hmm."

"Do you think we'll ever get married?"

He pulled himself up until he was resting against the pillows. "No, Mimi."

"You're sure?"

"I'm positive."

"Is it because I'm older than you?"

"That has nothing to do with it."

"Then what?"

"Can I trust you with the truth?"

"I'm much stronger now than I used to be."

"Because it will hurt."

"I have to know."

"Okay. Here it is. I don't love you, Mimi. I'll never love you the way you want."

She looked over at him. His swollen nose seemed to alter his entire face. Instead of the Noah she knew and loved, he looked like Shrek, the cartoon ogre who lived in a swamp. "I guess I needed to hear that."

"You won't . . . I mean, you're not planning to tell anyone about our . . . time together?"

She could see him sweating the answer and it gave her a welcome sense of power.

"This should probably be our last time together," he said.

Yes, she thought. It will be.

"But before I go, let's order up a fabulous dinner. An expensive bottle of wine. Something really special."

"I'd like that. And you know what? I bought a jar of that fig jam you like so much. I've got some brie in the refrigerator. And crackers. We can munch on that while we wait."

"You're a good woman, Mimi. If Ethan isn't the right man for you, I know you'll find him one day."

"Gee, Noah. That's nice of you to say."

"Yeah," he said, leaning his head back and closing his eyes. "No problem."

23

"Sharif actually hit Noah?" said Fi, sitting cross-legged in the center of the bed.

Annie had just returned to their room after spending the last half hour cleaning up in Cordelia's kitchen. Pacing in front of Fi, she seemed intent on wearing a groove in the rug. "After what Noah said—calling me a dyke and insinuating that it made me the same kind of moral scum he is—do you blame him?"

"I just wish I'd been there to see it," said Fi. She was elated. Score one for Sharif. "I wonder where Noah went?" It was going on nine and he still hadn't returned.

Annie didn't answer. She just kept pacing.

At least, thought Fi, things seemed to be moving in the right direction. With the exception of the note from Fi's stalker suggesting that he might have to give Annie a push out of her life— whatever that meant—Noah was soon to be history, and with the pipe bomber about to be arrested, they would be able to return home in the next day or two.

"Did you play poker with your dad today?"

"It's a standing date for as long as he's here. Four on the dot.

He bitched about Noah the entire time we played today. I've never seen him so angry. Have to say it warmed my heart. He has all these ideas about how to make Noah pay."

Fi had come up with an idea of her own.

"Look," said Annie, finally coming to a stop. "I've got to get out of here. I need some fresh air, and I don't mean in the rose garden."

Fi hid to admit that the rear of the house was more like a maze of tall hedges dotted with a few rosebushes than it was a garden.

"What do you say we go for a run?"

The thought of Annie leaving the safety of the mansion made Fi nervous. "I don't know. It's dark out."

"Exactly. Nobody will see us."

Annie's favorite times to run were early morning, before first light, and after the sun went down in the evenings. She always said that, in the dark, running felt like flying.

"Fi, come on. We could both use some fresh air."

"It's pretty hot out."

"We can shower together when we get back," she said, her voice dropping to a seductive register.

"What if we ask Sharif to go with us?"

"Sure, that works for me. You want to ask him or should I?" She stood at the chest and began pawing through one of the lower drawers.

"I'll do it," said Fi, climbing off the bed. When she opened the bedroom door, she found Sharif trudging toward his room, his shirt soaked with sweat. "Hey," she said, keeping her voice down. Bridget was sleeping in Tyrion's room tonight. She'd taken him up to bed shortly after finishing her nightly game of Scrabble with Ted. Fi figured that, by now, they were both asleep. Stepping out into the hall and closing the door behind her, Fi asked, "Where have you been?"

"Well—" He scratched the back of his neck. "Cordelia's got an elliptical machine in the basement. I decided to take it for a spin."

"Does that mean you won't go for a run with me and Annie?"

He hesitated. "I should be here when Noah gets back. I am, after all, the official bouncer. Then again, I suppose she's determined."

"Pretty much. If you went along, I'd feel a lot safer. We wouldn't have to be gone long."

He wiped the sweat off his forehead with the flat of his hand. "I'll go tell Ted where we're going, and that we'll be back soon."

Fiona spent the next few minutes changing into a T-shirt, running shorts, and finding her athletic shoes. When she was ready, she and Annie trotted down the central stairs to the great hall. Sharif came down a few minutes later.

"Ted wasn't in his room," he said. "You think we should look around for him?"

"He's probably watching TV," said Annie. "Let's leave by the back way, through the garden."

They ran down a side street until they came to the edge of Lake of the Isles. In the city, the stars never seemed as bright to Fiona as they did in Eden Prairie. She wasn't as fit as Annie or Sharif, so she lagged behind. Feeling entirely winded after only a couple of minutes, she called for them to stop. "This humidity is too much," she said, leaning over, hands resting on her knees. "Have you had enough air yet, Annie? Can't we call it a night?"

Annie trotted back to her, looking disappointed. She seemed to have so much nervous energy inside her that Fi figured she could have run happily around the entire lake.

Two men approached along the footpath, walking hand in hand.

"Hey," said the taller of the two, stopping just a couple feet away. "Aren't you Fiona and Annie. From the video? What a small world."

Annie took one look at the men and bolted across the grass toward the street. Sharif rushed after her.

"Did I upset her?" asked the man, turning to watch her run away.

"It's okay," said Fi.

"I'm right, aren't I? My boyfriend and I loved it."

"Thanks. The response has been a little overwhelming."

"Sure. I get it. We don't want to bother you. Just . . . you know . . . nice to meet you." They moved on quickly.

Fi took a couple of deep breaths and then took off after Annie and Sharif. She found them walking together down the center of the street. Sharif had his arm around Annie's shoulders. By the light of the streetlamp, Fi could see that she was near tears.

"I can't even step outside without someone hassling me," said Annie as Fi caught up to her.

Fi might have argued that the two guys were simply being friendly, but if Annie didn't see it that way, she'd take it as a criticism, and that would only cause more problems. Annie was on edge. Not even the good news they'd received today could shake her out of it.

Half a block from Cordelia's house, Fi pointed. "Isn't that Noah's van? Damn it. He came home while we were gone."

"I should never have left," said Sharif.

As they came nearer, Fi saw that the van had come to a stop at an odd angle. The lights were on, the motor was still on and the front driver's door was ajar.

"What the hell?" said Annie.

Sharif raced ahead. Ducking his head inside, he pulled immediately back out. "Call 911," he shouted.

Fi and Annie rushed up behind him.

Annie's hand rose to cover her mouth. "Oh—"

Fiona backed up a step. Noah was slumped forward and slightly to the right of the steering wheel, arms drooping forward. A huge chunk of his head was missing.

Sharif pressed his fingers to the bloody side of Noah's neck. "I think he's gone."

"God," said Annie, looking around wildly. "God."

"I don't have my phone with me," said Fiona.

Sharif reached for his back pocket. "I'll do it." He stepped away from the van and made the call.

In the darkness, the muggy stillness, Fi glimpsed the truth in Annie's eyes and let slip the word they both had to be thinking.

"Murder," she whispered.

Jane came home around nine thirty to let her dogs out, give them their evening kibble, and play with them for a few minutes. She had every intention of returning to the restaurant to work late. And yet, as she peeled herself an orange, watching the dogs play in the grass through the window over the sink, she felt worn out. Collapsing into a chair, she almost laughed. For weeks, she'd been working the restaurant like a gunslinger. When Wayne saw her coming, he made himself scarce. He was right to be afraid for his job. Jane had met today with her liquor distributor. The information she was given would be the final nail in his coffin.

Sitting at the table, Jane yawned so deeply that she shuddered when she finished. She suddenly felt incapable of movement. This had been her lot far too often in the last few months— exhausted by early evening, too tired to get up in the morning. Given a choice, all she wanted was to crawl into bed, pull the covers up and sleep, not until the alarm clock went off, but until she actually felt rested.

When the doorbell rang, Jane pried herself out of the chair. Julia stood on the steps outside her front door.

"I saw your car in the drive and decided to stop." She held out a new bottle of Ativan. "Here."

"Thanks," said Jane. After what she'd said to Julia last time, she was surprised that she'd come to the house with additional pills. What surprised her even more was that Julia was wearing sunglasses.

"Well, I guess that's all," said Julia. "Oh, one more thing." She reached behind her and picked up a sack. "Consider this a present. It's heavy, so be careful."

"What is it?"

"Several bottles of *good* wine. I hate to think of you drinking that bilge you served me a few days ago."

"That's really nice of you."

"I can be nice. On occasion."

"Why don't you come in and help me open one?"

"Are you sure you're not too busy? Someplace you need to be? A woman in your bed, counting the seconds until your return?"

"Lose the sarcasm."

"Who says I'm being sarcastic?"

As they entered the kitchen, Julia said, "Where are the dogs?"

"They're outside," said Jane, retrieving two wineglasses from the cupboard. She drew out the bottle of Carignan and found a corkscrew. "How come you're wearing sunglasses?"

Julia shrugged. "Sometimes bright lights hurt my eyes."

"You mean like the moon?"

"You're in a better mood tonight."

"You think so?"

Taking off the sunglasses and placing them on the table, Julia messaged her temples.

"If you've got a headache, I'm sure I could find you some aspirin."

"I'm fine."

Jane studied her while she uncorked the bottle. Something was wrong. She'd sensed it last time, too. She wondered if it was the reason for Julia's visit. "What's up? Come on. Tell me about it. Who knows? Maybe I can help."

"Don't be nice to me. I can't handle it."

"Why would you say that?"

"Because I know you don't really care."

Jane let out a frustrated breath. "Is that the way it is with us now?"

"It's the way you want it to be."

To some extent, she was right. Jane couldn't see herself in a relationship with Julia ever again, and yet, for good or ill, certain threads still bound their lives together. "I do care. Maybe not the way you want, but . . . if you're in trouble—"

"Why would I be in trouble?"

"You didn't come here tonight to give me a bunch of pills I don't need and didn't ask for. Just because we're not lovers anymore doesn't mean we can't be friends."

Julia gave her a half-lidded look. "That is such a lesbian cliché. We're not lovers, babe, but by golly, we can still be buddies."

"Are you really that bitter?"

"Let's just say my life hasn't turned out the way I planned."

"Very little turns out the way we plan."

"You sound like a fortune cookie."

"Look," said Jane, pouring the wine, "I'm here if you want to talk, but I'm not interested in arguing."

Elbows on the table, hands buried in her hair, Julia said, "I'm not in a very good place right now. To be honest, I would like to talk about it." She stopped when Jane's landline rang.

"Whoever it is," said Jane, "I'll make it quick." She leaned back and grabbed the cordless off the counter, ready to tell whoever had called that she would need to phone them back.

"Janey, this is an emergency," Cordelia shouted, just a note shy of hysterical. "There's been a murder."

"'Murder,'" repeated Jane. "Where? Who?"

"In my friggin' driveway. You've got to come. The police are on the way. I am freaking out."

"Okay," said Jane. "Just stay calm. I'm leaving right now."

Julia eased her chair back and stood. After Jane had hung up, she said, "Murder trumps me."

"I'm sorry," said Jane. She was torn. Julia was obviously in distress.

"No problem." She looked like she might cry. Picking up her sunglasses, she forced a smile. "I'll just show myself out."

"I'll phone you," called Jane. "We'll get together soon."

24

A police cruiser, lights flashing, had parked in Cordelia's circular drive. As Jane pulled her Mini into a spot across the street, she could see two officers examining the interior of a van that had missed the turn into the drive and had come to rest partway into the grass, its front end resting mere inches from two of Cordelia's garden gnomes.

Dressed in a pink terrycloth robe, Cordelia waved madly at Jane from her perch under the stone portico. No perimeter had been set up, so Jane gave the officers a wide berth and approached from the opposite side of the drive. "Are you okay?" she asked, taking Cordelia's trembling hands in hers.

"No," said Cordelia, her voice a strangled whisper. "Like a homicide happens on my property every day."

"Who was driving the van?"

"Noah. He's dead, Janey. Shot in the head."

Jane winced. "Have you spoken to the police?"

"They just got here."

As they stood and watched, a dark Crown Victoria rolled

down the street and parked behind the police cruiser. Two squad cars followed close behind and came to a stop at each end of the drive, blocking anyone from entering or leaving. A crowd of on-lookers had begun to gather out in the street. Two plain-clothes officers in suits and ties emerged from the Crown Vic. One headed immediately toward the van, the other walked up to the house.

"I'm Sergeant Eddy Vance, Minneapolis PD," said the homicide cop, his gaze shifting between Jane and Cordelia. "Either of you own this house?" Vance was middle-aged, with a wide tomcat face, a crew cut, and muscles that, even under his coat, looked as hard as concrete.

"It's mine," said Cordelia. "I am Cordelia M. Thorn. I own the Thorn Lester Playhouse in downtown Minneapolis."

"Uh-huh," said Vance, removing a notebook from his inner pocket. "You know the deceased?"

"Noah Foster. He was a houseguest."

"So he's a friend of yours."

"Not exactly. He's the brother-in-law of a friend." She was nervous, so she overexplained about the bomb at Fiona and Annie's house, her relationship to Fiona, and her reasons for inviting everyone to spend a few nights at her house.

Halfway through the spiel, Vance stopped taking notes. He eventually cut her off by asking, "Are they all inside?"

"In the great hall."

"The what?"

"The living room," offered Jane. "It's a really large room, with a vaulted ceiling and stained-glass windows. Standard medieval mansion stuff."

"And you are?" asked Vance, his attention now on her.

"Jane Lawless." She handed him one of her cards. "I'm a friend of Cordelia's. She asked me to come over."

"You're a licensed PI?" he said, holding the card up to the porch light so he could read the small print.

"I am."

He scrutinized her for a few seconds, then flipped back a page in his notes. "Someone named Sharif Berry made the 911 call. I need to talk to him."

"I'll go find him," said Cordelia.

After she'd disappeared into the house, Vance trained his eyes at Jane. "You here as a friend or an investigator?"

"Friend."

"Good. Keep it that way."

"Not a fan of private investigators?"

"Just saying I don't need your help."

One of the uniformed officers began stringing yellow police tape from one ancient elm to another. A second had gone into the street, encouraging people to go home. The strobe lights continued to be a beacon for curious neighbors.

Cordelia returned with Sharif trailing behind her.

"Sharif Berry?" asked Vance.

He nodded.

"See that Crown Vic behind the squad car? Go stand there. I have to check a few things and then I need to talk to you."

"Okay," said Sharif, nodding to Cordelia and Jane as he trotted down the steps.

"I'll come inside a little later to speak with the family," said Vance. "If you could keep everyone together, that would be helpful."

"Of course," said Cordelia, tugging Jane toward the front door. Once they were inside, she charged down the hallway to the back of the house and into her study. She shut the door extra quietly behind her and whispered, "Over there," pointing at a couch that sat under a series of mullioned windows. She grabbed her cell phone off the desk and joined Jane on the couch. "You wanted to get a look inside that van, didn't you. I could tell you were just itching to see it."

"Well, I—"

"So I took pictures."

Jane could have lived her entire life without seeing those photos and been perfectly happy.

"Here," said Cordelia. She brought up the first picture and shoved the phone into Jane's hands.

"Lord," said Jane. The inside of the car was covered with blood and human tissue.

"And it stunk to high heaven." Using two fingers, Cordelia enlarged parts of the scene.

"What's that on the passenger's seat and the floor?" It was a pinkish-looking mash.

"Vomit. He was sick all over the interior of the car, which obviously didn't happen after he was shot."

Jane repositioned the photo. The back of Noah's head looked like someone had taken a huge bite out of it. Cordelia was right. After he was hit by the gunshot, he'd slumped forward, his progress stopped by the steering wheel.

"So think about it," said Cordelia. "For reasons unknown, he's sick as a dog. He tries to turn the van into the drive, but because he's sick, he misses it and skids to a stop partway up on the grass. And then what? He's a victim of bad timing?

Somebody shows up out of the blue, right at that moment, and shoots him? How likely is that?"

"Meaning what?"

Cordelia swiped her finger across the screen, bringing up the next photo. "Look at his left hand, his left wrist. Somebody took his wedding ring and his watch. I admired the ring—it was a yellow diamond—so I remember it vividly. And a rose-gold Apple watch. Both were expensive. He also wore a rose-gold chain around his neck, and that's gone too."

"So, you're saying it was a robbery-homicide?"

"Why shoot a guy—a man who's been puking his guts out and is obviously in a weakened state—if all you want is bling? Most people would gladly hand it over to keep themselves alive. Makes no sense."

"Let me get this straight. You think someone set up the murder scene to look like a robbery, but in effect, it was an execution?"

"You tell me."

"Where was Noah this evening?"

"He never showed up for dinner. I asked about him, but nobody knew where he was. The weird thing is, they didn't seem to care."

"Did Bridget or anybody else try to get in touch with him?"

"Not that I saw."

Cordelia was right. It was odd. Then again, Jane had seen Noah come out of Cordelia's house earlier in the day sporting a bloody nose. After finding Bridget in tears and Annie muttering that she hoped Noah would never come back, Jane concluded she'd missed a family spat. Had it been worse than that? "Did Noah know anyone in the Twin Cities?"

"That's what we need to find out, Janey." Her eyes nearly bulged out of their sockets.

"The police will look into it. They'll figure it out."

"But what if they don't? Or what if *Eddy* gets a bad case of tunnel vision and targets the wrong person. Like *me!*"

"Nobody thinks you had anything to do with Noah's death, Cordelia."

"From your lips. I saw the way Eddy looked at me. He had a noose around my neck ten seconds after meeting me. I could hear the prison doors slamming, Janey. Even Perry Mason can't help me if he decides I'm the perp."

"Cordelia, that's not going to happen."

"Someone was murdered on *my* property, Janey. A guest in *my* house. This is not the time for 'cool, calm, and collected.' Oh, speaking of the detective, I better tell everyone to stay put in the great hall." She stood. "Are you coming?" she asked imperiously.

"I'll be along in a minute. I want to look at the photos one more time."

She tapped her head. "Always two steps ahead. That's me. The cops aren't going to finger me for this one, not with you on my side. I'm innocent, Janey. Innocent!" She stomped over to the door, turned around and gave Jane a salute, then left the room.

Jane tossed the cell phone on the couch. She had no desire to look at the crime scene again, but she did want a moment to catch her breath. Cordelia would eventually realize that she wasn't suspect number one. Until then, she would find new depths for the concept of drama. Reaching into her pocket for her cell phone, Jane tried Julia's number, but was put through to her voice mail. She felt terrible for the way she'd left things.

On her way to the great hall, Jane noticed that a top drawer of an antique credenza hadn't been closed properly. She tried to push it shut. When it wouldn't budge, she yanked it open. A wire-bound notebook appeared to be the problem. After removing it, the drawer closed perfectly.

As Jane took it back to Cordelia's office, she glanced through the contents. The name "Noah" jumped out at her. Closing the office door, she sat down behind the desk and flipped to the opening page. What she found was a series of letters Annie had written. It was clearly private. So who had put it in the credenza drawer? It must have been done quickly, stuffing it in, rushing away without looking back.

Taking her reading glasses out of her shirt pocket, Jane sat back and began to read.

ANNIE'S NOTEBOOK
Letter #4

This is my last letter to you, mother dear. My intent, at least initially, was never to send any of this. I've gone back and forth on it and still haven't come to a firm decision. The idea that you'd see my handwriting and toss the letters in the trash is pretty devastating. Equally appalling would be for you to read my words, the truth about what happened, and still refuse to believe them. I guess I shouldn't get sidetracked by any of this. I need to finish my story, if nothing else, for my own sake.

Back to that night. To my motel room. Standing at the mirror in the bathroom, dressed in clothing that made me feel like my normal self, and yet knowing that the person wearing those clothes was an imposter, that she would never be the old Annie, the one who was capable of trust, I knew I had to tell someone.

In a daze, in pain both emotionally and physically, I made my way down to your room. I was hoping you and Dad would both be there, but as luck would have it, it was just you. I came in and sat on the bed. You scolded me for taking off my beautiful dress, said I'd looked so lovely in it when I was making that toast at dinner. You went on and on about what a wonderful evening it had been, about how happy you were that Bridget and Noah were finally married, that you had such hopes and dreams for them, for the family they'd have one day. I don't think you even looked at me. If you had, you would have seen the bruise on my face. The other bruises were covered up, but they hurt like hell. When you finally realized I wasn't talking, you sat down on the bed next to me.

"Something wrong?" you asked.

I said yeah, there was. I said, "Noah came into my room a few minutes ago. He raped me."

You moved away, turned to look me full in the face. "That's ridiculous," you said. "Are you drunk? You're drunk, aren't you. Annie, why would you say something like that? Do you hate your sister—hate me and your father—that much?"

I said I didn't hate anyone.

"Annie, come on. What? Did he kiss you? You know how affectionate he is. And everyone's been drinking. You're making too much of . . . whatever happened. You need to go back to your room and sleep it off. Things will look different in the morning."

"He raped me. He pushed me down on the bed, pulled down his pants, and forced himself on me."

I can still see the look in your eyes. Part panic, part fury. You got up, began pacing around the room. I could see the wheels turning in your head. If you gave any credence to what I'd said, what did that mean for Bridget, for Noah, for the family, and for you? If you refused to believe me, what did that mean for me? The scales were loaded, and not in my favor.

"Did you flirt with him?" *you asked, as if that would explain it.* "Sometimes you flirt and you don't realize you're doing it. He's a handsome man, Annie. Sometimes we do things we're not proud of."

"You think I wanted him to rape me?"

"Why do you keep saying that word? You always make things seem worse than they are."

"You're saying I secretly wanted Noah."

"Come on, Annie. Everyone knows how much you care about him."

"Like a brother," *I screamed.*

"Keep your voice down."

"I did not ask for this. He raped me."

"Stop it. Stop saying that. I won't have it. Whatever happened——"

"I'm gay, Mom. I'm not attracted to men. I didn't flirt with him."

You finally stopped pacing and turned to me. "Don't be ridiculous," *you said. I can still see your lips twisting with revulsion at the very idea.*

"I've known I was gay since I was in my early teens. I have a girlfriend at USC. I can give you her name and telephone number. You can ask her about me. We've been dating for two years."

"I refuse to believe this," *you said, covering your ears.* "The extent to which you'll go to prove a point astounds me. Lying

*about something so important . . . I don't believe you." When
you saw me get up to leave, you said, "Where are you going?"*

"To tell Bridget."

*You flew at me, grabbed my arm. "You can't. I won't let you
ruin this night for her. Ruin her future. You're drunk. You
aren't making any sense."*

"Okay, then I'll talk to Dad."

*"No." Even though your face was inches from mine, you shouted
at me. "You've always envied your sister. I won't let you hurt
her. I won't!"*

*I squirmed away from you. I couldn't believe this was hap-
pening. It was all about Bridget and Noah—about Dad, and
probably, most importantly, about you. It wasn't possible that I
was a lesbian and you didn't know it. And if I was a lesbian, you
simply refused to hear it. Gays were perverted. Unnatural. Against
God's law. No daughter of yours was a lesbian. Noah wasn't capable of rape. He was a good man. Honorable. Men who raped
women were monsters, and Noah surely was not a monster. You
pleaded with me to go back to my room. To take some time and
think about the ramifications of my accusation. Bridget and Noah
were just starting their lives together. Didn't they deserve a
chance at happiness? Rape? It couldn't have been a rape. Noah
would never hurt me. Not like that.*

You kept hammering at me. You wore me down.

*I left you still babbling about Noah's innocence. I didn't sleep
that night, and for many nights thereafter. I told Dad the next
morning that I was gay. He took it about as well as you did. You
stood over by the window in the motel room, just waiting for me
to drop the bomb about Noah. I should have, but I let you have
your cheap dream. I was ashamed of you. I still am.*

*Noah raped me. That's a fact. Some use the word "violate,"
when describing a rape. You know what the word means?*

*Violate: To fail to respect. To treat with irreverence. To disre-
gard.*

*What do you call what you did to me that night, Mom? Maybe
you should give that some thought and get back to me.*

25

Ted Johnson tended to whistle when he was nervous. Fiona figured that if there was ever a time to be nervous, it was when you were waiting for a police detective to come talk to you. Ted had been whistling, off and on, for the last hour. It was always a ridiculously cheerful tune. He was sitting on the couch next to Bridget. Every now and then she would turn and glare at him, or Annie would, and he'd stop. But then he'd forget, or he couldn't help himself, and he was back at it. Except for the ticking of a grandfather clock, it was the only sound in the unnaturally quiet hall, which made it seem even more bizarre.

Eventually, Sharif, who'd been summoned by the detective, returned and sat down on the fainting couch. He eyed Annie briefly, then glanced at Bridget, who had a box of tissues in her lap to wipe tears from her eyes and occasionally blow her nose. She was the only one who seemed the least bit upset that Noah was gone. Everyone else, at least from what Fi could tell, sat grimly quiet, stunned perhaps, but not heartbroken.

"Listen up," said Cordelia, bustling into the room for the

second time that evening. A broad-shouldered man in a sweat-stained white shirt and striped tie came in behind her. "This is Sergeant Vance, Minneapolis PD."

Instinctively Fi and Annie, who were sitting on a brocade love seat under a tall triptych of stained-glass windows, moved closer to each other.

Vance settled himself into one of the wing-back chairs. "I'm sorry for your loss," he said, retrieving a notebook from his shirt pocket.

Bridget sniffed into a tissue. No one else moved.

Vance asked for everyone to introduce themselves and give their relationship to the deceased. After making a few notations, he said, "I realize it's late, and I know this is a terrible time for you, but I've got a few questions. Shouldn't take long. Okay," he said, looking around. "Let's begin. Do any of you know where Mr. Foster was this evening?"

Bridget shook her head.

"No," said Fiona. "He left around five. He didn't say where he was going."

"Was that usual for him?" asked Vance.

"He wasn't very good at keeping me informed about where he was," said Bridget.

"How would you describe your marriage?"

Looking down at her wedding ring, Bridget said, "It was troubled. Before we came to Minnesota, I contacted a divorce lawyer. I kept it from Noah. He knew I wasn't happy, but I doubt he believed I'd ever call it quits."

"Why were you unhappy?"

"He couldn't keep his pants zipped," said Ted, his tone defiant.

"So you knew your daughter was unhappy?"

"My daughter and I are very close." It wasn't really an answer, but Vance let it stand.

"Was it possible Mr. Foster had gone to see a girlfriend this afternoon? Someone he knew who lived here?"

"Anything's possible," said Bridget. "For all I know, he could have found himself a prostitute."

"Was Mr. Foster taking any sort of medication? Did he do any illegal drugs?"

Fi wondered at the question, why it might be important. Most likely, Vance was just covering his bases.

"None that I know about," said Bridget. "Except for the occasional antacid or ibuprofen."

"What about possible enemies? Someone who might have a grudge against him?"

Bridget shrugged. "He was a physician. Well respected, as far as I know."

"But not well loved within his family."

No one responded.

"Okay," said Vance, glancing down at this notes. "Where were each of you this evening between eight thirty and nine thirty?"

So that was his time line, thought Fi. When nobody responded, she decided to go first. "I came up to my bedroom after dinner. Annie came in around nine and said she wanted to go for a run. We invited Sharif to come with us."

"Did anyone see you leave the house?"

"I doubt it. We left the back way, through the garden." Out of the corner of her eye, she saw Jane come into the room and stand next to a suit of armor.

"Why was that?" asked Vance.

"Honestly? I don't remember."

"I suggested it," said Sharif. "It's closer to the lake. I didn't want to be gone long."

"How about when you were on your run?" asked Vance. "Did anyone see you?"

"A couple of guys stopped Fi and Annie," said Sharif. "They recognized them from the video—which I already told you about when we talked outside."

"Go on."

"Well, when we came back, we walked around to the front of the house."

"Why not the back?"

"We only had keys to the front door," said Fi. "That's when we discovered Noah's van in the drive."

"Do you remember what time that was?"

"Must have been around nine thirty. I didn't look at my watch, but we weren't gone more than fifteen minutes."

Vance regarded her skeptically. Turning to Sharif, he asked, "Where were you before you went for the run?"

"In the basement, working out on Cordelia's elliptical."

"Heavens," gasped Cordelia, a hand rising to her chest. "I dry my clothes on that monstrous object of torture."

"I removed them all carefully," said Sharif. "Nothing got wrinkled."

"Were you alone?" asked Vance.

"Yup. When I finished, I came upstairs to take a shower. Fi caught me in the hall and asked if I'd like to go for a run."

"When the three of you were coming back to the house, did you see anyone?"

"The streets were deserted," said Fi. "There were people over at the lake, like Sharif said, but because Cordelia's house is at the end of a cul-de-sac, I've never noticed much traffic or many people around here."

Vance leaned back in his chair. "What about you, Ms. Johnson? Where were you before you returned to your bedroom?"

"I was cleaning up the dinner dishes in the kitchen," said Annie.

"Alone."

"Yes."

"Did you hear anything unusual?"

"You mean like a gunshot? No. I was wearing earbuds, listening to music."

"The kitchen is where in the house?"

"Along the front, on the north," said Cordelia.

"Are there windows facing the driveway?"

"No."

"So what about you, Ms. Thorn?"

Cordelia sat up, looking as if she'd been electrocuted. "I was working in my office at the back of the house."

"Did you hear anyone leave?"

"I did not."

"Would it be normal for you to hear someone leaving by the back door into the garden when you were in your study?"

"I don't know. If they slammed the door I might have heard them. Not sure I would otherwise."

"And Mrs. Foster?"

Bridget pressed a tissue to her nose. "Well, I always play a game of Scrabble with my dad in the evenings. We probably finished around quarter of eight. Tyrion—that's my son—was watching a TV show, so I sat with him until it was finished, and then I took him upstairs for a bath. He's five years old. I was tired, so when I put him to bed, I'd crawled in next to him and fell asleep."

"And Mr. Johnson? How about you?"

Ted had on sweatpants and his Marine T-shirt, his face a study in crusty ill temper. When he began to answer, he seemed to lose focus. "I . . . I was in my bedroom."

"All evening."

"Yes . . . or, no. We played Scrabble, right?" He looked at Bridget.

"Yes, Dad. We played for almost an hour."

"And then I was in my room—until Annie came in to tell me about . . . about Bridget's husband."

"Noah?" said Vance.

"Yes. Noah. That's what I said. Didn't I say that?"

Bridget squeezed his hand.

Nobody's alibi, Fi thought with a sinking feeling, was all that strong.

"All right," said Vance. "Next question. Do any of you know a woman named Mimi Chandler?"

"Who is she?" asked Fi.

"That's my question."

Bridget lowered her head. She appeared to be pulling something from her memory. "I could be wrong, but she may be one of Noah's patients. He has . . . had . . . a psychiatric practice in Pasadena. I think we met Mimi and her husband at a charity event, maybe a year ago. I remember Noah talking to Mr. Chandler at some length. I believe he owns some kind of computer company."

"Was your husband currently seeing Mrs. Chandler?" asked Vance.

"You could contact his nurse. I'd be happy to give you the number."

"Can you think of any reason why Mrs. Chandler would call him a dozen times in the last few days?"

Bridget seemed at a loss. "Did she?"

Vance nodded.

"No. No idea at all. If she was in crisis, there's always an on-call doctor available through Noah's practice."

"So he wasn't in the habit of talking regularly to patients outside of therapy?"

"I can't imagine why he would."

"All right," said Vance. "Final question. Are there any fire-arms in this house?"

"Of course not," said Cordelia indignantly.

"I own a bunch of guns," said Ted with equal indignation. "All legal."

"Dad," said Annie, giving him a cautionary look. "He doesn't mean the guns you have in California."

Again, Sharif raised his hand. "I have a revolver. Thirty-eight caliber. I always travel with it."

Vance sat forward. "You own it legally?"

"Yes."

"Who, here, knew about the gun? Let me see a show of hands."

Slowly, silently, each hand in the room went up, with the exception of Ted and Cordelia.

"I see," said Vance. "I need to see this gun, Mr. Berry."

"That . . . could be a problem."

Stone-faced, Vance asked why.

"Because, when I came inside after finding Noah in the drive, I went upstairs to make sure it was secure. It wasn't there."

"When did you last see it?"

"This morning. I'd gone out for a motorcycle ride."

"What time? Specifically?"

"Around eleven."

"Did you see anyone go into your room after that time?"

He shook his head.

Vance gave himself a moment to digest the information. "Ms. Thorn," he said, "we'd like to take a look at Mr. Foster's room."

"Don't you need a search warrant for that?" asked Sharif.

"Not if the owner of the property gives her permission."

Cordelia regarded him with suspicion. "What do you think?" she asked Bridget. "Far as I'm concerned, it's your decision."

Annie knitted her fingers through Fi's and held on tight.

"I have nothing to hide," said Bridget.

Vance left the house and returned a few minutes later followed by two uniformed officers. "Would someone show us to the bedroom?"

Cordelia rose, and with a regal if annoyed countenance, led them upstairs.

When they were out of earshot, Ted said, "He thinks one of us did it."

Sharif put a finger to his lips.

It didn't take long before Ted began to whistle again. This time, Fiona was grateful for something to fill the volcanic silence.

Jane remained in the shadows on the second-floor landing until Cordelia and the police officers entered one of the bedrooms far down the hall. Moments later, Cordelia was ejected. In a low growl, Vance suggested that she wait in the hallway until they were done. He closed the door behind him.

Her posture rigid, her expression deeply aggrieved, Cordelia strode across the hall and sat down on an upholstered bench. She didn't seem even remotely surprised when Jane emerged from the shadows and walked toward her.

"What do we do now?" she whispered.

Jane sat down next to her. "Which bedroom is Sharif's?"

She cocked her head to the left, toward the door next to them.

"I'm going in. Any problems with that?"

"Under the circumstances, I have no moral compunctions whatsoever."

Jane twisted the door handle and found it unlocked. Once inside the messy room, she began a thorough search: First she pulled back the blankets and sheets on the bed, then turned her attention to the closet and all the drawers in the highboy, the nightstand, and finally the suitcase. She also checked under the mattress and the bed itself. If Sharif's revolver had been used to murder Noah, the murderer was probably smart enough to hide it. And if Sharif had been that murderer, the gun would be long gone from his room.

Easing the door back open, Jane poked her head into the hallway.

"All clear," whispered Cordelia, motioning for her to come out.

Jane moved swiftly to Cordelia's side.

"Find anything?"

"No. Since they're still busy, which is Ted's bedroom?"

"Already playing sleuth are we?"

"Just satisfying my natural curiosity."

"Of course you are." Cordelia pointed to a door across the hall, two doors down from Noah and Bridget's room.

"If the cops come out before I do," whispered Jane, "on your way back downstairs, try to bump Ted's door so I know my time is up."

"Never fear. I've made a career out of stumbling at just the right moment."

Jane rose and tiptoed across the hall. She tried the handle and was once again glad to find it unlocked.

Unlike Sharif's room, with its unmade bed and scattered dirty clothes, Ted's was a model of military perfection. Several magazines were stacked on top of a chest of drawers along with a small brown leather toiletry bag. Jane checked the bag and found pills, a shaving kit, nothing but the usual. The bed was so flawlessly made that after she'd felt under the mattress, she took great care to return it to its former glory. She searched through the chest of drawers, and then a large rolling duffel on a suitcase rack next to it. Again, she came up with nothing out of the ordinary. The closet was empty, except for an extra pillow and a couple of blankets. She lifted up the seat on an upholstered club chair, just to make sure nothing was hidden underneath. Moving at last up to the window, she saw that Ted's bedroom offered a perfect view of the circular drive, filled, as it was tonight, with powerful floodlights and people combing the area for information. It looked to Jane as if Noah's body might still be inside the van. The crowd in the street hadn't dispersed. If anything, it had grown larger.

Turning away, Jane drew open the top drawer of the nightstand. Inside were more prescription pills, a bottle of men's
vitamins and another bottle of ibuprofen. Next to them was a
pack of dental floss and a small digital alarm clock.

The second drawer down was empty. Jane expected the same
of the third, but instead spotted a black, soft-sided Moleskine
journal toward the back with a pencil tucked inside. It wasn't a
large journal—maybe five inches by eight. On the outside was
a taped note: "READ THIS EVERY MORNING."

Jane sat down on the club chair. The printing inside was precise and compact:

YOU ARE TED JOHNSON

YOU LIVE IN PASADENA CALIFORNIA

YOU ARE 68 YEARS OLD

YOUR ADDRESS IS: 15029 LOMA LINDA DRIVE

YOUR PHONE: 213-555-9302

YOU OWN JOHNSON GARDEN CENTER

MOIRA JOHNSON, WIFE, DECEASED

DAUGHTERS:

BRIDGET RACHEL 32, MARRIED TO NOAH FOSTER

ANNIE CLAIRE, 27

YOU HAVE ALZHEIMER'S

GO TO THE BACK OF THIS BOOK AND CROSS OFF

THE DATE FOR THIS DAY

ADDRESS AND PHONE NUMBER LIST IN BACK

So this must be why Ted hadn't remembered her this
afternoon. She was saddened to learn he was struggling with

such a terrible disease. Switching to the back of the book, she found a list of names followed by phone numbers and addresses. Removing her cell phone from her back pocket, she took several pictures.

Returning to the front of the book, she read:

June 1, 2016

Started this so I can keep track. Doctor suggested it. I feel good. A little arthritis, but that's to be expected. Bridget has given me a list of rules. Go to the refrigerator in the kitchen to see the list.

One rule I won't keep. She says I can't go for a walk alone. That's bullshit. I go for walks every morning, before my handler gets here and makes me breakfast. I know my way around. I'm not an invalid. I realize I have a disease, but it doesn't control me—not yet. Neither does my daughter. Enough said.

June 5

Forgot to write in this the last few days. All good. Bridget and Tyrion and I went to the park today.

June 6

Good day. Bridget and I started playing Scrabble in the evenings. She won. Rematch tomorrow.

JUNE 7.

PLAYED GOLF WITH TOM AND ANDY.

WON AT SCRABBLE.

JUNE 11

HAVE TO REMEMBER TO WRITE IN THIS.

FUZZY TODAY. I FEEL LIKE I'M LIVING

UNDERWATER.

JUNE 12

GOOD DAY. WON AT SCRABBLE. DINNER

AT VINCENT'S.

Jane skimmed the rest until she came to the day when Ted first saw the video.

JUNE 26

FOUND ANNIE!

GREAT DAY.

JUNE 27

LEAVING FOR MINNESOTA.

Ted was apparently a man of few words, though on the day when he and Annie were finally reunited, he wrote half a page before, and an entire page after.

Hearing voices in the hallway outside the bedroom and then a thump against the door, Jane knew her time was limited. Vance would likely make a quick statement to everyone gathered in the great hall and then return outside to the crime scene.

Ted might stay down in the hall, or he might choose to return immediately to his room. Jane had only a few minutes to finish up. Flipping to the spot marked by the pencil, she scanned the page. Instead of his usual precise letters, Ted had scrawled in all caps:

SCREECH OF BRAKES OUTSIDE
WENT TO WINDOW
NOAH'S VAN
MUZZLE FLASH
A WOMAN????
BASEBALL CAP

Underneath the paragraph he'd written:

ANNIE????????
BRIDGET?????

And then he'd crossed out Bridget's name, leaving Annie's to carry the weight of his damning conclusion.

26

Jane was stretched out on the couch in Cordelia's study, a snifter of brandy resting on her stomach, waiting for her friend to finish Annie's letters. It was going on two in the morning. She was glad now that she'd contacted her neighbor, Evelyn Bratrude, as she was driving over to Cordelia's place. She explained that she wasn't sure when she'd get home, and asked Evelyn, if she had the time, to take care of the dogs. As usual, Evelyn jumped at the chance to invite Mouse and Gimlet over to her house for the night. She told Jane to come get them whenever it was convenient. They were welcome to stay as long as needed.

"This is astonishing," said Cordelia, looking up from the notebook as if she'd just emerged from a deep reverie. "Appalling on every level. That poor kid. You found this where?"

Jane explained that someone had stuffed it into the top drawer of Cordelia's antique credenza out in the hallway. "If it hadn't been done so haphazardly, perhaps so quickly, the drawer wouldn't have been sticking out."

"So," said Cordelia, tapping her long red talons on the arms of her chair, "who do you think put it there?"

"More importantly," said Jane, "who's read it? Because, who-ever knows about the rape had a clear motive for murder."

"You don't believe Ted's conclusion then? That Annie's the responsible party."

Jane had thought of little else since she'd read Ted's journal. "I don't know what to think. It was dark out. He was on the second floor and he wears glasses. He obviously couldn't see the person well enough to be certain about who it was."

"Just that it was a woman."

"But what does that mean?" asked Jane. "That the person had long hair? Was wearing a dress?"

"And a baseball cap. If it was a woman, we're obviously talk-ing about someone with *no* fashion sense."

"Have you ever seen Annie wearing a baseball cap?"

"Not that I recall. But then, who doesn't own a few baseball caps?" Answering her own question, her face brightened: "*Me*."

"I suppose it's possible that Noah's demise could be for some other reason."

"He was sleeping with Willow Lewis, Tyrion's nanny. Fi con-fided to me that she'd seen Willow coming out of Noah and Bridget's bedroom. She said something to Annie and Annie passed it on to Bridget. That's why Bridget fired her this after-noon, gave her enough money so that she could hop a bus back to LA, and told her she never wanted to see her again. Annie said that Willow didn't even try to deny she'd been sleeping with Noah. In fact, she insisted Noah loved *her*, not Bridget."

"So you're saying Bridget did it?"

"Maybe."

"What a mess," said Jane, rubbing her eyes.

"Do we turn that notebook over to the police?" asked Cordelia.

"The police might jump to the same conclusion Ted did—that Annie did it. They might even arrest her based solely on the notebook."

"To quote Ingrid Bergman," said Cordelia, " 'Uff da.' "

"Did she use that word?"

"She was Swedish. All Swedes say 'uff da.' "

"I believe it's Norwegian."

"Did anyone ever tell you that you're a font of useless information?"

"Probably," said Jane, finishing her brandy. "I think I should go home."

"You've been drinking. You should stay here tonight, in the safety of Thorn Hall."

Jane didn't exactly feel like getting up. "If you'd find me a blanket and a better pillow, I would gladly curl up right here. Why don't we sleep on it and see what we come up with in the morning?"

"Sounds like a plan," said Cordelia, slapping her knees and thrusting herself out of her chair. She removed a blanket and a pillow from the closet, tossing them at Jane. "Nighty night," she said on her way out. "Don't let the bedbugs, proverbial or literal, bite."

In a breathless rush, trembling into each other, Fiona and Annie made love just before sunup. It was a fearful thing to love someone as much as Fiona loved Annie. A love as deep as marrow. Fiona lost herself gladly for those minutes, but the festering inside her returned as Annie rested her head against Fi's stomach. Fi played with Annie's hair, smoothing it, brushing it this way and that. If only they could stay like this, away from the oppressive glare of a day that promised nothing but more anguish.

"What's the best thing you've ever done?" Fi asked Annie.

"That's easy. Saying yes to your proposal."

Fiona closed her eyes and smiled. "What's the worst thing?"

"Are you asking me if I murdered Noah?"

"Good Lord, no."

"Okay, so who do you think did it? Had to be one of us. Sharif. Dad. Bridget. You. Me."

"The police have no idea what Noah did to you," said Fi.

"They'll find out. Somehow. And then they'll arrest me. It's only a matter of time."

"You're wrong."

"Am I?" She swung her legs out of bed and got up.

Fiona stayed under the covers while Annie went to take a shower. It was still early, barely day, when Annie returned and dressed quickly. Bending over Fi, she said, "I love you. Nothing will ever change that."

"I know. And I love you."

"I'm going for a motorcycle ride with Sharif."

"Now?"

"We'll stop somewhere for breakfast. I need my friend, Fi. It's not that I don't need you, but I need him, too."

All she could force out was, "Okay."

Annie kissed her softly. "Don't worry. Sharif's a good driver. We'll be safe."

As Fiona came into the kitchen several hours later in search of coffee, her cell phone buzzed inside the front pocket of her shorts.

208

"Hello," she said, taking a mug down from the cupboard. The house was quiet. Nobody else appeared to be up.

"Ms. McGuy?" came a man's voice.

"Yes?"

"This is Sergeant Bill Larson, Bloomington Bomb Squad."

"Oh, hi. Have you learned anything more about the bomb in our front yard?"

"That's why I'm calling. We arrested a young man last night. He admitted his guilt, so there's no chance we got the wrong person."

"Who is he? Why did he do it?"

"Name's Gerrit Moss. He's eighteen, just graduated high school. This isn't his first bomb. He's apparently fascinated by explosives. Thank God, he's not very good at making them. His dad is a minister."

"Oh. I get it."

"No, the dad is very gay friendly. He's been marrying gay and lesbian couples for the past year. The son is the one who has problems with it. Between you and me, I think his problems are mostly with his dad. The kid posted some comments on his Facebook page that were pretty explicit. He's in lockup and will remain there until he either pleads or goes to trial. His parents want him moved to a mental health facility, but that's unlikely to happen any time soon."

Fi felt some small part of herself unwind. "Thanks so much for calling."

"You have a good day."

Carrying her coffee mug into the breakfast room, Fiona sat down at the table and gazed out the multipaned windows at the rose garden. She couldn't wait to give Annie the good news.

209

Checking her watch, she saw that it was going on ten. Annie had left just after six. Fiona couldn't help herself—she was impatient. She understood Annie's need to talk to Sharif, and yet she needed to talk about what had happened last night, too.

As she sipped her coffee, she heard the sound of clattering dishes in the kitchen. A few seconds later, Cordelia, dressed in faded jeans and baggy T-shirt, her auburn hair hanging in uncombed curls around her shoulders, dragged herself into the room with her own mug of coffee and a bowl of Froot Loops. It was hard not to notice that Cordelia had an almost Armageddon-ready level of cereal stored in the kitchen.

"Ugh," said Cordelia by way of greeting. She set her breakfast on the table, pulled out a chair and dropped onto it. "Didn't sleep much last night."

"Me either," said Fi.

Cordelia pulled her mug closer, peered into it. "We're out of cream so I had to use milk. Milk in coffee is disgusting. A crime against nature."

"But it's okay on Froot Loops?"

"Marginally."

Fiona watched as Cordelia slowly, laboriously slurped up the cereal. "You're not a morning person, are you?"

She took a sip of her coffee and grimaced. "Nope."

"I just found out that the Bloomington police arrested the guy who tried to blow up our house."

"Super."

Cordelia said nothing more until she'd finished the cereal and downed the entire mug of coffee. "There," she said, wiping a hand across her mouth. "I will become human again any second now." She glanced up at Fi as if taking her in for the first time.

"So. About last night. I know about the rape. What Noah did to Annie."

"Wait? What?"

"Jane happened across an old notebook of Annie's. Someone tried to hide it in the hall credenza, but made a bad job of it. We probably shouldn't have, but both Jane and I read it. I assume you've seen it."

"I haven't," said Fi. "But Annie told me about it."

"Why did she bring it to my house?"

"She didn't. Sharif did." Fi explained how it had happened.

"So, I'm curious. Who had it last? Who hid it in the credenza?"

"Sharif said Ted took it from his room. Ted was the one who finally broke the news to Bridget."

"Oy. How did she take it?"

"How do you think?"

Cordelia rose from her chair and went into the kitchen. She returned with a can of Coke. Sitting back down, she cracked it open and said, "Is it fair to assume that everyone in Annie's family knew about the rape before Noah's murder?"

"I'm afraid so," said Fi. Her eyes drifted back to the garden. "Are you going to give the diary to the police?"

"I expect we'll have to."

Fi felt a sense of dread so strong, it was as if someone had whispered the blackest of futures into her ear. "Annie should be home by now."

"Where'd she go?" asked Cordelia.

"For a motorcycle ride with Sharif. They left early."

"Jane stayed the night, such as it was. She's sleeping on the couch in my study. She's been looking so ragged lately I couldn't bring myself to wake her. That said, I think we'd both like to talk to you and Annie when she gets back."

"Of course," said Fi. "I better go call her and see where they are."

Cordelia waved her off.

Holding her cell phone to her ear, Fi walked out into the foyer. She'd just crossed under the arch into the great hall when the front door opened and Sharif came in.

"Oh, God, you're back," said Fi, flooded with relief. "Where's Annie?"

He stood motionless, arms at his sides.

"Sharif?"

"Come up to my room."

"Why?"

He held out his hand. "Please, Fi. Just come with me. I'll explain everything, but not here."

"Is she okay? Is she hurt?"

"She's fine."

"You have to tell me. *Now*. What's going on?"

Sharif stepped forward and put his arm around her, gently guiding her toward the stairs.

27

While running on one of the hotel treadmills, Mimi's brain was operating like a LaserSaber, unsheathed and ready to melt or slice through anything or anyone who got in her way. She was so amped that she was only partially listening to the morning TV news when a picture on the screen caught her attention. All expression died on her face. She jumped to the sides of the moving treadmill and turned up the sound on her earbuds. She listened for another few moments before switching off the machine, ripping the buds from her ears and heading for the elevators.

Up on the top floor, she raced to her door, which she found standing open. Two cleaning women were working on the bedroom.

"Stop," cried Mimi. "Don't touch those sheets. Get your hands off them, I mean it." Those sheets were the last thing she'd have to remember Noah by.

"No clean?" asked one of the Hispanic women.

"No," shouted Mimi, yanking a pillowcase out of the woman's hands. "No more cleaning. You can leave now."

"Bathroom?" asked the other woman.

"Don't touch anything. I'll take care of it. Thank you." She kept thanking them as she herded them out the door. Once they were gone, she ran back to the bedroom and dove for the bed, covering herself up until she was completely cocooned in the bedding. She could still smell his scent. She'd been angry at him last night. She had every right because he'd treated her badly.

"Oh, God," she groaned. "Why does everything bad have to happen to *me?*"

Sharif pressed play and handed Fiona his cell phone.

Annie's face filled the screen. "I'm a coward," she said. "I couldn't tell you this in person. It was just too hard. I'm leaving, Fi. I'll be back, but for now, I need time away. The police will undoubtedly take my flight as just one more sign of guilt. If they do, there's nothing I can do about it.

"Please, sweetheart, don't look for me. I'm good at hiding. Last night, when I was looking in your briefcase for your iPad, I found the latest note from your stalker, the one where he asks if he needed to push me out of your life. It's all too much. I can't live like this.

"Give me the time I need. When I think about going, my heart breaks. There are no words to express how much I love you. Remember that. Remember *me.*"

Annie's face disappeared.

Dazed, Fiona sat down on the bed.

"Please don't shoot the messenger," said Sharif. "I tried to talk her out of it."

"How?" said Fi, searching his face, trying to understand. "Why?"

He sat down on the window seat opposite her, leaned forward and rested his arms on his knees. "Annie asked me last night if we could go for a motorcycle ride early this morning. I said sure. I figured she wanted to talk. We found a café and had some breakfast. While we were eating, she told me about the stalker notes you've been getting. The newest really upset her. She told me she didn't feel safe *anywhere* and didn't see how it would ever change. All she did was worry. And then last night . . . when Noah was murdered, she made a decision. She had to get away."

"But . . . why didn't she come to me? We could have discussed it. Figured out another way."

"She knew you'd try to talk her out of leaving and that she'd cave because it would hurt so much to go. She felt trapped, Fi. Overwhelmed. Can you understand that? There was no good option, one that would make you both happy."

Fiona pressed a hand over her mouth. "But how could she just leave? She's right. The police will see it as a sign of guilt."

"I tried to talk through the situation with her. We went over different options. In the end, it was her decision to go. As a friend, I have to support that decision."

"Where, Sharif? She must have told you where she was going."

"She didn't."

He was lying and they both knew it. "So, you're saying you understand but I couldn't possibly. You're her knight in shining armor and I would have insisted she do something against her will."

215

"You're putting words in my mouth because you're angry."

"You support her. And me, I'm a critical bitch."

"Stop it."

She burst into tears. "*Remember me?* That sounds like she's leaving for good."

"She promised me she'd be back and I believe her."

"Right. You know her better than I do. I'm just her wife."

"Look," he said, the muscles along his jaw tightening. "You've never been raped. You have no idea what it can do to you—to your head. How it changes you."

"And you do. Like you're all-knowing."

"I do know, Fi."

The certainty in his voice stopped her.

"All I'm saying is, cut her some slack."

"Sharif? You know what it's like? What's that mean?"

He rose from the window seat and turned to look outside. "Leave it alone."

"Who? When? How?"

"It's something I don't talk about."

"Oh, God." She'd guessed correctly.

He lowered his head, pressed his fingers to the glass.

"Please, tell me. I need to understand."

"You act surprised, like it's not supposed to happen to men. Not big men like me. Thing is, I didn't always look like this. Maybe it's one of the reasons I worked so hard to build up my body. If anybody ever tries it again, believe me, Fi, I will fucking obliterate him."

"You were young?"

"Fourteen. My brother and a couple of his army buddies were home on leave. I worshipped my brother, thought he was the coolest guy in the universe. I felt the same way about his two friends."

"One of them did it?"

"Let's leave it there."

"It wasn't your fault."

Through clenched teeth, he said, "I know that. But it nearly ruined my life anyway. It's why I lost whole years of life, why I entered my junior year of high school when I was nineteen. Why I . . . *felt like a freak.*" Turning around, he said, "One in five women are raped during their lives. One in five. Ask around. More women you know have been raped than you can even imagine. Twenty percent of college females are raped before they graduate. But it's men, too. Except men and boys report it even less than women. Most of us aren't predators, but the guys who *are* do it over and over and over, and rarely get caught. Either the women in their lives give them a pass—or the cops do. You can't prove rape, according to way the hell too many people in our so-called justice system. It's an epidemic and nobody wants to talk about it. So, yes, I do understand Annie better than you do. Deal with it."

Fi felt like she was seeing him clearly for the first time. Beneath the smart-aleck, easy-going exterior was a man who carried deep scars. "Does Annie know?"

"Absolutely not. And I don't want her to."

There was so much she didn't understand. "I'm glad you told me."

"Really? Why?"

She had no idea how to respond.

On his way to the door, he said, "Annie will do what she has to do. I suggest you give her the space she needs. Otherwise, you'll lose her." Throwing a glance over his shoulder, he added, "You feel me?"

"I do."

"Good. I don't want to talk about this again."

28

Cordelia's voice rumbled through the dreamy mists. "Wake up, sleeping beauty."

When Jane cracked open one eye, she saw that her friend was sitting on the couch next to her, filing her fingernails. Jane hovered for a time between sleep and full awakening, and then everything came back to her in a rush. Noah's murder. Annie's rape. Ted's journal.

"It's noon, Janey. Time for the dead to rise and walk."

"Why did you let me sleep this long?" said Jane, running a hand over her eyes.

"Because you need some extra Zs."

"Have the police called?"

"Not a word from the good sergeant or any of his minions."

"I need a shower," said Jane. "Wish I'd thought to bring along some clean clothes."

"I've still got plenty of your clothes from when you stayed with me last winter."

"Oh, wonderful. A bulky ski sweater is the perfect thing to wear in ninety-degree heat."

"Don't be disagreeable," said Cordelia, pushing off the couch and looming over her. "I'm sure we can dig up the perfect frock for you. So, come on. Chop, chop. Much to do today."

Later, freshly showered and dressed in clean jeans and a light chambray shirt, Jane joined Cordelia in the breakfast room. She was actually feeling rested. "Where is everyone?" she asked, setting her mug of coffee on the table and pulling out a chair.

"Last I heard, Annie and Sharif had gone for a motorcycle ride. Fi roared out of the drive in her Beetle a few minutes ago. I have no idea where she was headed. Bridget, Tyrion, and Ted are back in the nook watching TV."

The nook was what Cordelia called the family room. It was hardly a mere nook as it was bigger than Jane's kitchen and dining room combined. Then again, compared to other rooms in the house, it was definitely smaller. And because it was lined with bookshelves and filled with comfortably overstuffed chairs and couches, it did feel cozier than much of the rest of the house.

"So, what's our first move?" asked Cordelia, unwrapping a stick of bubble gum.

"Don't you want to have teeth when you're eighty?"

Cordelia held up the pack. "Sugarless," she said, flashing Jane her pearly whites.

Jane gazed out the windows and sipped her coffee. "I should get back to the restaurant."

"Not until you figure out who murdered Noah."

"I'm unlikely to do it in the next fifteen minutes. Besides, that's what the police are for."

"Don't worry, Janey. I'll give you the benefit of my high-octane gray cells. We need to get this resolved so that Fi and I can get back to work."

"What if Fi did it?" asked Jane. "Did that occur to you?"

"Piffle." Cordelia blew a bubble.

While Cordelia assuaged her nervous energy by blowing bubble after bubble, Jane's thoughts returned to Ted's journal. She'd gone over and over his final note in her mind. Ted hadn't said he was positive he'd seen a woman approach Noah's van, just that it *might* have been. There were four question marks after the word "woman." It was hardly proof. Beyond that, Ted wore glasses. Who knew how well he could see the circular drive from the second floor. And it was dark out. The nearest streetlight was half a block away. Of course, the outdoor portico was fitted with lantern fixtures, but they didn't cast much light on the spot where Noah had stopped his van. Jane couldn't exactly question Ted about what he'd seen without letting on that she'd read his journal.

Since everyone in the family either knew or had recently learned that Noah had raped Annie, Jane assumed they all had an emotionally compelling motive. If Ted had seen a woman, there were two other women at the house last night that he'd failed to mention: Cordelia and Fi. It was possible he couldn't remember their names. It seemed more likely that his own fear had driven him to write his daughters' names down, not that he'd actually seen one of them. Still, Jane couldn't be certain, and because of that, the question remained open.

The next issue for Jane was why Noah had pulled into the drive at such a weird angle. Where had he gone after he left the house? From the photos Cordelia had taken, it looked as if he'd been sick, vomiting all over the front seat of the van. Was it food poisoning? Cordelia said the van had smelled rank.

Or, and this was an even bigger question, had he been

poisoned? Was he actually murdered twice last night? Some poisons act quickly. Others take hours, even days, to begin working. Had someone in Cordelia's house slipped something into his food? And then, later, had a different someone been waiting with a gun for him to return home? Where was Sharif's revolver? The police would have ballistics evidence soon, which might eliminate it from contention, though until then, Sharif was also a prime suspect.

"I'm sure the cops went over Bridget and Noah's bedroom with a fine-tooth comb," said Jane. "But I'd still like to take a look. Just in case they missed something. We better go find Bridget and get her permission."

Cordelia sucked a bubble into her mouth. "A plan of action," she pronounced. "Not a major plan, to be sure, but forward progress." She stood up and all but hurtled past Jane on her way out of the room. Jane finished her coffee, following at more leisurely pace.

"Where's the fire?" asked Ted, glancing up sharply as Cordelia burst into the nook. Jane smiled down at the little boy, who was sitting on the carpet with his mom and grandpa, playing blocks. "Bridget, I wonder if you'd mind if I examined your bedroom."

"Didn't the police already do that?" asked Ted.

"I'd still like to take a look."

"I suppose. Tyrion, honey, I'm going upstairs to Mommy and Daddy's bedroom. If you need anything, just come upstairs."

"I can take care of him," said Ted, bristling.

"Tyrion, did you hear me?"

"Yeah, Mommy." He set a block on top of a precarious look-

ing stack. When the stack didn't fall over, he looked up trium-
phantly.

Jane spent the next few minutes searching the bedroom.

Cordelia seemed content to let Jane do all the work. She po-
sitioned herself at the window overlooking the circular drive.
"You probably haven't said anything to Tyrion yet."

"No," said Bridget. "And I don't intend to." She stood in the
doorway, hands in the pockets of her tan slacks. "Not until I can
talk about Noah's death without completely coming apart. I
knew he was unfaithful to me, but until yesterday, I had no idea
what he'd done to Annie. How could I love someone like that?
How did I not see who he really was?"

"Rapists don't come with signs attached," said Jane, opening
the closet door. "I wish they did so we could herd them all into
a cell and throw away the key. Speaking of yesterday, what happened before Noah left?"

Bridget sighed. "I asked him to come down to the great hall.
We were all waiting for him because we wanted to have it out.
But he saw it as a trap. He knew something major was up."

"Who hit him? I saw his bleeding nose when he came out of
the house. I was on my way up to the front door."

She looked down. "It was Sharif. Noah made some snide comment about Annie and Sharif decked him. I think Sharif would
have beaten him senseless if he hadn't left. After he was gone, I
used Cordelia's landline to call my divorce lawyer. I told him
to go ahead with it. I wanted to erase him from my life. I expected the lawyer to tell me I wouldn't have any problems with
custody of Tyrion now that we all knew about the rape."

"But there was no definitive proof," said Jane.

"That's what he told me. I couldn't believe my ears." She turned and walked out into the hallway, clearly too upset to continue the conversation.

Jane and Cordelia glanced at each other.

"You said you lost your phone," said Cordelia a few minutes later when Bridget had come back to stand in the doorway. "Did you ever find it?"

"Haven't had the energy to look. Tyrion could have dropped it anywhere. There are so many calls I need to make. I guess I'm putting off the inevitable."

Cordelia stepped over to the closet and angled her way in front of Jane. "You have absolutely no idea where Noah was last evening?"

"No idea at all."

"Cordelia," said Jane. "You're in my way."

"Well alert the freakin' media."

Jane gave up and went to look under the bed. "Maybe we could help you find your phone."

"I suppose."

"What's your ring tone sound like?" asked Cordelia, fishing her cell out of her pocket.

"It's pretty boring. It's just the standard telephone ring."

"And the number?" As Bridget repeated it, Cordelia punched it in. Cupping a hand around her ear, she said, "Don't hear anything."

"This is a huge house."

"Are we done with the bedroom?" asked Cordelia, tapping her foot impatiently.

Jane was lying flat on her stomach, examining dustballs under the bed. "Yes," she said, climbing to her feet and brushing off her clothes. "We're done."

"Excellent. I'll keep hitting redial. You two spread out."

They began on the second floor and worked their way downstairs to the entrance hall. Cordelia continued to punch redial as Bridget headed through the butler's pantry into the kitchen and Jane went into the great hall.

The longer they looked, the more Jane wondered if losing the cell phone had some larger implication. Did it contain evidence Bridget didn't want anyone to see?

Moving slowly down the wide central hallway, head bowed, listening intently, Jane eventually heard a muffled ring coming from the billiard room. If the door hadn't been open, she might never have heard it. Once inside, she found a wicker basket on the floor between two leather chairs. She bent down and pulled off a red scarf. Sure enough, a cell phone with a bright pink case lay on top of an assortment of unrelated objects. Jane clicked the phone on and said, "Hello?"

"Hello?" replied Cordelia. "Who is this?"

"Who do you think it is?"

"Janey? Where are you?"

"In the billiard room."

"Don't move. I'll be right there."

Kneeling down on the carpet to take stock of the basket's contents, Jane removed one of Cordelia's most egregious pieces of costume jewelry—a pin the size of a grapefruit, covered in fake diamonds and rubies. There were two nails, one of them bent. Three screws. Five white rocks of varying sizes, probably taken from the rose garden. A small yellow onion. Two shiny silver pens. Three jelly beans that had seen better days. A cloisonné egg from one of the curio cabinets in the great hall. A piece of bright yellow ribbon. A square of blue billiard cue chalk. An unused tea bag. A dime. A quarter. And finally, at the very bottom, Jane found a tiny glass salt shaker. What the hell?

Hearing the patter of feet, Jane looked up as Tyrion rushed at her from the doorway.

"That's *my* treasure," he cried, his face puckered with rage. "You can't have it. It's mine." He dropped to his knees and began tossing everything back into the basket.

"You must have been collecting that treasure for a long time," said Jane.

"Years," said Tyrion.

"You like beautiful things."

"I *love* them."

Cordelia sauntered into the room, followed by Bridget.

"Tyrion," said Bridget, coming to a stop just inside the door. "What are you doing in here?"

Cordelia peered into the basket. "Goodness. He has a stash."

"It's *my* treasure," he said, gazing up at her defiantly.

Bridget crouched down next to him. "Honey, you can't take things just because you think they're pretty. Remember, we talked about that. If you want something you have to ask, otherwise it's stealing. You know what stealing is, right? It would be like me taking your set of blocks and hiding them from you."

"They're *my* blocks," said Tyrion, picking up the basket and holding it tightly against his chest.

Glancing at Jane and Cordelia, Bridget said, "I think we're going to need a time-out." She reached for Tyrion's hand. "Come with Mommy."

"No. I want my daddy."

His words caused her to flinch. "Tyrion, we need to go up to your room. If you don't come with me, you won't have any dessert tonight."

"You're *mean*," he said, scuttling out the door.

"I'm sorry," said Bridget, staring after him. "I'll make sure you get everything back."

"See that you do," said Cordelia. "That onion is exceedingly valuable."

29

Fiona was glad to find her house still standing when she pulled into the driveway on Saturday afternoon. With the engine running and the air-conditioning churning out barely cooled air, she sat motionless, thoughts of Annie jabbing at her like needles. She had to get away from Cordelia's place because, if she'd stayed, everyone would have asked her where Annie was. She didn't want to talk about it, not when her feelings were so raw.

What would it be like to live without Annie—for days, weeks, perhaps even months—while a murder investigation went on around Fi and some deeply disturbed individual continued to write her mash notes? She felt like a human teakettle building steam, only moments from releasing a piercing whistle.

As hard as she tried to believe that everything would turn out okay in the end, one thought refused to go away. Annie had asked Fi who she thought murdered Noah. She could easily have assured her that she had nothing to do with it. And yet she hadn't. She'd never once said, "I hated him, Fi, but I didn't kill him." It would have been so easy. Was her comment about finding the stalker's note in Fi's briefcase simply a way to deflect?

Had Annie's motivation for running away been her guilt, her very real fear of being arrested? Fi didn't want to even consider the idea that Annie had done it, and yet, because she'd thought about it herself, it didn't seem impossible. If Annie was responsible, Fi wasn't likely to ever see her again.

Startled by a rap on the driver's side window, Fi turned to see Phil Banks, her neighbor from across the street, standing next to the car, holding his dog in his arms and looking deeply relieved. She rolled the window down. "Hi."

"Gosh, Fiona, I'm so glad to see you. Where did you go? I thought once the police removed the bomb, that you'd be back. I was so worried about you."

At least someone was worried. "Annie and I have been staying with a friend."

"Yeah, I saw her over at your house early this morning."

"Annie? She was here?"

"She was with that big black guy, the ex–football player. They seemed pretty busy."

Fiona cut the engine and slid out of the front seat. "Busy doing what?"

"They were loading up Annie's car. A couple suitcases. Some bags of food. Looked like she was getting ready to take a trip. She going somewhere?"

"You didn't speak to either of them?" asked Fiona.

"If you'd been with her, I would have come over. Baxter really likes you, you know."

"He does?"

"Didn't I ever tell you? He sits on the couch in the living room and watches your house."

How did Phil know what Baxter did unless he'd been watching, too? Like so much else these days, the very thought made her skin crawl. "Uh-huh," she replied, eyeing him suspiciously. "Well, I better get inside."

He didn't move. "Have you been crying?"

"Allergies."

"Oh, yeah, I have those, too. Would you like to come over to my house and get your mail? I've been collecting it for you. Or, I could bring it over to your house. Either way."

Fi had forgotten about the mail. "Is there much?"

"Maybe half a bagful," he said.

An inner voice warned her away from going into his house alone. She tried to brush the feeling away. What would the world be like if she could never trust anyone again? "If you wouldn't mind bringing it over."

"Love to," he said. He set Baxter down. "Be right back."

Phil used to be such a quiet neighbor, mostly keeping to himself. Lately, he was morphing into glue.

Fi hustled up the front walk carrying her briefcase. She pressed her key into the lock. Once inside, a foreign smell—perfume, aftershave—assaulted her. Was someone in the house? She began to panic. That's when Roxy, holding a small watering can, emerged from the living room.

"What the hell are you doing here?" demanded Fi.

"What's it look like? I'm watering your plants. You want them to die?"

"How did you get in?"

"I'm not breaking and entering," said Roxy, examining a fern on the console table. "If you recall, you gave me a key so I could look after your house while you and Annie were in Colorado. Even if I didn't have one, you guys weren't very cagey about

230

where you hid your extra key outside. Under a potted plant is pretty standard. Might want to do something about that." She removed a few brown leaves. "You okay? You look kind of funny."

"Allergies," said Fi. "I didn't see your car."

"Nah, it's down at the park. I came with my sister and her kids. Thought since I was so close, that I'd walk up and see if everything was secure around the old homestead."

The doorbell rang.

"Expecting someone?" asked Roxy.

"It's my neighbor, Phil Banks. He's been picking up the mail. Will you handle that for me?" She had something she needed to do.

"Sure. I'm totally at your service."

Fiona entered her study and set her briefcase on the desk. Opening the two gold hasps, she removed Annie's notebook. She'd taken it from Cordelia's office back at the mansion because she didn't want it to be handed over to the police. That had been her primary reason for coming here today. If the police found out it existed, she might have to move it again——or perhaps destroy it. For the time being, she felt it would be safe in the bottom drawer of her desk. She also intended to spend some time reading it.

Roxy bustled into the study carrying a paper bag. "You hit the jackpot again."

Fi wondered if one of the letters was from her stalker.

"Phil wanted to stay but I told him you were busy."

"Thanks."

"Want some help sorting through this?"

"I'll look at them later," said Fi. "You know, I don't mean to be inhospitable——"

"But you're throwing me out," said Roxy, adjusting one of the straps on her overalls.

"Yeah. Hey, one last favor?"

"For you, babe, anything."

"Will you remove that house key from under the pot by the front door and leave it on the console table?"

"On my way out." She grinned. "Sure."

"I'll see you at the theater on Monday morning."

"Will do, chief."

Once Fi heard the front door click shut, she opened Annie's notebook and began to read.

Sharif opened the fridge and grunted with disgust. Only one beer left. He screwed off the top and then spent the next few minutes walking through the house looking for Bridget and Ted. He'd taken Ted on a short walk yesterday afternoon. The old guy seemed to like sitting by the lake. Maybe they'd take another walk today.

Sharif finally found them in the Nook. "Where's Tyrion?" he asked, easing down on one of the recliners.

"Taking a nap," said Bridget, looking up from a magazine.

"Isn't he a little old for naps?"

"Actually, he cried himself to sleep. He's been stealing things again."

" 'Stealing'?" repeated Sharif.

"It's not stealing," said Ted, turning the sound down on the TV. "It's not like he's going to keep any of that stuff. He likes the adventure. What kid wouldn't like the idea of secret treasure? I even help him sometimes."

"You knew where he kept it?" asked Bridget.

"Of course. Don't be so hard on the boy. It's just a phase."

Sharif wasn't sure what they were talking about and didn't really want to know. "Listen, I need to talk to you two. It's important."

Ted switched off the TV. "Does it have anything to do with the police canvassing the neighborhood? They've been at it all morning. I stood at the window in my bedroom and watched them."

The comment seemed to make Bridget nervous. She twisted her wedding ring. "So, what's up?"

"Annie left this morning. She'll be gone . . . for a while."

"Left," said Bridget. "You mean she went back to the house in Eden Prairie?"

"No. She took off for parts unknown. She needed to get her head straight. Needed to get away from all the turmoil. It wasn't something she wanted to do, it was something she had to do. Since we don't live inside Annie's skin, I don't think it's our place to judge."

Ted erupted. Thrusting himself out of his chair, he blurted out, "This is absolute bullshit. I don't believe a word of it."

"Dad," said Bridget, reaching for his hand. "Please."

"Annie and I made a date to play poker *every* afternoon. Four on the dot. You got that? She wouldn't miss it. It's our time together. I don't know who you think you are, coming in here with that load of crap, but you're dead wrong."

"I'm not making this up," said Sharif. He couldn't believe the old guy's attitude. There was a murder investigation looming and all he was concerned about was a poker game?

Ted cocked a fist. "I thought you were my friend."

"Dad," said Bridget, rising and taking hold of his arm. "You have to calm down. This isn't good for you."

"You believe him?" demanded Ted. "You buy that Annie left and never even said good-bye to us?"

"Why would he lie? I knew Annie was frightened, that she was barely holding it together. She won't stay away forever. We owe it to her to give her some space."

"She did *not* leave," said Ted through gritted teeth. "I will not let you two say that. You'll see. We'll be playing cards together at four."

"Where are you going?" asked Bridget, watching him stomp toward the door.

"Up to my room. Just leave me the hell alone."

Sitting back down, Bridget looked utterly worn out. "I'm sorry, Sharif. He never used to get angry like that. It's the Alzheimer's. He's on medication and, thank God, it's helping. He's been so happy here, seeing Annie again, spending time with her and getting to know Fiona."

"Until he found Annie's notebook hidden in my suitcase," said Sharif. Secrets always bit you in the ass eventually. He should have learned that lesson long ago. "I'm responsible. I should never have brought it."

Bridget dipped her eyes. "We've all made mistakes. I wanted to resurrect my relationship with her as much as Dad did. I needed her forgiveness for the way I behaved. Now, I wish we'd never come. I could have divorced Noah quietly and gone on with the rest of my life and none of this would ever have happened."

"The video brought you here."

"That and the shame we felt for the way we treated Annie." Her eyes welled with tears. "I don't want to cry," she said, pinching the bridge of her nose. "Look, I need to get upstairs to check on Tyrion, but before I go, tell me the truth: Was part of the Annie's reason for running off because she was afraid she'd be arrested for Noah's murder?"

"She didn't murder Noah," said Sharif.

"You sound so sure."

"I am."

"Does that mean you know who did it?"

He couldn't help himself. Once a smart aleck, always a smart aleck. "Cordelia," he said gravely. "Have you noticed that she has shifty eyes?"

Bridget's reaction was no reaction at all. "I better see about Tyrion."

Oops, thought Sharif. She apparently had no appreciation for gallows humor. Or maybe she didn't find murder funny. Come to think of it, neither did he.

30

Jane spent part of the afternoon pouring coffee for her customers in the main dining room. For a summer Saturday, the late-afternoon turnout was pretty good. Seeing one of her regulars calling her over, she wove her way through the tables.

"Did you know Le Tartine is closing?" asked Colin Elefson, a local restaurant critic for the *Skyway Daily Post*.

Le Tartine was a French restaurant in downtown Minneapolis, one that had never quite lived up to expectations. Jane didn't know the owner, but she did know the manager quite well. "I'm sorry to hear that."

"Five Twin Cities restaurants have shuttered their doors in the last six months."

"It's a perilous business."

"Glad the Lyme House is solid," said Colin.

"We appreciate all our customers."

As she continued on to the next table, she caught sight of Wayne. He was standing inside one of the wait stations, talking heatedly to one of her best broiler cooks, poking a finger at the guy's chest. Jane refreshed each person's coffee, then made straight for the station. "Is there a problem?" she asked. "Wayne? Bruno?"

"I quit," said Bruno, ripping off his apron and forcing it against Jane's stomach. "That man is a bastard."

Wayne grabbed the front of Bruno's shirt. A stupid thing to do because Bruno was a foot taller and a good fifty pounds heavier. Bruno brushed Wayne's hand away like it was a feather. "Fire his ass, Ms. Lawless, before he wrecks the place. I'm outta here."

Everyone in the restaurant appeared to be watching the scene.

"Let me explain," said Wayne, giving Jane one of his best car-salesman smiles.

Jane placed the coffee carafe back on the burner. Lowering her voice, she said, "Get in the kitchen and talk to the head chef. Tell her what happened and then figure out how to cover Bruno's station."

"Sure, but I should explain."

"I don't want explanations. I want you to *fix* this."

"Just so you know, we're better off without him. Trust me on that one."

She fought the urge to fire him on the spot. "Give me half an hour and then come down to my office."

"Right. Will do."

Before dropping by Cordelia's house yesterday afternoon with the good news about the pipe bomber, Jane had met with her liquor distributor, Grunwald Wines & Spirits. After being invited into the wine distributor's office, she'd placed a copy of the company's most recent price list on the desk in front of the assistant manager. She informed the man, whom she knew to be the nephew of the owner, that she'd highlighted prices on the sheet that were higher than other local distributors. She asked him to explain. He gave her the usual blather about shipping costs, stocking costs, et cetera. When she said that she knew he'd given her manager gifts—in other words kickbacks and bribes, though she refrained from using those words—to continue to buy from them, even with the higher prices, the guy vehemently denied it.

Jane didn't know for sure that Wayne was dealing under the table, although when he'd taken it upon himself to oversee the liquor and beverage ordering in May and the costs had begun to rise, she'd considered it, but hadn't followed up. Using that info, she bluffed. She informed the guy that if he refused to tell her the truth, she'd go straight to the owner, his uncle. That's when he began to backtrack. Yes, he said, he may have given Wayne some Twins tickets, a case or two of free booze. Nothing major. She told him to send her a new price list. Once she'd had some time to study it, she might continue to order from them or she might not. Whatever her ultimate decision, she now had her hands on the final nail in Wayne's coffin.

Back behind her office desk, Jane looked up the phone number for Le Tartine online and phoned the restaurant. She asked to speak to Meg Auster. A moment later, Meg came on the line.

"Hi, it's Jane Lawless."

"Wow, nice to hear from you."

"This may be a little unorthodox, but I just heard that Le Tartine may be closing."

In a more confidential tone, Meg asked, "Who told you?"

"Colin Elefson. Any truth in it?"

"Afraid so."

"Look, I know this comes out of the blue, but if you're looking for another manager position, I'd love to hire you."

"Seriously?"

"You were the best assistant manager I ever had. I was glad for you when you were offered a better position at Le Tartine, but I certainly felt your loss."

"That's nice to hear." She paused. "You're actually offering me the manager position?"

"I am."

"When would you want me to start?"

"Five minutes from now. Tomorrow? Monday?"

"Really? That quick."

"I'm about to fire my current manager. I need someone I can trust. The fact that I trained you, that you know this restaurant back to front, pushes you to the top of my list. We can talk salary when you get here. I'm sure I can match what you're making now, or even sweeten the deal a little. I really want you."

"Let me talk to the owner. I'm sure I can make it work."

"Great. Get back to me when you have something firm."

"Thanks, Jane. I think you just saved my life."

"Consider it mutual salvation."

Usually, Jane hated letting people go. Firing Wayne, however, would be pure joy. As soon as he sat down in front of her desk and saw the look on her face, he knew he was toast. Even so, he tried to talk her out of firing him, first with feigned indignation that there was anything wrong with his job performance, and finally with arguments about why others were to blame. She listened to his justifications, but they only made her angrier.

Much to Jane's horror, she ended up completely losing it.

She'd never behaved this way with an employee before. She accused Wayne of stealing. Of taking bribes under the table. She shouted at him that he'd turned the restaurant into his personal fiefdom. That he was abusing his power and good employees were leaving, or on the verge of leaving, because of it. She went down the list, point by point. By the end of her tirade, she was on her feet, gesturing toward the door. She called upstairs and asked for one of the waiters to stand with him in his office while he cleared it out.

"I suppose this means I won't get a letter of recommendation," said Wayne.

"I wouldn't recommend you to take out the freakin' trash," she shouted at his retreating back.

Jane picked Cordelia up from her house just after five.

"Where are we going?" demanded Cordelia, stuffing herself into the passenger's seat of Jane's Mini. "This car belongs in Lilliput, not on the streets of a human-sized city."

"It's cozy," said Jane.

"It's microscopic."

All Jane had said to her on the phone was, "Change into something more presentable than a baggy sweatshirt and jeans. I'm picking you up in fifteen minutes." Assessing Cordelia's current attire—black leggings, her new Lucchese Renaissance-inspired boots that came to just below her knees, and a red taffeta flamenco blouse with a frilly, deeply plunging neckline—Jane felt that the ensemble, as usual, exceeded not only expectations, but possibly good taste. Cordelia wasn't a fan of fading into the woodwork.

"I had an inspirational moment," said Jane.

"Oh, goody."

"Don't you want to know what I figured out . . . or, at least, think I've figured out?" Sitting at her desk after firing Wayne, attempting to turn her thoughts to something less fraught, an idea had occurred to her.

Cordelia offered a quick, cold appraisal. "Dazzle me with your brilliance."

"It was those two shiny silver pens; the ones we found in Tyrion's treasure stash."

"I don't remember any pens."

"They had the words 'Maxfield West' printed on the side."

"So?"

"Have you been to the Maxfield West lately?"

"I've never darkened that particular door."

Neither had Jane. "Someone in your house must have spent some time at the hotel, otherwise, why would those pens be there?"

"Seems axiomatic."

"If it wasn't you, and if Annie hasn't gone out, nor has Bridget, and Fiona's been driving with you to the theater, that leaves Ted, Sharif, and Noah. I put my money on Noah."

"And why would he visit there?"

"Remember that woman who kept calling him? His patient, Mimi Chandler? The one Sergeant Vance told us about?"

"But she lives in California."

"I figured it was possible that he flew her in. Family reunions can be boring. Maybe he thought he'd have some free time."

"You really think he'd get involved with one of his patients?"

241

"Why all the phone calls from her if they weren't? So . . . I called the hotel. Asked to be put through to Mimi Chandler's room."

"And?"

"No Mimi Chandler listed. I asked if they had a Noah Foster staying at the hotel. Turns out, they did. He'd booked the penthouse suite for himself and his wife. They even gave me the number of the suite."

"Okay," Cordelia deadpanned. "Consider me dazzled."

Jane was lucky enough to find a parking space directly across the street from the hotel. The Maxfield West was downtown Minneapolis's newest luxury hotel. It was built by the same family who owned the historic Maxfield Plaza in Saint Paul.

Walking through the ultra-modern interior with its mushroom gravy—colored walls, marble floors, and raw silk drapes, Jane had to admit she was impressed.

As they came off the elevator on the top floor, Jane cautioned Cordelia. "Let me do the talking."

"Why on earth would I do that?" She marched up to the door and knocked. It was opened by a woman wearing nothing but a bra and panties. She was thin but generously endowed, with a helmet of glossy black hair, perfectly trimmed bangs and an impish expression partially hidden behind extra-large black-rimmed glasses.

"I thought you always brought one of those tables with you," said the woman.

"Tables?" replied Cordelia.

"I'm not sure why I need *two* masseuses, but you might as well come in." She turned and walked back into the room, where it

242

appeared she was in the midst of three games of solitaire at the dining room table. "I suppose I could lie down on the bed. Is that how you do it?"

"We're not here to give you a massage," said Jane.

"You're not? Then who the hell are you?"

"My name's Jane Lawless." She offered Mimi one of her cards. "I'm an investigator looking into Noah Foster's murder. And this is Cordelia Thorn."

Mimi smiled. It wasn't a friendly smile.

"I have a few questions I'd like to ask you," said Jane. Some people didn't understand the role of a private detective and assumed that they were required to cooperate. Jane hoped Mimi might be in their number.

"It was a mistake," said Mimi, flicking edgy glances at them as she returned to the solitaire games.

"I hardly think a gunshot to the head was a mistake," said Cordelia.

Mimi staggered slightly as she moved around the dining room table examining the cards.

"May we join you?" asked Jane, nodding to a couple of chairs.

She ignored the question. "Who would want to kill such a wonderful man?"

"Did you know him well?"

"I loved him," she said, looking up with defiance. "He loved me. We were getting married, you know."

"You were?" said Cordelia. She moved behind Mimi, joining her in scrutinizing the cards.

"Oh, yes. It was a shared understanding, nothing verbalized, but that doesn't make it any less real. He was my therapist. Not always an ethical therapist, I grant you, but if he had been, we would never have fallen in love. He infuriated me sometimes. I admit that. I'm not a nice person when I'm angry. But you have to understand. He was *everything* to me."

"You knew he was married?" asked Jane.

"He wanted a divorce."

"How long have you been . . . together?"

"Since my seventh therapy session, eight months ago."

"Would you mind explaining how you became . . . intimate?" asked Jane. She knew it was an intrusive question, and yet she was curious how a therapist seduced a patient.

"Well," said Mimi, seeming to warm to the topic. "From the very first, Noah was able to read my mind. It was uncanny. He told me right off that I didn't trust men. He was right, of course. He said it was an issue that would be vital for my future happiness. We would work on it together. During the third session— we met twice a week—he asked me to take off all my clothes. He told me not to worry, that nothing was going to happen."

Cordelia nearly fell over. "You actually did it?"

"I didn't really want to. I took off my sweater first. My shoes. Eventually, I took everything off. He asked me to lie on his couch. He sat behind me, where I couldn't see him, and we talked. He asked a lot of questions, mostly about the guys I'd dated. What we did together. How it made me feel. When the session was over, I dressed and left."

"You're saying he never touched you?" asked Cordelia.

"Not so much as a handshake. After that, I simply came in and took off my clothes. Sometimes he'd bring his chair close to the couch so I could see him. He'd place a hand on my thigh, just let it rest there. To be honest, several weeks into the therapy, I was dying for him to do more. Being with him was all I thought about. And then one afternoon, instead of pulling his chair over, he knelt down next to the couch and put his hand on my stomach. As we talked, he moved the hand lower." She looked up at Cordelia. "You're an adult. You can figure out the rest. After that, we made love every session."

"You didn't think it was wrong?" asked Cordelia.

"Of course it was wrong. I'm not an idiot. But it turned into true love. You can't argue with true love."

Jane and Cordelia exchanged glances.

"And so he booked this room for you so you could be together while he was in town," said Jane.

"Yeah. Well, sort of."

"You two talked on the phone a lot."

"I needed to hear his voice."

"And he spent time with you here."

"We made love, had dinner together."

"Last night?" asked Jane.

"He left around eight thirty." She went from game to game, pushing cards around. "Now, I'm bereft. I don't know what to do."

"You've got two plays," said Cordelia. "Put the seven of clubs on the eight of hearts. And the two of spades on the three of diamonds."

Mimi smiled. "Yeah, that works."

Jane felt like she'd entered the Twilight Zone. "Do you have any idea why Noah might have become sick last night? He'd been vomiting in the car."

"Really? How awful. No idea at all."

"What condition was Noah treating you for?"

"I'm a bunch of stuff. A salad of psychiatric disorders. Mainly,

I'm bipolar. A bipolar narcissist." She laughed. "According to the great doctor."

"Put the jack on the queen," said Cordelia.

For someone who'd just lost the love of her life, Mimi seemed awfully chipper. "I wonder," said Jane. "Would you mind if I used your bathroom?"

Mimi tapped her black nails on the table. "I've got a gown hanging in the one in the hall. I'm steaming the wrinkles out. Use the one in my bedroom."

"I don't see another play on that game," said Cordelia, winking at Jane.

"Then it's time to redeal," said Mimi. "I adore solitaire. I could play it all day."

"What time was your massage scheduled for?" asked Cordelia, keeping the conversation going.

"Five."

"Shiatsu? Swedish?"

As Jane passed into the bedroom, she noticed Mimi's purse lying on the nightstand. With Cordelia keeping her busy in the living room, Jane sat down on the bed and opened it. Inside were several sheets of paper all folded together. Studying the top sheet, Jane saw that it was a car rental agreement. Mimi had rented a red Ferrari Spider three days ago. Jane took a picture of the page with her cell phone.

Next, she checked inside Mimi's pocketbook, where she discovered some cash, a California driver's license, a Santa Monica library card, and two credit cards, one belonging to Noah H. Foster. Once again, she took a photo. Had Noah actually given Mimi his credit card? From what Jane knew about bipolar disorder, she doubted he'd trust her with it. After spending a few minutes in the bathroom looking for Mimi's medications and finding nothing but a bottle of Aleve, she returned to the front room.

"Why don't we order dinner?" said Mimi, jumping up from a chair to go dig through a drawer in the kitchen. "Here's the hotel menu." She held it up. "The chef is a magician. Come on, you two. My treat."

"I suppose we could at least *look* at the menu," offered Cordelia.

"We can't stay," said Jane. "Remember? We're heading up to Duluth tonight."

"Duluth?" said Mimi, frowning as she appeared to inspect the word for its true meaning. "Never heard of it. Hey, why don't I come along? We'll make a night of it."

"A friend of ours is in the hospital up there," said Jane, motioning for Cordelia to cease playing cards. "Wouldn't be much fun for you."

"Yeah, not my scene."

"We're very sorry for your loss," said Jane.

"Loss? Oh, you mean Noah. Thank you." Mimi might not look the least bit sad, and yet, as she sat there, her attention focused on the cards, tears began to trickle down her cheeks. "I miss him, you know? I don't understand any of this. I don't think I'll ever get over it."

"Will you be flying back to California soon?" asked Cordelia, rising from her chair.

"I'm not sure. I don't like to have too many definite plans. Best to keep options open. I wonder where Noah's body was taken?"

"The Hennepin County medical examiner does the forensic autopsy," said Jane.

"Where's that?"

"In downtown Minneapolis. Chicago Avenue, I think."

"Oh." She stared off into space.

"Thanks for your time," said Jane.

"Um, when you get back from Duluth," said Mimi, adjusting her bra, "give me a call. If I'm still here, let's go clubbing. Or to a movie. I love summer movies, don't you? Or we could order dinner up here in my suite. It's always great to make new friends."

31

After returning to the mansion, Jane and Cordelia's first order of business was to locate Bridget. They found her in the dining room, setting the table for dinner.

"We decided to order Chinese tonight," she said, standing at the foot of the table, folding a stack of paper napkins. "Sharif didn't feel like cooking. Nobody did."

Jane, hoping for some privacy, asked her to come back to the sunroom. "It's important."

"But first, I have something to tell you," said Bridget as they made their way through the great hall. "Annie's gone. She left this morning. Nobody knows where she is."

Jane stopped and turned around. "Gone?"

"Apparently, the pressure was too much. Noah's murder. The pipe bomb. She confided to me yesterday that she felt marooned here, completely cut off from all the moorings in her life. She woke every day filled with nothing but dread."

"Oh my stars and garters," said Cordelia, throwing herself dramatically over the fainting couch. "I don't care what motivated it, it was a stupid move. The police will take it as a sign of guilt."

Jane had to agree.

"I was sure the police would call us today," said Bridget. "That, you know, they'd want to interview us individually."

"From what I understand," said Jane, "the MPD is pretty backed up with two other high-profile murder investigations right now. Three U of M college kids were murdered in their dorm room last weekend. And then, on Tuesday, the wife of one of our state senators was found dead in her garage. It may take a while before they get to you."

Bridget just shook her head.

Sensing that Cordelia wasn't likely to move from the couch any time soon, Jane pulled over one of the wingback chairs and nodded for Bridget to do the same. "Back to Annie for a moment. Did Fi know she was leaving?"

"Nobody did. Dad's really upset about it. In fact, I don't think he believed it until she didn't show up for their poker game. Connecting with Annie again has had such a positive effect on him. Now . . . I just don't know. I've never seen him so down. Anyway, you said you had something important to tell me."

Jane quickly explained about finding Mimi Chandler, and about Noah's credit card. "Do you think he gave it to her?"

"No way on earth," said Bridget. "His parents died in a small plane accident when he was nine. He was raised by his aunt. She worked at a dry cleaners in the valley, never made much above minimum wage. Money was a huge deal to him. He liked to spend it on himself. When it came to others, he was usually as cheap as they come, unless he wanted to impress."

"Is there any way you could check online at the Visa site and see what was billed to the card?" asked Jane.

Bridget fished her phone out of the pocket of her slacks. "I'll bet anything she stole it from his wallet. It's my card, too. Let me see what's what." She clicked the phone on and began tapping on the keypad with her thumbs. "Oh, my God," she said after a couple of minutes. Her lips tightened into a thin, angry line. "You won't believe this. In the past week, she's charged over thirty thousand dollars."

"For what?" asked Cordelia, pressing the back of her hand to her forehead and looking wan.

"First-class plane tickets to Minneapolis. A ridiculously expensive rental car. The penthouse suite at the Maxfield West. A round-trip plane ticket to New York. Hotel room at the Marriott Marquis. A nine-thousand-dollar charge for something at Bergdorf Goodman. A seventeen-thousand-dollar, thirty-six-day Mediterranean cruise from Taylor and Waverly Travel. A case of wine from Haskell's. The list goes on. If Noah wasn't already dead, I'd kill him."

"You better contact Visa and let them know the card was stolen," said Jane.

"God, if I have to pay this, it will take a huge chunk out of Noah's life insurance."

"His life was insured?" said Cordelia, raising an elegant eyebrow.

"We both took out large policies after Tyrion was born. I better go take care of this," she said, thanking them for bringing her the information, and then rushing out of the room.

When Jane looked over at Cordelia, she found her friend staring back at her.

Sharif stood under the stone portico, smoking an illegal Cuban cigar and glancing down every now and then at his cell phone.

He had something even more felonious—a blunt—in his back pocket and would much rather have been smoking that, but figured Cordelia's neighbors were watching the property after what happened. A few minutes ago, he'd tapped in the words, "Are u there?" It was the sixth time in the last three hours he'd sent the same message. So far he'd received no response.

Sucking in a rounded mouthful of smoke, he blew it out slowly and watched it curl and drift away. He didn't consider cigars mass suicide the way he did cigarettes. Not that they were good for him. Then again, nobody lived forever.

Sharif had left his ex-girlfriend, Tamika, several voice and text messages in the last couple of days, hoping she might have forgiven him. He missed her. The idea of living in that big house in Ohio without her in his life depressed him. He'd always controlled his emotions, made sure he was riding on steel rails where his love life was concerned, but for some reason, Tamika had gotten under his skin. He'd long ago given up his adolescent fantasies of outlaw glory with an endless stream of sexy women. He wanted to settle down. With her. But he'd ruined it again, just like he always did.

In the heavy gray evening gloom, Sharif thought he detected a slight cooling in the air. Or maybe the humidity had gone down. Whatever the case, it was welcome. Feeling his cell phone buzz, he looked down and saw that he had a text.

HERE. SAFE. TIRED.

He was instantly relieved. A second later, another text came in.

252

He typed back: UPSET.

        Annie: ANGRY?

        Sharif: YEAH.

        Annie: I AM PATHETIC.

        Sharif: STOP THAT.

        Annie: POLICE?

        Sharif: NO WORD. RELAX. THEY KNOW
                  NOTHING. U GOT ENOUGH FOOD?

        Annie: TOO MUCH.

        Sharif: BEAUTIFUL LAKE, YEAH?

        Annie: PEACEFUL.

        Sharif: THE HOUSEBOAT?

        Annie: SERIOUSLY MANLY DECOR.

He laughed. The place belonged to one of his football buddies.
It was up on Rainy Lake, right on the border with Canada.

He'd spent many happy hours on that manly houseboat, fishing, swimming, reading, and partying. It was about as far away from the Twin Cities as a person could get and still be within the state. All it had taken to set it up was a phone call.

Sharif: FEEL SAFE?

Annie: YES.

Sharif: KEEP IN TOUCH.

Annie: LOVE U.

Hearing the crunch of footsteps on gravel, Sharif was surprised to see Willow Lewis, Tyrion's former nanny, making her way up to the house.

"Hi," she said, stopping a few yards from the portico.

"Thought you'd gone back to California."

"Not yet."

Removing the cigar from his mouth, he said, "What are you doing back here?"

"I came . . . because I left a pair of shoes behind."

It seemed less of a reason and more of an excuse to him. "You heard about Noah?"

She gave an almost imperceptible nod. "Is Bridget here?"

"Yeah."

She seemed uncertain. "Maybe I better forget about the shoes."

He sat down on the steps, sweeping his arm wide and saying, "Why don't you step into my office?"

"I don't think so."

"What kind of shoes?"

"Huh?"

"You said you left a pair of shoes here."

"Oh. Right. Flip-flops."

Had he heard her right? "You came all the way back here for two-dollar flip-flops?"

Her gaze roamed the drive, coming to rest on the spot where Noah had died. "Doesn't make a lot of sense, does it. But then nothing I've done recently makes much sense." Offering him a weak smile, she turned and walked away.

32

"When Annie gets back tomorrow," Ted piped up, pushing his moo goo gai pan around, "I think we should celebrate and all go out for a special meal."

Everyone at the table in Cordelia's baronial dining room appeared jarred by the comment, and that included Jane. It was the first time anyone had mentioned Annie's name. She wondered if he was confused and really thought Annie would be back tomorrow, or if he was just keeping a positive attitude.

"That's a nice thought," said Fi.

"Why don't you make the reservations?" replied Ted. "My treat."

Fi toyed with the food on her plate. She'd spoken little since returning to the house. Nobody at the table seemed all that keen on talking, with the exception of Cordelia and Sharif, who were arguing about movies.

After trying a piece of lemon chicken, Tyrion climbed out of his booster chair and raced off, no doubt headed for his favorite place—the nook, with its sixty-five-inch TV and the Xbox One.

"I better go after him," said Bridget, looking defeated as she pushed her chair back and left the room.

"Just let him be," shouted Ted, apparently oblivious to Cordelia's raptorlike gaze as he wiped a clean spoon with a napkin.

"Our silverware isn't tidy enough for you?" she asked.

"Just prefer everything spit and polish."

"Probably wouldn't have mentioned this around Bridget," said Sharif, most likely making a stab at changing the subject before Cordelia threw a carton of fried rice at Ted, "but Willow stopped by a few minutes ago."

"I thought she was headed home," said Jane. "Didn't someone tell me she was taking a bus?" It occurred to her that she'd failed to add Willow's name to the list of women who might have had a reason to be in the drive last night.

"Guess not. She only stayed a minute. Not really sure why she came."

Since nobody was talking much, the food was dispatched in short order.

While Cordelia and Sharif carried empty cartons and plates into the kitchen, Ted excused himself, saying he wanted to go join Bridget and Tyrion in the nook.

Jane and Fi were left alone at the table. "How are you doing?" she asked.

"Not well," said Fi.

"Have you heard from Annie?"

"No, and I don't expect to."

"You sound angry."

"I don't know what I am." Removing a folded piece of paper from her back pocket, she handed it to Jane.

"Don't tell me. A new letter from your stalker?"

"I drove down to my house in Eden Prairie this afternoon. It was in with the mail. I was hoping you'd take a look, tell me what you think."

Jane unfolded the note and read:

WHEN I'M AWAY FROM YOU IT'S SO HARD.
I BEGIN TO WONDER IF WE'LL EVER BE
TOGETHER. I KNOW WHEN I LOOK INTO
YOUR EYES THAT YOU FEEL THE SAME WAY
I DO, BUT THIS IS TAKING TOO LONG. I NEED
A SIGN FROM YOU, SOMETHING THAT WILL
GIVE ME HOPE. HERE'S WHAT WE'LL DO.
I WANT YOU TO WEAR SOMETHING RED TO
THE THEATER EVERY DAY THIS WEEK. I
DON'T CARE WHAT IT IS. A RED SCARF. A RED
DRESS. RED SHOES OR A RED PURSE. WHEN
I SEE IT, I'LL BE OVER THE MOON WITH
HAPPINESS. WE NEED TO MEET SOON TO
PLAN OUR FUTURE. I'LL GET BACK TO YOU
WITH MORE DETAILS. UNTIL THEN,
XXX AND A FULL BODY O

Every time Jane read that over-the-top signature, she felt a wave of revulsion.

"What should I do?" asked Fi. "I have to say, I'm getting pretty sick of this. Do I play his little game or don't I? Honestly, at this point, I wish he'd show himself so I could tell him to get the hell out of my life. I mean, he wants me to wear something red? Do you see how ridiculous that is?"

"So don't do it," said Jane. It wasn't a good enough answer, but unless she pursued Fi's stalker full time—something she couldn't do—she didn't know what else to say.

"Good. That's what I thought." Fi stuffed the note back in her pocket.

"Sweets?" chirped Cordelia, carrying a plate of crispy cream cheese and banana–filled wontons covered in chopped peanuts and powdered sugar out of the kitchen. They were Cordelia's current favorite dessert. Jane actually found them mildly disgusting. She took it as her cue to leave. She needed to get back to the restaurant.

"You're not going," said Cordelia, licking her fingers.

"I'm afraid work calls."

"But the scrumptious banana wontons."

"It's a sacrifice," said Jane.

"Never fear. I'll fight off the salivating hordes and save you one."

"You're awesome."

"I *used* to be awesome," Cordelia corrected her. "Now I'm epic."

At the restaurant, Jane found a voice mail message waiting for her from Meg Auster. She'd spoken to the owner of Le Tartine and could start working as the Lyme House's new manager tomorrow. She wouldn't be able to make it until noon. That was fine with Jane. Sunday brunch was usually the busiest day of the week. Trial by fire for poor Meg.

Jane sat at her desk for the next hour making notes, looking through the statement of manager responsibilities she'd compiled, a list she'd restructured over the years, prioritizing the information Meg would need to hit the ground running. When she was finished, she made two phone calls, one to Evelyn to ask how the dogs were doing and to see if they might be able to spend another night at her house, and the second to Julia. Once again, she was put through to voice mail. It appeared the good doctor was out.

As Jane was about to head upstairs, an idea struck her. She flipped through the photos she'd taken of Ted's journal. Specifically, she was looking for Willow Lewis's phone number. Sure enough, she was there, seventh on his list. Jane tapped it in and, when the call went to voice mail, left Willow a message. As it happened, Willow had been upstairs with Tyrion on the night Jane visited with the family so they'd never actually met. Jane left a message, saying she was part of the investigation into Noah Foster's murder and needed to talk to Willow before she left town. She included her number and asked Willow to call as soon as possible. And then she mentally crossed her fingers. If Ted had seen a woman approach Noah's van on the night in question, Willow should have been added to the list of potential suspects.

Mimi Chandler was another name for this list.

Knowing that tomorrow would be unusually hectic, Jane left the restaurant shortly after ten. Instead of going home, she drove over to Julia's loft, thinking that making a personal appearance might persuade Julia to talk to her.

Jane entered the front lobby and used the security phone to call upstairs. Julia lived on the top floor, with wonderful views of Lake Calhoun to the west and downtown Minneapolis to the north.

It only took a moment before Julia answered.

"It's me," said Jane.

260

"You assume I recognize your voice?"

"Come on. Buzz me in."

"I'm on my way to bed."

"Fine. Go ahead and crawl in. I'll pull up a chair."

"You are absolutely no fun at all."

The elevator doors opened and Jane got on. Once up on the fifth floor, Jane had to wait, as usual, until Julia got around to answering the door. She was still dressed. In fact, she looked like she'd just come home. Her raincoat had been tossed over one of dining room chairs. Her purse was on the table.

Kicking off her heels, Julia led Jane into the kitchen, where an open bottle of vintage Trinidadian rum sat on the counter. "I was just about to pour myself a nightcap. Care for one?"

"If it's small."

Julia removed two glasses from the cupboard and filled Jane's almost to the brim.

"Funny."

"Have you ever tried this brand?" She handed the glass to Jane and then padded into the living room, sitting down on a white leather couch with the best view of the downtown city lights. "It's good."

Jane poured three-quarters of the rum back into the bottle.

Except for candles lit and placed here and there throughout the loft, there were no lights on. Adele's latest album played softly from the stereo.

"Looks like you've been out," said Jane, choosing the same couch.

"If you must know, I had a hot date tonight."

Jane glanced toward the bedroom.

"Not that hot."

"Are you serious about her?"

"If I were, would you be jealous?"

Jane tried the rum. Julia was right. It was lovely. "Very smooth."

"I read about the murder at Cordelia's house. Have they arrested her yet? By the way, if she needs a character witness, better not call me."

"I wish you two could get along."

"Never going to happen."

"You were about to tell me something important last night," said Jane. "I felt bad that I had to leave so abruptly."

"I'm used to it."

"For crying out loud, will you stop that. We may not be together anymore, but we're still friends."

"Let's unpack that," said Julia, crossing her legs. "Unless you need something, do we ever see each other? Are you ever anywhere but somewhere else? Do we exchange e-mails? Do we go out to dinner? If you've sent me a birthday present or a Christmas gift in the last five years, I should tell you now, I never received them."

"Do you want me to leave?"

Julia sipped her drink.

"I may not know *what* we are exactly," said Jane, "but we're not strangers."

"I could say the same for the woman who cuts my hair."

"You don't make anything easy, do you."

"Why should I? You haven't exactly made my life a joyride."

As the song "All I Ask" came over the speakers, Jane felt suddenly ashamed of the way she'd treated Julia. And then, just as quickly, she was ashamed of being ashamed. Julia was impulsive and manipulative. She had a huge ego, lacked any normal sense of remorse when she crossed a line, moral or otherwise, and lied more often than she told the truth. She was hardly a great candidate for a long-term relationship. And yet, Julia had been there for Jane whenever she'd needed her. And not only for Jane, but for her father, when he'd been ill. Nobody, as Jane knew well, was all good or all bad.

"Humans feel things in their muscles and bones, not just in their minds and hearts," said Julia, holding the snifter to her lips. "When you left me, I began to bleed internally. Sometimes I think I'm still bleeding. I know you can't understand why I haven't let go of you because, frankly, I don't understand it myself."

"Tell me what's wrong," said Jane. "You were about to last night."

She took a sip of rum. Then another. "Sure. Why not? I was recently diagnosed with a sphenoid wing meningioma. It's an intercranial tumor."

"A brain tumor?"

She nodded, setting the snifter on the end table next to her. "It's growing on my optic nerve, behind my eyes."

"So that's why you were wearing sunglasses."

"Light bothers me, which is an unusual symptom. I may lose my vision entirely. In fact, I've already begun to experience dark patches in my field of vision. The larger the tumor becomes, the more it impinges on the optic nerve."

"Is it—" Jane couldn't bring herself to say the word.

"Cancer? Mine is classified as atypical. That means it's not benign, but it's not malignant. Yet. I won't go into all the details. Because I'm an oncologist, the diagnosis is alternately horrifying and fascinating. The main problem is, because of the location, surgery to remove it comes with serious risks. And even if I did decide on surgery, it would likely only be a partial resection because of the placement, and that means it would likely grow back. The flip side is, my doctors think the tumor may be having an impact on how blood reaches my brain."

"Oh. God."

"Yeah. Not pretty."

"I honestly don't know what to say."

Julia gazed out the windows. The silence stretched. "Remember, Jane. Nothing can trip a person up like compassion. Better reel yours back in before you do something you'll regret."

"Such as?"

"I don't know. Why don't we get married?"

Jane began to laugh.

"I'm serious."

"You never stop."

"No, but someday, something will stop me."

"Look, I want to help if I can."

"Why don't you find me a new brain?"

Jane slid a bit closer.

"Careful. I might actually tell you the entire truth for once."

"That's what I came to hear."

Julia pressed a finger to her lips, thinking it over. "Okay. Again, why not? You want to know my greatest fear?"

"Yes."

"My greatest fear, the one that keeps me up at night, is that . . . I will have to go through this alone. I have friends, but nobody . . . I mean, there isn't anyone—"

"I understand," said Jane.

"I don't know how long I have. Could be years and years. Could be far less. If I do lose my sight, I lose my profession. Not many blind cancer doctors out there."

"You won't be alone," said Jane.

Julia turned to face her. "How do you figure that?"

"Because I'll be there for you."

"I'm not asking for your help."

"No. I'm offering."

Julia took another couple of sips of rum. Hesitantly, she reached out and touched Jane's face. "The idea that there may come a time when I can't see you, that all I'll have are memories, God, you don't know how much that hurts."

Was Jane being a total moron, rejecting a woman who clearly loved her so deeply? Were the candles, the rum, and Adele's voice mixing together, causing her better judgment to elude her? "I'm not offering romance, Julia, but . . . this time . . . I am offering real friendship."

Julia laughed. "That's nice of you, but I'm not interested in pity."

"It's not pity," said Jane. Maybe middle age had made her reckless. Or maybe it was simply too hard to keep erecting barriers. "Whatever happens, we'll face it together."

33

The following morning, Jane met with Willow at the Nicollet, a coffeehouse in the Stevens Square area of Minneapolis, just south of downtown. A young woman wearing a low-cut pink tank top and black jeans walked in shortly after ten, her expression tight and watchful. Her gaze roamed the room until Jane held up her hand and motioned her over.

"Are you Willow?"

She nodded.

"Can I buy you a cup of coffee?" She already had a macchiato on the table in front of her.

"No, thanks," said Willow, removing the strap of her backpack from her shoulder and pulling out a chair. "I don't have a lot of time."

"You're headed back to California?"

"I called my parents and they don't want me taking a bus home. They were furious when I told them the Fosters brought me here and then fired me. Dad said I should fly back to San Diego standby and he'd reimburse me. I'm hoping to get out today."

"This won't take long," said Jane. She waited for Willow to get comfortable. "I have a few questions."

"Like what?" she asked, touching the tip of her little finger to the edge of her glossed lips.

"I'm wondering why you stayed in town so long?"

"Well, I mean, I was hoping to see Noah one more time. I left him several phone messages, but he never called me back."

"You two were—"

"I loved him. He loved me."

"I'm curious how it happened. How you got together."

"Um," she said, brushing a lock of her hair behind her ear. "I used to work at the Johnson Garden Center in Pasadena."

"Doing what?"

"I helped one of the guys who cared for the plants. I loved that job. I like helping things grow, you know? Sometimes he'd give me stuff that he thought was too far gone. I'd bring the plants back to my apartment. It was an efficiency, so not lots of room. After a while, it was so filled with greenery that I could hardly move around. I don't know," she said, folding her hands. "There's just something inside me that wants to nurse things back to health. Noah was like that. He needed caring for."

"How so?"

"Like, he'd come into the garden center with Bridget sometimes. I thought she treated him bad. I felt sorry for him. While she was busy in the office, he'd wander back to the stock area and we'd talk. He was the one who convinced her to give me the nanny job after their old nanny . . . well, let's just say she wasn't a happy camper by the time she quit."

"Why was that?"

"I probably shouldn't say."

"Something Noah did?"

She looked away. "I suppose you'll find out anyway, whether it's from me or someone else. See, when the old nanny—her name was Tiffany—found out I was about to take the job, she, like, called the garden store and asked to speak with me. She warned me about Noah. Said to watch out, especially when he'd been drinking. At first all she said was that he had grabby hands. I told her I didn't believe her. That's when she informed me that he'd . . . forced himself on her. She said Bridget paid her off so she'd keep her mouth shut. She said she got ten thousand in cash. I never entirely believed it because I knew Bridget and Noah were having money problems. But whatever happened between Noah and Tiffany, it was ugly."

"That didn't make you think twice about taking the job?"

Willow blinked a couple of times and looked away. "It's possible that . . . that I was already falling in love with him a little. I wanted the job because it meant I could be around him more."

Noah was a predator. Willow was just one more innocent fly he'd caught in his web. "I just don't understand why he wouldn't return my calls," said Willow. "I know he didn't like confrontations. He'd get really upset if he thought he was being criticized."

"Did you ever criticize him?"

"No, I wouldn't do that. But I did do a bad thing. I opened his cell phone to see what calls he was getting. It seemed like, the last few days, it just kept ringing and ringing. Turns out, it was a woman. Mimi something or other. When I asked him about her, he said she was a patient. But, I mean, why would a patient call him?"

"You didn't believe him?"

"I wanted to. I probably shouldn't say anything, but the thing

268

is, for the past few months he's been telling me he's going to leave Bridget, that we would be together. As far as I could see, it wasn't happening and it probably never would. I was fed up with his excuses, so I asked him if he was sleeping with Mimi."

"And? Did he admit to it?"

"He said I didn't deserve his love and walked away."

"How did that make you feel?

"Small," said Willow. "Like I didn't really matter to him. Like . . . maybe he'd been lying to me all along just so I'd have sex with him."

Willow might not look like a murderer, but she'd just offered up a strong motive.

"Where did you go on Friday after Bridget fired you?"

She traced a scratch on the table with her index finger. "She gave me a check, like that did me any good. I didn't even know where a bank was, and without an account, I never could have cashed it. I had twenty-two dollars in my purse. Thankfully, I had a credit card that wasn't totally maxed. I walked over to Hennepin Avenue and got on a bus. I found a hotel for sixty-two dollars a night out by the Mall of America."

"Did you ever go back to Cordelia's house?"

"No, never. Why would I?"

"To see Noah."

"No," she said, shaking her head.

"So you didn't come back yesterday afternoon either? Sharif said he saw you."

"Well, I mean—" She knew she'd been caught in a lie and began to wring her hands. "Okay, maybe I did go back. But only the one time."

"Why?"

"I was drawn back. I don't know how to explain it. I wanted to see the driveway, where he'd been shot. Maybe that's ghoulish, but it's the truth. As soon as I got there, I knew it was a mistake."

"Where were you on Friday night?"

"In my room at the hotel. I ordered a pizza."

"What time?"

"Around nine. I don't have a receipt, but it was from Domino's. You can check it. I used my credit card. Willow S. Lewis."

If the pizza order checked out, she was off the hook. Still, Jane had one last question. "Were you aware that Sharif had a gun with him?"

"What? No."

"You didn't take it from his room?"

"*No.*" This time, she almost jumped out of her chair. "Look, can I go now? I need to catch a bus to the airport."

Jane didn't really think Willow had anything to do with Noah's murder, and even if she did, she had no way to make her stay. "Go ahead."

"Really? That's it? I can leave?"

"Thanks for talking to me. I hope you have a good flight home."

34

Fi found little reason to get up on Sunday morning. As each hour passed, with no word from Annie, the knife of realization sank in more deeply. She understood Annie's need to keep things from her, and yet she couldn't help but wonder if there was some lack in *her* that had caused it. Guilt was a volatile thing. If Fi gave into it, it could easily eat her alive.

Throwing on a bathrobe around noon, she went downstairs. The coffeepot was still on, so she poured herself a mug and went into the breakfast room, where the morning paper was scattered over the table. Hearing clattering in the kitchen, she assumed the other late riser was up.

Cordelia shuffled into the room with a can of Coke.

Breakfast of champions, thought Fi. "Morning."

Cordelia mumbled, "Who wants worms?"

"Excuse me?"

"Early birds. What kind of idiot wants worms?"

Finding the front page, Fi began to scan the stories. She didn't find anything on Noah's murder until she turned to the "local news" section. There, above the headline "Possible Connection between Local Lesbian Video and Kenwood Homicide" were pictures of Annie and Fi. "Freakin' hell."

"Damn straight. No yucky worms for this girl."

"No, no," said Fi. She folded the paper in half and pushed it across the table.

Cordelia held it up, squinting to see the small print. "Bloody rise and shine."

"How can the paper print that when the police haven't even talked to us?"

"Good thing they haven't. If they had, they'd know Annie's in the wind."

Fi jumped when the doorbell rang. "We mention the police and they arrive?"

"With our luck it's a SWAT team with a battering ram."

"Don't tell them about Annie," said Fi. "Please. I'll go hide upstairs. If they want to talk to Annie or me, just say we're out."

"I can't answer the door like this." She glanced down at her ripped T-shirt and gray sweatpants, and then pointed to the scrunchie holding up her hair. "Cordelia Thorn does not appear in public looking like a bumpkin."

"Someone's got to answer it. What about your butler?"

"The truth is, he's really an old actor friend who needed a job. He bought a uniform to look the part, but that's as far as it got. I see him occasionally, flitting here and there, though with his rheumatism, answering doors would be out of the question."

They tiptoed through the kitchen. As they peered into the hall that led to the front foyer, they saw Ted pulling the door back. Bending over, he hauled a heavy package inside and set it next to a bench.

Withdrawing into the kitchen and drooping against the counter, Cordelia said, "That's just my weekly provisions from Zabar's. But in case Vance does stop by, I better change into something more presentable." Drawing herself up to her full six foot height, she stared down her nose at Fi and added, "Seems like combat fatigues are in order."

"You actually own combat fatigues?"

"Doesn't everyone?"

The doorbell didn't ring again until shortly after nine that evening. Fi was in her room, lying on the bed reading. She stepped out into the hallway, lowering her head and listening.

"Evening," said a voice Fi recognized as Vance. "I need to speak with Annie Johnson."

"She's not here," came Ted's voice.

Fi tiptoed to the stairway and sat down on the landing, watching the scene through the heavy balustrades. Ted and Bridget blocked her view of the front door.

"When will she be back?" asked Vance.

"I don't know," said Bridget, her hand pressed to Ted's back. "Perhaps you could come back another time."

"If I find out you're hiding her in there—"

"We're not," insisted Bridget. "Look, maybe I can help you." She stood to the side and invited him to come in. "Dad, why don't you go back to the nook, make sure Tyrion's okay. It's late for him to be up. I'll take Sergeant Vance into the breakfast room. I'll only be gone a few minutes."

"Stay," said Vance, moving inside. "I might as well ask both of you a question." Hooking a thumb over his belt, he continued, "We received an anonymous tip a few hours ago. According to the caller, Mr. Foster sexually assaulted Annie. Any truth in that?"

Ted's posture became ramrod straight. Neither he nor Bridget responded.

"This caller also said there was a written record of the incident."

"Sergeant," said Bridget, stepping between Vance and her father, "I think . . . if this is something you want to pursue . . . we'll need to contact a lawyer."

"I'll take that as a yes."

"Take it however you want. I'm sorry, but we have nothing more to say."

Fi thought Vance looked like a man who'd just swallowed ground glass. "Have Annie call me as soon as she gets home."

"I'll do that," said Bridget. She held the door open for him and shut it after he was gone.

Ted collapsed onto a bench. "It's all my fault," he said, covering his face with his hands. "I should have protected her. I should have seen Noah for what he was."

"None of us saw it," said Bridget, rubbing his back.

"I can't live like this, with Annie gone." He broke into sobs.

"You won't have to. She'll be back. She didn't murder Noah. It's not in her."

"But I wrote something in my journal. That night. The night Noah died. I must have been standing at my window. I wrote down that I saw a woman."

Bridget stiffened and removed her hand.

"What if it was Annie?"

"Who knows what you were thinking that night? Come on, let's go back to the nook."

Fi didn't have a minute to lose. She rushed back to her room, found her keys and her wallet, and then, moving ever so quietly, crept down the steps and out the front door. She needed to destroy Annie's notebook before Vance got his hands on it. She should have done it before she left her house. Without written proof, Fi prayed that anything Vance learned would be considered hearsay, or even less credible, gossip.

Flying down I-35W, Fi was careful to keep to the speed limit. She couldn't imagine a worse time to be stopped by a traffic cop. As she eased her old VW onto the exit ramp for Highway 62, her cell phone rang. Digging it out of her pocket, she saw that it was Charlotte Osborne. Charlotte had an almost comical knack for calling at all the wrong moments. She tossed the phone onto the passenger's seat and forgot about it.

The fourteen-mile drive from Minneapolis to her house in Eden Prairie felt endless. Taking the exit ramp onto Highway 169, she hoped to cut a few minutes off her travel time, but immediately ran into a stretch of roadwork that slowed the traffic to a crawl.

"Damn it," she said, pounding the steering wheel. Glancing at her phone, she clicked it on and saw that Charlotte had left her a voice mail.

"Ah, hi? It's me. Charlotte? I thought you
might answer. Sorry for bothering you, but
I have something important I need to tell
you. You're probably busy. But if you have a

minute, call me back? You've been so great.
Please, please, call me when you can. Maybe
tonight? I so need to talk to you.
Bye.

Right, thought Fi, like she was going to call in the midst of
this chaos. She stuffed the phone back in her pocket.

Twenty minutes later, Fi turned onto her street, drove up the
hill and into her drive. As she passed the red clay flowerpot on
the front porch, she remembered that she'd asked Roxy to remove the hidden front-door key. Checking under the pot, she
found that it was gone. Score one for Roxy. A friend she could
count on.

She stood in the foyer for a moment, sniffing the air. She
could still smell the spicy scent of Roxy's perfume. Boy, thought
Fi, she really must have doused herself with it. Making straight
for her study, she was surprised to find her desk lamp on. She
didn't remember turning it on earlier in the day. She wouldn't
have needed it because of all the afternoon light flooding in
through the windows. As she came around the edge of her desk,
she saw that the bottom drawer was pulled out. It was where
she'd hidden Annie's notebook. She jumped when she heard a
noise. The sound of the patio doors in the kitchen opening and
closing.

For an upside-down second, Fi was paralyzed. Several moments passed. And then . . . Phil sauntered past the room,
stopped and turned slowly toward her.

Fi could hardly believe her eyes. He had on a Speedo and
nothing else.

"You're here," he said, a grin spreading across his houndlike face. "I said a little prayer, you know. I'm not a religious man, but I was aching to be with you tonight."

With her breath growing fast and shallow, she said, "What are you doing in my house?"

"I just had a swim." He used the towel he was holding to dry his hair. The ease with which he carried himself seemed to indicate that he found nothing unusual about being here.

"Were you in my study?"

"Yes, I had quite the reading experience."

"You read—"

"Annie's letters. And then I called the police. I thought they needed to know that Annie was likely a murderer. In fact, I don't blame her. Oh, by the way, I've opened a bottle of wine in the kitchen. Now that you're here, you can join me. Unless you want to take a swim first."

Fi's skin felt suddenly too tight. "Do you . . . often use my pool?"

"Oh, sure. I wish I had a nice pool like yours, but then I'd have to maintain it. This arrangement suits me much better. Actually, I should show you some of the photos I've taken of you and Annie skinny-dipping. My God but you're hot." He mimicked striking a match and then blowing it out.

Fi swallowed back her revulsion and forced herself to smile.

"I thought you might be back tonight, now that Annie's gone for good. It's what I've been waiting for. We can be together now."

Her eyes widened and froze. So *this* was her stalker? Phil. Her rotund retired-banker neighbor.

"I'm thinking it might make sense for me to move in here. I'm several months behind on my mortgage. Getting fired from my last job really did me in financially."

"You were fired? I thought you said you'd retired."

"Well, I might have said that. I was pretty angry. I mean, I was the loan operations manager at that bank for six years, until one of the female tellers accused me of stalking her. *Me*." He laughed. "But the president of the bank and HR thought it was easier to get rid of me than to challenge some ball-busting feminazi. It was bullshit. She had it in for me from day one. And because her allegation went on my record, I've had zero luck finding another position."

"Gee," said Fi. "That's . . . too bad."

"Yeah, but the upside is you. I never would have realized that the woman of my dreams lived right across the street if I hadn't had all this free time."

"Right," whispered Fi. "Kismet."

"Huh?"

"Nothing." She had to think fast. "Look, you're right. I'd like to take a swim. You interested in a second round?"

"With you? That's an offer I can't refuse."

He came into the room, walked right up to her.

Fi's legs began to tremble. "And I've got another idea. I have a bottle of champagne in the basement refrigerator. Why don't you go sit out on the patio. I'll open the champagne, make us up a plate of cheese and crackers, and I'll meet you outside."

"On one condition: Leave the bathing suit in your closet." He touched his index finger to the tip of her nose. "I'll be waiting."

She stayed in her study until she heard the patio doors scrape open and then shut again.

In an instant, she was out the front door, running for the safety of a high hedge two houses away. Ducking down behind it, she took out her cell phone and called 911. When a woman answered, she blurted out, "There's a man in my house. He's been stalking me for months. He won't leave. You have to send someone right away." She gave them the address, repeating it twice to make sure they had it right.

"Are you safe where you are?" asked the dispatcher.

"I think so," said Fi. "But *hurry.*"

35

Mimi wasn't sleeping well. She'd been existing on carafe after carafe of coffee, and food from the vending machines two floors down. She wasn't even sure what day it was. She stood in the bathroom in her wedding dress, examining herself in the mirror while eating from a sack of Famous Amos chocolate chip cookies. Night was day and day was night. Noah was gone and nothing seemed to matter anymore.

She'd forgotten to plug in her cell phone. She couldn't remember the last time she'd used it. Mainly, all she ever got were calls and texts from her husband. The poor guy didn't have the slightest idea where she'd gone or why. Weird as it seemed, she was beginning to miss Ethan. She should go home. But then she remembered she couldn't. Not yet.

The one phone that never rang was the hotel landline next to her bed. She was applying a new shade of lipstick when, out of the blue, she heard it. Holding up the folds of her gown, she rushed out of the bathroom.

"Hello," she said, sitting down carefully on the unmade bed.

"Mimi? It that you?"

It was Ethan. He'd found her. "Yes, hon, it's me."

"God, I've been so worried." He sounded close to tears. "Are you okay?"

"I'm fine. Thanks for asking."

"Oh, God. I can't believe I finally found you. I called all of your friends to see if they'd seen you. You've been gone since last Wednesday, Mimi. That's five days. Five freakin' days."

"What day is it?" she asked, hoping for enlightenment.

"What? It's Monday. I called all the local hospitals. I even hired a private detective."

"How did you get this number?"

"Hell, Mimi. How do you think? The Minneapolis Police called me. They told me Noah Foster had been murdered and that they wanted to talk to you in connection with his death. In *Minneapolis*. He was there for some sort of family event. They thought you might be in town, too."

"Did they? Will you excuse me for a second?"

"Mimi, no, don't hang up."

She slithered out of the wedding dress, draped it carefully over a chair, then climbed back in bed and pulled up the covers. "I'm back. How did you find me?"

He shouted, "I want to know what's going on."

"Answer my question first."

"Oh, hell. I called every hotel and motel in the city. You weren't listed anywhere. The PI I hired suggested you and Noah might be . . . that you were—"

"We were," said Mimi.

"Shit," he said, more of a moan than a shout.

"You found Noah Foster's name listed on the hotel register."

"Yes. And I had the front-desk guy put me through to his room."

"And up I pop," said Mimi throwing off the blankets and sweeping her arms wide.

"Why do you sound so cheerful?"

She glanced over at her wedding dress and smiled. "Life is strange, isn't it, hon?"

"I want you to stay put. I'm coming to get you."

"There's really no need." She wondered if Ethan might be interested in going on that adventure cruise.

"Do you have your medication with you?"

"It's poison. Without it, I soar like an eagle."

"It's called mania, Mimi."

"Right. Like you'd know pure joy if it bit you in the ass."

"Please, Mimi. Just stay in the hotel. I'll get the first flight out. I love you. Just remember that. We'll get through this."

Mimi wasn't so sure she'd still be alive by the end of the day. "Check the jails before you come to the hotel."

"What? Why? Mimi, what are you saying?"

"Think about it, babe. When you're a kid, everyone tells you to follow your dreams. When you're an adult, the same people call it madness. I'm on a search for the holy grail of love and happiness. I go wherever my dreams lead."

With Phil Banks behind bars, unable to come up with enough money to post bail, Fi could finally rest more easily. She'd handed over all the notes Phil had sent her to the cops last night, after they'd handcuffed him and led him out to a waiting squad car. She would give a full statement to the police later today.

Before returning to Cordelia's house, she'd burned Annie's notebook. She ached to talk to Annie, to tell her that the stalker had been caught, and yet as long as Annie remained the prime suspect in Noah's murder, it was probably best that she stay lost.

Instead of catching a ride to the theater with Cordelia, Fi drove herself. It seemed like the right time to begin moving back to a more normal life. Not that her life would ever feel normal without Annie in it. In the last few days, Fi had disconnected from the video and its aftermath. She still intended to give interviews. Requests continued to come in. Tonight, she would announce that it was time to move back home. Annie's family, along with Sharif, would need to stay around town a while longer, until the police gave them the okay to leave. Cordelia had been incredibly generous, considering what had happened, but she would undoubtedly welcome their departure.

Fi stopped at the Italian deli at the corner of the theater building for a latte and her favorite pastries, a sfogliatella riccia and sfogliatella frolla. As she was standing at the counter, paying for her order, she noticed Charlotte sitting at a booth, staring intently into a cup of coffee. Thinking this might be a good time to talk, before the workday began, Fi approached.

"Oh, gosh, it's you," said Charlotte, looking up. "I'm sorry I bothered you last night."

"May I sit?" asked Fi.

"Oh, sure, sure. I'd like that."

Fi slid into the other side of the booth. "So what's up?"

Charlotte turned the coffee cup around in her hand. "You've been so nice to me, listening to all my travails with my mother. I was truly at the end of my rope with her. I mean, I started daydreaming about pushing her wheelchair out the window."

Fi winced. "But you didn't."

"No. I'd never hurt her. What I did was call my aunt Marie, my mother's sister-in-law. Uncle Nick died a few years back. She lives outside Green Bay, in this big old drafty farmhouse. The longer we talked, the more I let my hair down. She told me that Mom was abusing me, that I had every right to be angry. She and my mom have always gotten along. I have no idea how she does it, but Mom actually behaves around her. She drove to Minneapolis yesterday and invited Mom to move in with her."

"Wow."

"Yeah, wow is right."

"How did your mom react?"

"Well, you know how she is. She began listing all the reasons why it wouldn't work. She thought her trump card was me—that I needed looking after. I almost gagged. But, somehow, Aunt Marie convinced her. By the end of the month I will be free."

"Can you afford the rent all by yourself?"

"Heck I'm the one who's been paying the rent, the utilities, the insurance. Mom takes care of some of the groceries, but mostly she watches QVC all day and buys crap."

"I'm so incredibly happy for you," said Fi, reaching across the table and squeezing Charlotte's hand. "You're a good person. A hard worker. I'm sure you love your mother, but you don't need someone browbeating you like that."

Charlotte sipped her coffee. "Can I tell you something?"

"Sure."

"I don't love her. I never have. I asked her to move in with me because she was so lonely and I felt sorry for her."

"When she moves in with your aunt, will she abuse her, too?"

Charlotte almost cackled. "I'd like to see her try. I wish I was more like Marie. She doesn't take crap from anyone. Like I said, Mom actually behaves around her. When she doesn't, Marie ignores her."

"Sounds like the new arrangement might work," said Fi.

"Even if it doesn't, Mom's never moving back in with me."

"You're sure about that? You're kind of a soft touch."

"I feel as if I'm finally growing up," said Charlotte. "Finally seeing that I need to take responsibility for my life and my decisions. I credit you for that. I've been watching you, the way you handle people, the way you negotiate your work life. I've got a long way to go, but I feel I'm on the right path now. Who knows, maybe one day, I'll be a stage manager somewhere." Her face radiated happiness.

"I hope that happens," said Fi.

Good things were happening all around. If only Annie could come home. The problem was, the Gordian knot that was Noah's murder would never be resolved without far more pain than the booting out of Charlotte's mother.

Standing outside the hotel waiting for the porter to find her a cab, Mimi adjusted her wedding veil, noticing the envious stares of other people waiting for a ride. When a large van pulled up next to her, she nodded her approval. She'd already determined that her wedding gown and her rented Ferrari didn't mix well. The porter opened the sliding door and helped her in. She handed him a tip and gave the driver her destination.

"The Hennepin County medical examiner's office?" he repeated, turning around to look at her.

"You know where it is?"

"Um, no."

She was glad she'd memorized the address. "It's 530 Chicago Avenue."

"Are you sure that's where you want to go?"

"Quite sure." She felt for the credit card she'd stashed in her bra to make sure it was still there. She held a single red rose to her lips as the cab sailed along the downtown streets, finally stopping in front of a boring-looking building. "Wait for me," said Mimi, sliding out. She held up the front of her gown on the way up the steps, across the sidewalk and into the building. An older man in blue scrubs stopped her almost immediately.

"Can I help you?" he asked, trying his best to peer through the veil.

"I want to see my husband," she said, looking around. She wasn't sure what she'd expected, but this wasn't it. It was all so businesslike, and at the same time, sterile.

"Does he work here?" asked the man.

"Work here? No. He's dead. I want to see his body."

The man hesitated. "Did someone call you, ask you to come over?"

"Is there a problem? Where do you keep the cadavers?"

"I'm . . . a bit confused," said the man. "You're wearing a wedding dress."

"A couture wedding gown. If you can't help me, who can?" She began to walk away.

"Miss?" said the man.

She whirled around. "What?"

"Tell me your name. I'll see what I can find out."

"Foster. Mrs. Noah Foster. My husband died last Friday night."

"'Foster,'" repeated the man. "Please, if you'll come with me."

Finally, thought Mimi. She followed him down a brightly lit hallway into a small room, one that looked like a doctor's office. He nodded to a chair, but she remained standing. "My husband?" she asked.

"Typically, we don't allow next of kin to see the body after an autopsy has been performed. I'm assuming you've contacted a funeral home."

"I want him cremated."

"Yes, well, that's usually handled by the funeral home."

"We're from California."

He picked up a phone and punched in a number. "Sly, will you bring me Noah Foster's file. I'm in one twenty-four." A woman came in a few moments later and handed the man a folder. He thanked her, adjusted his glasses, and then sat down at a desk to examine the contents. "Bridget Foster. Is that right?"

"I'm in kind of a hurry," said Mimi. "Can't you just let me see him. I need to be with him one last time. You can understand that. He was the love of my life."

"But . . . are you getting married again?"

"What? Of course not. Look, whoever you are, Noah belongs to me, not you. I demand to see him."

"As I said—"

"Okay, okay. So tell me how he died. The police said it was a gunshot to the head."

"Without going into detail, I believe that is correct."

"Anything else?"

"Excuse me?"

"Did he *die* from anything other than the gunshot wound?"

"I'm not sure what you're asking."

"Poison," she almost yelled. "God, but you're dense."

He studied her openly. "I wonder if I could see your ID."

"Do I look like I have a purse with me?"

He stood. "If you'll give me one more minute, I'm sure we can help you." He kept his distance, eyeing her as if she were made of plutonium on his way out of the room.

"Screw this," Mimi muttered. She gave it a minute, then stood in the doorway looking both ways down the hall. Rushing for a door marked EXIT, she pushed through. The instant she did, warning bells went off. Mimi kicked off her high heels, tossed the rose away, picked up her dress, and bolted for the cab.

36

The longer Jane spent with her new manager, Meg Auster, the more certain she was that she'd made the right decision. Meg would work the evening shift tonight, which left Jane free to pursue two questions concerning the Noah Foster homicide.

First, she wanted to examine the red Ferrari that Mimi Chandler had rented—if, that is, she was still in town. Jane had no illusions that it would tell her much, but it seemed like one of the bases she needed to cover. Her second, and perhaps more important mission, was talking to Ted Johnson.

With Annie missing in action, perhaps running from a murder charge, Jane had come to the conclusion that telling Ted she'd read his journal in order to get him to open up about what he'd seen the night Noah died was the lesser of two evils. If he'd glimpsed a woman through his second-floor window, perhaps, if she could help him pull the scene from his damaged memory, she might learn something that would point to one of the women in Noah's life.

Leaving the restaurant shortly after seven, she headed downtown and entered the Maxfield West's parking garage.

The first two levels were open to the pubic. The top three were for guests only. If she had to, she would park and walk into the guest-only area.

She drove slowly through the dank concrete interior, her tinted side windows rolled down, scanning the stalls for the Ferrari. She assumed, with a car that expensive, that Mimi would opt for the more secure, hotel-only parking. As she came around the second curve, there it was, parked third from the end. Jane pulled into an empty spot and got out. She hated parking garages. The central areas of this particular building were reasonably well lit, but with night coming on, the dimly lit corners expanded, providing perfect hiding places.

Clicking on her flashlight, she shined the light into the front seat. She almost stopped breathing when she saw a billfold, an Apple watch, and a diamond ring scattered across the passenger's seat. A gold chain hung from the rearview mirror. Letting out a gasp, she felt certain she'd found Noah's murderer.

Backing away and switching off the flashlight, she returned to her car and called 911. She explained who she was, where she was, what she'd found, and asked the dispatcher to contact Sergeant Eddy Vance from the homicide unit to let him know. The dispatcher said a squad was on its way.

Hearing a police siren in the distance, Jane leaned back and waited. Mimi had said she loved Noah. If so, why had she murdered him? Beyond that, what was she thinking, leaving the evidence right there in her rental car in plain sight? It was an invitation to any passerby who happened to notice the expensive bling to break the window and snatch it.

A squad car roared in behind Jane's Mini a few minutes later, lights flashing. She introduced herself to the two officers, who asked her to stand back while they examined the Ferrari. Before they finished, Vance's Crown Vic had swung around the corner and stopped. Jane remembered his comment on Friday night, that he didn't need her help. She wondered if he remembered it.

Half an hour passed. Vance questioned her more aggressively than she thought absolutely necessary, though since he seemed to alternate between excitement that this discovery might move the murder into the solved column, and annoyance that Jane had been any part of it, she let him have his moment. He eventually let her go. If he felt any gratitude at all for her part in the investigation, he never let on.

Jane drove straight to Cordelia's house. She was elated. Annie could come home now. The world finally made sense. She slowed her Mini to a stop when she saw a cab sitting in the street just outside Cordelia's circular drive. A woman in a wedding gown got out. She spoke briefly to the driver, then lifted the front of the dress and rushed up to the house. Because it was getting dark, Jane couldn't see the woman's face, but the oversized black-rimmed glasses were unmistakable. It was Mimi.

Inside the mansion, Cordelia slouched in front of the refrigerator, tutting with disgust. Tyrion had made off with her last can of black cherry soda. She wasn't sure how she was going to get through an entire evening of work in her study without the sustaining elegance of her favorite elixir. When the doorbell rang, she hip-bumped the door shut and slogged out into the front hall to answer it.

The woman outside under the portico blinked. "It's you."

"Mimi," said Cordelia. "You're the last person I expected to see on my doorstep."

"But it's a happy surprise, right?"

"Are you on your way to a wedding?" With a black backpack slung over her shoulder, the costume didn't add up.

"Can I come in?"

"*May* I."

"May I come in?"

"Why?"

"Because I want to."

It seemed like an honest answer, if lacking detail. Cordelia stood back, touching the fabric of Mimi's gown as she entered. "Couture?"

"Marchesa."

"Ah."

"Bridget Foster lives here, right?"

"She doesn't live here. She is, however, staying with me."

"You're so literal."

Cordelia was instantly offended. "Am I?"

"Can you go get her?"

Just then, Bridget, Fi, and Sharif came into the foyer from the great hall.

"We're the munchies brigade," said Sharif, a toothpick dangling from his mouth. All three stopped when they saw the woman in the wedding gown.

"Perfect timing," said Mimi.

"You look familiar," said Bridget. "I can't quite place your face."

"We met once. I'm Mimi Chandler."

Bridget's smile turned to horror. "What are you doing here?"

"I came to explain," said Mimi, lifting the backpack off her shoulder, dipping her hand inside and removing a semiautomatic.

"Whoa," said Sharif, holding up his hand. "Why don't you . . . put that away."

"I don't want to."

"Tell me there's no bullet in the chamber."

"Maybe there is, maybe there isn't."

"But the safety's on, right?"

"This particular gun doesn't have a safety. No one mentioned that little fact when I bought it at a gun show last Wednesday."

"You were at a gun show?" said Fi.

"In Saint Cloud. You gotta love a state that doesn't require a background check."

At least, thought Cordelia, Mimi knew enough to keep her index finger pressed to the side of the weapon, away from the trigger. "Mimi," said Cordelia, her tone stern. "This is a gun-free establishment."

"Is there somewhere we could sit down and talk?"

"*We* can talk," said Sharif, pulling Fi and Bridget behind him, "but why don't you let everyone else go."

"May I say you are one fine-looking dude. Ever thought about taking a Mediterranean cruise?"

"Huh?"

"We can talk about that later. Right now, let's find a cozy little spot and all sit down for a chat."

Throwing worried looks at her compatriots, Cordelia led the way. They all settled at the table in the breakfast room. Mimi stood at the head of the table, the gun, mercifully, held at her side. By now, Cordelia was hyperventilating. "Can you make this quick?" she asked, using the newspaper to fan air into her face.

"Sure. I'll get right to the point. Noah and me, we were in love. We were Tristan and Isolde. Rhett and Scarlett. Antony and Cleopatra. Lancelot and Guinevere."

"We get the point," said Cordelia. "Move on."

Mimi adjusted the front of her gown. "Okay, so we sometimes had our moments. He could drive me crazy. There were times when I wanted to strangle him. Metaphorically. But that's all part of the package, right? True love never travels in a straight line."

"Mimi, please," said Bridget. "My son is in the other room watching TV. What if he walks in on this . . . this, whatever it is."

"It's an explanation of certain . . . aspects . . . of an event," said Mimi. She pointed the semiautomatic at the ceiling and, in a tiny, Mickey Mouse–like voice, said, "Bang."

Cordelia flinched.

"So we made love on Friday night. Like rabbits." She laughed. "Sorry. Private joke. I saw it as the pinnacle of our time together. But then, during the afterglow, he got mean. And he stayed mean. He wrote out a list of my 'issues,' like I don't already know them. I'm bipolar. Big deal. That doesn't make me evil incarnate. Next on the list was 'narcissist.' I could easily build a case that narcissists are the only people truly in touch with their feelings. It's an incredibly useful character trait. We're the movers and shakers. The people with passion. And then, at the bottom of the list, he wrote something I didn't understand. Something he'd never called me before. A . . . 'sosoligistaptath.' Or . . . oh, I can't remember."

"Sociopath," offered Cordelia helpfully.

Mimi pointed at her. "That's it. I meant to look that up. Whatever. Back to Friday night. I don't mean to brag, but I have a master's degree in organic chemistry. I may not know a lot about psychology, but I know my poisons. I only gave him a little, just enough to make him sick. But then I got to thinking, maybe he ate too much of the jam on an empty stomach. Not that his stomach was completely empty. He'd eaten a sandwich before we went at it. My sandwich. I'd ordered it for *me*, but he gobbled up the entire thing without even offering me a bite—except for a piece of kale. He thought that was hilarious. I thought he was a dick."

"I'm about to dissolve into a puddle of nerves," said Cordelia. "Have pity." Out of the corner of her eye, she caught a fluttering motion.

Everyone looked up as Jane appeared in the doorway.

"Heavens," said Cordelia, hand flying to her chest. "Is this a ghost I see before me?"

"Why, Jane," said Mimi, a brittle smile spreading across her face. "I didn't know you lived here. Welcome to our little gathering."

"What's going on, Mimi? What is this?"

Cordelia silently cheered. The marines had freakin' *landed*.

"I'm making my case."

"For what?"

"For innocence. Have a seat." When Jane remained standing, Mimi issued an order. "Sit." She waited for Jane to pull out a chair.

"Right. Where was I? Okay, so, when Noah left the hotel, I followed him back here. I wanted to make sure he was okay, that I hadn't overdosed him. When I saw the way he parked in the drive, I got worried. I went up to the van. The door was open. He was puking all over himself. It was totally disgusting." She gave a dramatic shiver. "I know you may not believe the next part, which is why I brought the gun along." She swung it toward the rose garden, cupped her palm over the slide, racked it, and sighted down the barrel.

Cordelia grabbed Jane's arm and hung on for dear life. "Save me," she whispered.

"I had it with me that night," said Mimi, turning her head and taking in the group.

Her words came tumbling out, almost too fast to comprehend. Cordelia wanted to cover her ears, to slither to the floor under the table and hide. If only she could rip off her clothes and reveal her superhero costume underneath. Extremely plump but pale skin was hardly going to cut the mustard when it came to real bullets.

"I'm not sure why it was in my hand," continued Mimi, her voice rising to an almost theatrical level. "I never meant to use it. But I did want to scare the living shit out of him, so maybe that's why. I waved it at him. And then . . . it, like, jumped in my hand. It was this living thing with a mind of its own." She paused. When she resumed her tale, her voice had returned to normal. "The dang thing has a hair trigger. Who knew. I looked up the make and model online the next day and read account after account of people firing off rounds they never intended. It wasn't just me. I mean, look." She swung the gun toward a decorative plate hanging on the wall just above Fi's head. "Watch my finger. I barely have to touch the—"

Fi ducked as a bullet blew a hole in the wall next to the plate.

"See? I never meant to hurt Noah. Scare him, yes. Murder, no."

Cordelia shifted her head ever so slightly toward the door, hearing footsteps coming toward the kitchen.

Mimi seemed oblivious. "So that's my story and I'm sticking to it. Am I forgiven?"

Men in SWAT gear burst into the room, weapons drawn.

Mimi was so startled, she dropped the gun. Another round went off. When Cordelia felt a bullet whiz past her ear, she jumped into Jane's lap.

Everything moved quickly after that. Mimi was handcuffed and led out to a waiting squad car. Vance breezed in, thanked Jane this time for calling and letting him know where Mimi was.

"We'll need a statement from all of you," he said. "But we can do that later."

Once he'd left, Jane explained what she'd found in Mimi's rental car. "Annie's off the hook," she said. "The police have enough evidence to put Mimi behind bars until she's an old woman."

Fi gave Jane a hug. "You did it."

"Not without a little luck."

"But you were the only one looking for a piece of luck."

As everyone scattered from the breakfast room, Cordelia turned to Jane. "Didn't mean to hurt you when I jumped in your lap."

"I'll live. The bruises and broken bones will heal."

"Cute. Tell me, how did the SWAT team get in?"

"When I saw Mimi go into the house, I called 911, told them what was happening, and said I'd leave the front door open."

"Thank God I gave you a key. This calls for a celebration, yes?

I'm thinking a muscular little Bordeaux. Maybe some salty nibbles."

"It's over," said Jane. "Now, if we could find a way to pass the word to Annie."

37

Fi sat on the steps outside the mansion, smoking a cigarette and watching the last of the police leave. She was too keyed up to stop smoking today, as had been her plan. More of a wish than a plan, really, as long as Annie wasn't around to read her the riot act for her stupidity. Then again, she'd give anything to hear Annie's voice, angry or otherwise.

With so many emotions tangled up inside her, Fi could hardly form a coherent thought. All she knew was that Annie was safe. It was hard to admit that she'd ever considered Annie a suspect, and yet she had. She'd always believed that people were capable of almost anything, given the right impetus. She wondered about Mimi, if what she'd told them was the truth, or simply the story she'd convinced herself was true.

Flicking ash into the dirt, Fi settled back against a pillar. She would move home tomorrow. Annie's family had no real reason to stick around, now that the murder had been solved, and especially now that Annie was gone. Fi hoped Sharif might stay for a few more days. Without Annie, the house would seem incredibly empty.

"Fi," came a whispered voice.

Fi gripped the edge of the step. She held her breath.

Annie stepped out from behind one of the tall arborvitae. "I'm back. Are you angry?"

"Oh, God," said Fi, tossing the cigarette away. She rose and wrapped her arms around Annie, kissing her, caressing her hair, breathing her in and holding her tight. "God, are you real?"

"I'm real. I'm sorry I ran away. It seemed like the thing to do six years ago, but it didn't work this time. I should have stayed and faced my demons."

"There were so many, you must have felt outnumbered."

"Yeah."

"I have so much to tell you."

"I saw the police take someone out of the house. Was she—"

"The one who murdered Noah? Yes."

"I kept thinking it might have been my dad. That thought alone was driving me crazy."

Fi kissed Annie's forehead. "He's fine. We're all fine now that you're back. We should go tell everyone."

"Not yet," said Annie. "Just stay here with me a little longer." She placed her hands on either side of Fi's face and kissed her eyelids, her cheeks, and finally her lips.

It was a long, lingering kiss, just the kind Fi had been longing for.

"I love you," said Annie.

"And I love you."

"There should be more words for love. For different grades and levels. So we could be more precise."

"Spoken like a future lawyer." Nuzzling close, Fi whispered,

300

"But sometimes there are no words, especially for what's really important."

"Except for this." With her voice breaking, Annie said, "Through life, past death, and into the hands of God."

Fi's eyes welled with tears.

Jane was helping Cordelia find a bottle of "muscular" Bordeaux in the wine fridge when Bridget and Sharif burst into the kitchen.

"Have you seen my dad?" demanded Bridget. "I thought he was in the nook playing a video game with Tyrion. That's why I was pretty sure neither of them would come into the breakfast room while Mimi was holding us captive. They get lost in those stupid games. But we can't find him anywhere."

"We've looked all over the house," said Sharif.

As they were talking, Fi walked in, followed by Annie.

Cordelia did a double take. "My stars and garters, the prodigal hath returned." She clapped her hands and hooted.

Annie was surrounded, everyone trying to hug her at once.

"I have so much I need to explain," said Annie.

Bridget cut her off. "And we all want to hear it, but first, we've got to find Dad."

"Is he lost?" asked Annie.

"He was beyond upset last night after the police left. I've never seen him that depressed before."

"It's all my fault," said Annie.

"I think," said Cordelia, hands rising to her hips, "we've all earned the right to blame Noah from now unto eternity for everything, including global warming."

"Works for me," said Bridget. "Sharif thinks Dad might have gone over to the lake."

301

"We've taken a couple of walks over there together. He loves sitting on this one particular bench."

"Did anybody try his cell phone?" asked Fi.

"It's in his nightstand upstairs," said Bridget.

When the doorbell rang, everyone groaned.

"I'm no longer living in a mansion, I'm living in a madhouse," muttered Cordelia. "I'll go see who it is."

"Someone's got to stay with Tyrion," said Bridget.

"You stay," said Annie. "The rest of us will head over to the lake."

"Call me if you find him. Maybe I should phone the police."

"We've had enough police for one night," said Fi. "He hasn't been gone that long."

Jane agreed with Fi. "Let's wait."

Jane, Fi, and Annie all rushed for the back door, with Sharif leading the way. Because he was the fastest runner, he quickly outdistanced everyone.

A beautiful, deep purple twilight had settled over the lake. As they reached the grass by the walking path, Jane saw a man on a bench near the water. Sharif had stopped a good fifteen yards away, waiting for everyone to catch up.

Breathing hard, Annie said, "Let me go talk to him. Find out what's going on." She trotted up to the rear of the bench, slowing as she came around the side.

Jane whispered for Sharif and Fi to stay put, and then followed. She didn't think Annie was in any danger, but wanted to be within earshot, just in case.

Annie bent over her father. "Dad," she said. "It's me. I'm back."

He seemed to be miles away.

"Everything's good, Dad. Let's go back to the house." She hesitated. "What's that under your hand?"

"What? Oh, nothing."

"It looks like Sharif's revolver. Why don't I take that."

"You go away now, honey. Leave me alone with my thoughts."

"But I just got home. Don't you want to spend some time with me?"

"Well, I—"

"Sure you do. Come on. I missed you."

He reached for her arm. "Annie, listen for a second. I need to say something. I should have said it the other night. I . . . I was a failure as a father. I see that now. I'm glad I have this last chance to talk to you."

"Last chance?"

"I have to make it up to you. You're in trouble. I can be the solution."

"Dad, no. The police found the person who murdered Noah. It's over. I'm no longer a suspect."

He smiled. "Nice try, Annie. Just so you know, there's a piece of paper in my jacket pocket. It's a confession. Give it to the police after I'm gone."

"Gone? Dad, you're not making sense—and you're not listening."

He glanced down at the revolver. "It's a gift. Please, go on home now. Let me do what I have to do." He picked up the gun, moved it from his left hand to his right. "I'll be leaving you anyway, Annie. Might as well make my death worth something."

"I don't want this," she said, arms at her sides, helpless and intense. "I don't want you to die."

"My mind is disappearing. *I'm* disappearing."

"But not yet."

He looked up at her. "No. Not yet."

She cupped her hand over the gun. "I'm not in danger anymore, Daddy."

"You called me Daddy. You haven't done that since you were a little girl."

"I'll always be your little girl. If you want to give me a gift, then I want you. For as long as I can have you."

"But the police."

"Listen to me." Ever so carefully, she removed the gun from his hand and stuffed it in the back of her jeans. Hands on his shoulders, looking him straight in the eyes, she said, "The police are gone. They arrested someone for Noah's murder. They're not coming back. I'm fine. I want you to come back to the house with me. Bridget's there. And Tyrion. They need you. I need you."

He dropped his head. "How can I fight all of you?"

She drew him up by his hands. Slipping her arm around his waist, she walked him away from the bench and back toward the street.

Fi followed close behind, giving Jane and Sharif a thumbs up.

"Well," said Sharif, bending down to retie one of his athletic shoes. "That was close."

"If he'd gone somewhere else," said Jane. "If we'd waited just another couple of minutes—"

"We got lucky. Or maybe there really are angels looking out for us. Can't say this was much of an anniversary weekend for Fi and Annie, but at least they have a chance now."

Jane reached down and picked a blade of sweet grass to chew

on. "It all goes back to that video. This whole chain of events was like a watching a line of dominoes fall."

"Funny that something so powerful can also have such negative consequences." He straightened up and they began walking toward home.

"There can be lots of dominoes in our lives," said Jane.

"Meaning?"

"Well, take guns. You buy one because you think it will solve a problem. It's the first domino. But then, it becomes part of the problem, not the solution. You have no idea, when the final domino falls, which it eventually will, what it will be."

"You own a firearm?"

"I used to. I got rid of it last winter."

"Because you hated it."

"Actually," said Jane, "the first time I held a gun in my hand, I was astonished by the feeling of power it gave me. That feeling scared me more than the gun did."

He laughed. "Yeah, I hear you."

"It makes me think about Mimi. About Noah."

"Hell, I'm not giving that asshole another second of my time. Far as I'm concerned, it was karma. He got what he deserved."

Jane sometimes wished she could view life that way. Flat on. No need for analysis. The problem was, she was always looking for context, for something to help her understand.

Sharif kicked at a rock. "Before I left Ohio, my girlfriend dumped me because she found a revolver in my bedroom drawer. Her brother was killed in a gang hit. She hates guns. She said, 'Sharif, it's me or that gun.'"

"And you chose the gun?"

"I'm an asshole." Looking up at the stars, he added, "When I get back, I'm going to beg her to come back to me. No more guns in this brother's bedroom drawers. Think she'll forgive me?"

"I'd say you're worth a second chance."

"Think so, huh?" He gave her a playful shove. "You are so right, girl. So seriously right."